ELSIE SZE grew up in Hong Kong and cu
husband, Michael. They have three sons, Benjamin, Samuel and Timothy. A former teacher and librarian, she is an avid traveller, often to remote places which form the settings for her stories. Her first novel, *Hui Gui: a Chinese story*, was nominated for Foreword magazine's Book of the Year Award in Fiction, 2006. Her second novel, the *Heart of the Buddha*, was published in the United States in 2009 and was shortlisted for the Foreword Magazine 2009 Multicultural Fiction Book of the Year Award. In 2013, Elsie won the inaugural Saphira Prize, a literary prize offered by Women in Publishing Society, Hong Kong, for unpublished writing for her manuscript "Ghost Cave".

Praise for *Ghost Cave*

"*Ghost Cave: a novel of Sarawak* contains surprises at every turn. A long-ago tragedy, a buried treasure and a harrowing guerrilla war are just part of what makes this exceptional tale a highly recommended read. More importantly, it explores the heart and heartbreak of a family bound to each other across a turbulent time."

Shannon Young, editor of *How Does One Dress to Buy Dragonfruit?* and author of *The Art of Escalator Jumping*

"In the tradition of the folklorist, Elsie Sze presents a multigenerational tale of Sarawak past and present. Rich in historical detail, *Ghost Cave* unearths long-forgotten secrets and promises, to reveal the timelessness of human bonds."

Ania Szado, author of *Studio Saint-Ex* and *Beginning of Was*

"Elsie Sze writes an engaging story of Sarawak that is both wonderfully detailed and informative. Each chapter of this compelling novel takes us deeper into the history of Borneo and into the lives of the characters."

Leanne Lieberman, author of *Gravity, The Book of Trees* and *Lauren Yanofsky Hates the Holocaust*

Also by Elsie Sze

Hui Gui: a Chinese story
The Heart of the Buddha

GHOST CAVE

A novel of Sarawak

GHOST CAVE

A novel of Sarawak

ELSIE SZE

WOMEN IN PUBLISHING SOCIETY
HONG KONG

Published in 2014 by Women in Publishing Society
Hong Kong
GPO Box 7314

Copyright © Elsie Sze 2014

The moral right of the author has been asserted.

All rights reserved. No part of this publication may be reproduced, stored in a retrieval system or transmitted in any form or by any means without the prior written permission of the publisher, nor be otherwise circulated in any form of binding or cover other than that in which it is published and without a similar condition being imposed on the subsequent purchaser.

Cover design: Angela Ho
Cover photograph of Mau San © Elsie Sze
Typeset by Polly Yu Production Limited

While the traditional Wade-Giles romanization system for Chinese words is generally adopted for use in the novel, certain Chinese names are romanized using the Pinyin system due to the familiarity of present-day English language readers with them.

To my father and mother, Hon Ngi and Elizabeth Chin,
with love and gratitude

Acknowledgements

To the Women in Publishing Society, Hong Kong, thank you profoundly for the Saphira Prize, and making this publication a reality for me.

I am immensely grateful to my family and friends in my father's homeland of Sarawak, especially Alice Chin Li Yee, Desmond Chin Lip Fong, Chin Oi Yee and Florence Lai Nyuk Lee, for their unrelenting and enthusiastic assistance during my research for the novel, to the extent of getting me to the exclusive premises of Ghost Cave. Warmest thanks to Katherine Chin for reading early versions of the manuscript and giving me invaluable input on the Hakka and Bidayuh cultures.

For my writing group in Toronto – Leanne Lieberman, Elizabeth MacCleod, Dianne Scott, Roz Spafford, Ania Szado and Anne Warrick – for their insightful comments and feedback on the manuscript, and standing by me over the years with staunch encouragement and unfailing moral support, my gratitude and affection.

To Carol Dyer, my editor, my deep appreciation for her most proficient editing, the close attention to every detail, the countless candles burned at both ends working on the edit. Thank you, Carol, for caring for my story as your own.

To Sam Sze, my son, who took time off his busy workday to produce the custom maps I requested with efficiency and promptness, a big, heartfelt thank you!

For Michael, who braved the tropical heat and rain forests of Borneo with me, as we continue our life's multi-faceted adventure, my love for ever.

Contents

Kuching Encounter	1
The Journal: 1849	20
Guerrilla Days: Indoctrination	44
The Journal: 1850–1856	55
Guerrilla Days: The First Insurgency	74
The Journal: 1857	79
Guerrilla Days: Life in the Jungle	99
The Journal: 1857–1858	104
Guerrilla Days: Tragedy at Camp	134
The Journal: 1858–1860	139
Exploring Black Magic	151
The Journal: 1861	153
Guerrilla Days: Ambush	170
The Journal: 1861–1913	175
Family Misfortune	201
Guerrilla Days: Times of Darkness	203
The Face in the Bark Painting	212
Return to Ghost Cave	218

SOUTHEAST ASIA
WITH SARAWAK, BORNEO

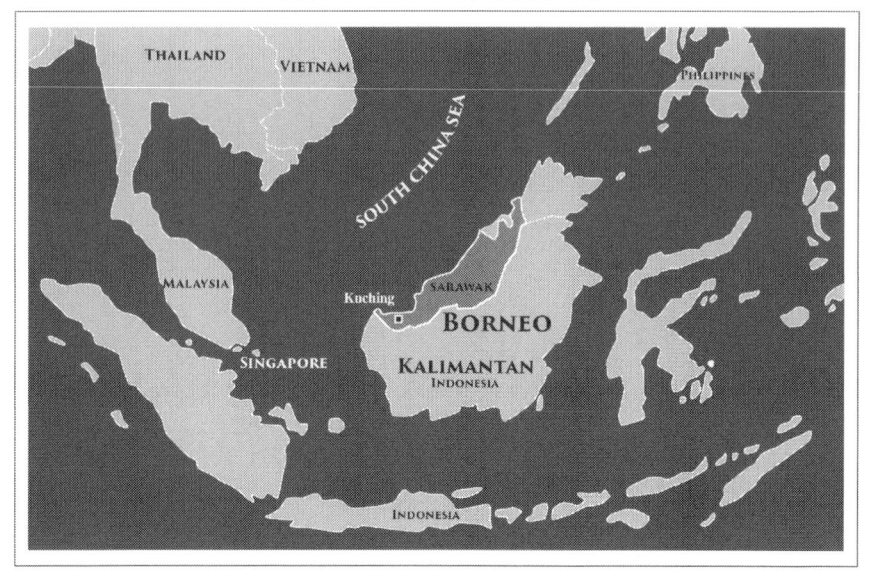

BORNEO

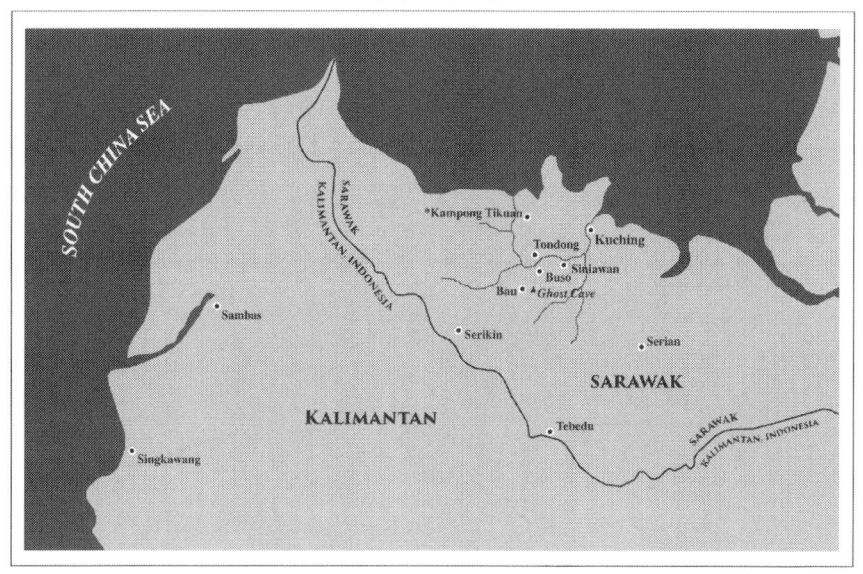

*Fictitious place

"I believe in the spirits of our ancestors, who protect us from harm and whose primary concern is our welfare. Mostly, they are not seen, only felt by the sensitive among us. And, very occasionally, when these spirits choose to manifest themselves to the human eye, for reasons that are important to them, we call them ghosts."

Liu Hon Min

1

Posted on July 29, 2012

One more sleep and I will be embarking on an adventure of a lifetime, to Sarawak, home of my paternal grandfather. Does everyone know where Sarawak is? A small clue: Grandpa Liu was a guerrilla who fought anti-communist troops in the 1960s, in the tropical jungles of northern Borneo.

Therese recognizes her grandfather as soon as she sees him at Kuching Airport, the same sunken face and eyes, those pronounced ears. She has only met him once, when he visited Toronto for a month in 2001 when Therese was ten. She remembers him as a tall, gaunt man, with deep-set eyes and large, protruding ears, which then she thought of as "elephant ears". He is seventy-one now. His hair is still amazingly dark and he seems perhaps thinner, and slouches a little. He speaks surprisingly good English, having studied the language at university in Singapore, a convenience for Therese who speaks only a smattering of Cantonese, and no Hakka. Therese never met her paternal grandmother. She died after a prolonged fight with cancer in 1993 when Therese was just two. Her father, who left Kuching for Toronto to pursue his studies in medicine and has worked in Toronto as a doctor ever since, returned home for his mother's funeral, but Therese was too young to travel the long distance and remained with her mother, a Canadian-born Chinese whom her father met while a student at the University of Toronto. Since his wife's death, Grandpa Liu has lived on his own with the help of a Malay manservant who takes care of his two-storey terrace house and garden off Kuching's 7th Mile Bazaar.

As Therese grew into her teens, her father told her how her grandfather had been exposed to communist ideology, first in the Chinese secondary school which he attended in Kuching, then at Nanyang University in Singapore during the period of the communist insurgency in Sarawak in the Sixties. Liu Ka Ming later became a militant radical and joined the guerrilla force in the jungles of Borneo to fight against the government of the then young Malaysia for communist control in Sarawak. All that is behind him. He has been for years now a respected member of the Chinese community in Kuching, having sold his father's country store in Buso, a bazaar twenty miles upriver, and moved into the city. He ran a business in Kuching exporting local produce, pepper, cocoa, sago and the like, while keeping a retail store on the Main Bazaar selling swiftlets' nests, sundry spices and dried seafood. He retired five years ago, and now spends his time with friends, playing bridge and practicing t'ai chi, "going gentle into the good night", as he describes it.

To Therese's remembrance of Grandpa Liu is added a sense of awe, bordering on respect, which she associates with guerrillas, having romanticized the figure of Che Guevara from books and a recent movie of the radical Argentine icon. Apart from her family interest in visiting Sarawak, she intends to gather material for the journalism programme she will be pursuing at the University of Toronto. She sees her grandfather's story as a communist guerrilla a worthwhile and fascinating subject for her Master's thesis.

Settling into her hotel room at the Santubong, a modest local establishment on Wayang Street in downtown Kuching within easy walking distance of the riverfront, Therese locks her passport, other IDs, credit cards and most of her money into the room safe. As Grandpa Liu has warned, she's not taking chances with muggers in a strange city where she must stand out as a fresh, foreign visitor on her own, especially with her short, dark bob highlighted with streaks of auburn red, not a common phenomenon for an Asian woman even in her part of the northern hemisphere. She loves her hairstyle, a little funky, cool on all counts, while the colouring and side bang lend an air of playful charm to her otherwise tomboyish looks. She will be picked up by Grandpa Liu for dinner later in the evening, but it is now only mid-morning. With many hours to spare, she is wasting no time in starting to explore the city. After a much-needed shower, and wearing a white halter top, khaki shorts and open-toe leather sandals, Therese steps out into the hot and humid inferno of Sarawak's state capital on the grand island of Borneo, a place where, according to what she has read on the internet, indigenous groups headhunted not too long ago, orangutans abound and voodoo is believed to be still practised.

Kuching in 2012 is a bustling city with tall new constructions, modern hotels, trendy shopping malls, but whose main attraction is still its old town, most of which dates back to the early nineteenth century. Leaving the hotel, Therese ventures forth on foot along the esplanade that runs beside the Sarawak River in the newer section of town where old historic temples and shophouses are dwarfed by multi-storeyed hotels. The esplanade is clean and pleasant, with shady trees, benches intermittently placed along the way and a couple of food stalls with signs picturing mouth-watering *laksa, popiah* and *nasi lemak*, and their respective English explanations of spicy vermicelli in soup, spring rolls and Malaysian coconut rice. There are just a handful of pedestrians on the promenade, it being early afternoon on a weekday. Some workers are hanging up coloured lanterns between lamp poles along the brick-paved walkway in that stretch of town that must come alive at nightfall.

The river is calm and clear, an occasional chugging sampan breaking its mirror stillness. Therese walks past the more glamorous part of town along the riverside promenade to the busy thoroughfares reeking of salted fish, dried shrimp paste and human sweat. She weaves along the congested "five-foot ways" in front of shophouses of the Main Bazaar and Gambier Road, walking between displays of local produce and merchandise that have made their way out of the stores into those spacious covered pedestrian passages, items such as barrels of salted fish and sundry spices, racks of native beaded jewellery, rattan baskets and mats, even cartfuls of the colourful Malaysian layered cake, *kek lapis*. The shopkeepers and shoppers are mainly Chinese and Malay, and some Indian. The men are in shorts and singlets, a good number bare-chested, while the women wear their native *samfu*, sarong or sari, according to their ethnic origins. Hakka is spoken among the Chinese, as are the Hokkien and Teochew dialects. Therese can speak none of these, but she recognizes Hakka when it's spoken, having heard her father using the dialect whenever he calls Grandpa Liu on long distance.

From the congested marketplace, Therese turns into a side street called Bishopgate Road, a misnomer as what she sees is really a small, short street coming to a dead-end at a doorway framed by a red wall some fifty yards from the marketplace entrance. She passes the rear of some two-storey buildings whose back doors open into the street. She soon reaches the doorway. A brass plaque on the wall reads "Bishopgate", describing it as the pedestrian gateway to access the bazaar and the waterfront from the Anglican Mission complex in the eighteenth and nineteenth centuries. The original gate is gone, but a small part of the wall has remained, freshly painted red, in which is set the present doorway. As Therese steps through into the back street leading to the Anglican Mission complex, she hears footsteps behind her and instinctively looks back into Bishopgate Road. Sunlight is casting shadows on the street, but the only people she sees are a woman hanging washing from the second-floor window of a building, a couple of kids playing hopscotch and a street vendor with his stall where the street enters the marketplace. Feeling uneasy, Therese quickly makes a left turn and walks fast until the back street rejoins a wide road.

She soon comes to the white-walled Bishop's House, quite a mansion, though a modest one even by today's standards; a sign on the fence identifies it as the oldest surviving dwelling in Kuching, dating back to 1849, the time of the first White Rajah, James Brooke, who gave the land that is now the Mission complex to the Anglican Bishop Francis Thomas McDougall. Walking along the main road that encircles the wide expanse of the complex, Therese comes to St Thomas' Cathedral, the earliest version of which dated back to 1849 when Bishop McDougall ordered the erection of a wooden church at the behest of James Brooke. As Therese crosses the churchyard, she hears the sound of movement near her and has an uncanny feeling that she's being followed. She looks up and down the path, which winds from the Cathedral to the graveyard, and along the rows of tombstones all around her. A bare-chested gardener wearing rolled-up kung fu pants and a wide-brimmed hat is tidying the ground by a grave. No one else is in sight. Perhaps it's the idea that she's on burial ground that gives her the jitters. Therese has been afraid of ghosts from an early age. Since her late teens, she has tried to dismiss them as ungrounded figments of her all-too-imaginative psyche.

She picks up her step towards the front of the Cathedral and the gate opening onto one of the main roads with a long Malay name that is difficult to pronounce. From the Bishop's House and the Cathedral, Therese heads to the riverfront. Directly across the river is a white fort with two towers, each of which has a pair of dark crescent-topped windows, like eyes scrutinizing activities on the river and on its opposite bank. A covered sampan, which the locals call a *tambang*, is moored at a wooden dock on the south bank, opposite the fort. Therese walks up to the boatman and indicates her intention of crossing the river. For fifty sen she is rowed across to a cement jetty leading up to the grounds of the fort. It takes just six minutes to cross from one bank to the other. Therese walks up the footpath to the gardens. Facing the river at the top of the slope is a notice on a wooden stand introducing the historic building.

> The Astana was built in 1870 by the second White Rajah, Charles Brooke, as a home for his bride, the Ranee Margaret. Charles' uncle, James Brooke, lived in a residence on this site called The Grove, when he became the first White Rajah of Sarawak in 1840. The Grove was burned down during the Chinese Rebellion in 1857. On the site where The Grove had been, James Brooke built a new residence which was later demolished by his successor Charles Brooke to make room for The Astana. Today, The Astana is the home of the State Governor of Sarawak.

Perhaps in the nineteenth century the two towers with their sinister windows were meant as watchtowers. The White Rajah could remain safely in his grand domain, the river separating him from his subjects, the indigenous people of Sarawak, as well as the Malays, and the Chinese and Indian immigrants. At least the present government is generous enough to open the gardens to the public. Such rich history the place holds, Therese muses. If only the earth beneath The Astana and its predecessors could talk, it would tell tales of high seas' adventures and native conquests, the romance and perils of an exotic empire, and the horror and tragedy of a rebellion.

Therese is suddenly conscious of there being someone behind her. Turning her head, she looks right into the dark glasses of a young man of brown complexion with short spiky black hair. She gives him a spontaneous once-over. He has on a white *I love New York* T-shirt and blue jeans. His sneakers must have accounted for his quiet advent. The fellow has no unusual features, except for a distinct mole to the left of his upper lip. Therese assesses people by their eyes, but it's hard to see his behind those sunglasses. She is uncomfortable with his somewhat close proximity to her, unnecessarily close as they are the only two reading the board. Is he a pickpocket? Or worse, a sex maniac looking for cheap thrills? Without hesitation but with measured steps, she makes her way towards the well-groomed gardens of The Astana, self-consciously aware that the man might be eyeing her as she does so.

2

The pungent smell of fried garlic and chilli fills the night air as Therese and Grandpa Liu emerge from the elevator to the Top Spot, an open-air food court on the rooftop of a building not far from the riverfront. Grandpa takes Therese on a tour of the stalls that encircle the dining area, stopping at the ones with exotic food items and culinary activities that catch her fancy. They order and are seated at one of the tables in the centre. A waitress soon brings over a plateful of *midin*, the wild jungle fern stir-fried with *belacan*, a shrimp paste mixed with chilli pepper, and a deep-fried oyster pie looking like a thin-crust pizza studded with baby oysters.

"I won't fit into my jeans if I'm to eat like this every day, Grandpa," Therese says.

"If you come and stay with me, my Malay cook can make very good curries and kek lapis for you," Grandpa coaxes. Grandpa Liu has repeatedly asked Therese to stay with him but she thinks his house at 7th Mile on the outskirts of Kuching too inconvenient.

"I'd love to, but I also want to explore the town and go to museums and historic sites. It's easier for me to stick around here. I'll see you a lot anyway, Grandpa. You're the reason I've come to Kuching. Besides, I want to hear the story of your guerrilla days for my thesis, remember?"

At mention of the past, Liu Ka Ming gives a faint, thoughtful smile, the furrows on his forehead accentuated by his pensive, faraway gaze. "That was long ago, when my blood was hot with patriotic idealism and my heart pulsing for what I believed to be equality and freedom for my people. I will tell you my story. But," he pauses, sipping through a straw the cool, fresh juice from a green coconut, before continuing, "I have another story for you, one that you will probably want to read first and use for your journalism studies."

"What is it?"

"It's the story of my great-grandfather who came to Borneo from China in the mid-nineteenth century. It was written as a journal by an English woman in Kuching, as told to her by my grandfather."

"Your grandfather could speak English back then?"

"I never knew him for he died before I was born, but according to my father, my grandfather was sent to Kuching to study English as a young man because my great-grandfather, the ancestor who came from China, believed English would be useful for his son's future. As a result, my grandfather could speak English reasonably well. However, he needed someone better versed in the language to write his father's life story for him."

"That must be some story. It's amazing it's been preserved."

"My grandfather passed it to my father, who, as far as I know, never read it. In fact, my father never told me about it. The journal was tucked away in the attic in our shophouse in Buso. I only found it while clearing out the place twenty years ago when I moved to the city after your grandmother was diagnosed with cancer. I brought it with me to Kuching. I must confess that I have never read it either."

"Weren't you curious? I'd be dying to read it," interjects Therese.

"Well, my eyesight was already getting very poor, the result, I was told, of the early onset of some form of macular degeneration, and reading a whole manuscript written in cursive English was too much for me, although I must say the script was beautiful." Grandpa Liu pauses, then, looking tenderly at Therese, continues, "I want to pass the story on to my descendants because the struggles and sacrifice of our forefathers migrating from China and building a home here on foreign soil should be known and remembered. I want you to read it."

"It sounds so interesting, Grandpa. Why don't I read it to you?"

"I'll like that, but you should first make the most of your time here sightseeing, and doing your research. I need to tell you my tale too."

"Of course, I want most to hear that! The manuscript can be my night-time reading at the hotel for now. I'm so lucky. Just think, how many of my peers can boast that they have a grandfather who had been a guerrilla?"

"Lucky for you, but not so for me back then," Liu Ka Min laughs. "I tell you, being a guerrilla is like living in a shit dump. There's nothing glamorous about it, contrary to what you may see in movies. You are cut off from the outside world, from your family and loved ones. You are in constant danger of being shot at or blown up. And you are completely at the mercy of the jungle in the tropics, getting drenched by torrential rain, burned by the sun, and sick from the dirty water you drink, or from insect bites. As if that's not enough, you are always hungry, because the food, if there is any, is never enough." There is a tremor in Grandpa's voice, as his mind seems to wander off into the distant past. "What is most painful is watching your loved ones die, from injury, illness or starvation."

"I am thankful you survived that time," Therese says, nodding slowly, sobered by her grandfather's words.

"I was so close to being killed once, I thought my end had come." Grandpa gazes into oblivion. "To this day, I still think about that time, and am grateful. I'll tell you all about it in my story."

That evening, Grandpa Liu gives Therese the handwritten journal, dated 1920, of the life of his great-grandfather. It is quite thick and the paper has yellowed heavily at the edges. The cover reads *The Life and Times of Liu Hon Min: A Journal, by Mary Ann Warrick, as told to her by Liu Nan Sun*. A letter is attached to the front.

> To my descendants and anyone who may set eyes on this manuscript:
> This is the extraordinary life story of my father, Liu Hon Min, who journeyed from Guangdong to Sarawak in 1849. A small part of the story was based on my own recollections and experience, but most of it was told to me by my father. I am very grateful to Mrs Mary Ann Warrick, an English teacher and writer in Kuching and a good friend, for writing my father's story for me in the fine words of her mother tongue. I believe for my father's story to reach across time and space, it should be written in English, the language of the future. Though his story is entirely factual in content, I have given Mrs

Warrick the liberty to tell it with embellishment of style, language and details, as her literary discretion dictates, for it is my hope that the story will be read and appreciated not only by our descendants but by many readers here and in distant lands for generations to come.

Liu Nan Sun
August 3rd, 1920

3

Therese drags her blistered feet into the air-conditioned lobby of the Santubong. It's been a very long and eventful few hours, and only her first day in Kuching. Tonight, she is too tired to start on the journal about her ancestor Liu Hon Min. That will have to wait. She'll turn in as soon as she has taken another shower, her third of the day. As she nears the reception desk, a man walks towards her. In the split second their paths cross, Therese notices the *I love New York* T-shirt he is wearing, and the mole above his upper lip. He does not have his sunglasses on. He casts a sweeping glance in Therese's direction, avoiding her eyes, then diverts his face from her as he aims for the nearest exit from the hotel. Disturbed, Therese makes her way briskly towards the elevators and frantically pushes the "up" button beside them.

Her hands still shaking, she opens her room door with her key card. Once inside she immediately locks the door. Can that man be staying in the same hotel? Perhaps he is just a visitor. Surely, he is not after her. Even so, seeing him at the Santubong, which means he knows she is staying there, unnerves her. Then she sees the red light blinking on her hotel phone. A message for her. She picks up the receiver and dials for messages. An envelope has been left for her at reception.

Afraid to have it delivered to her room, lest it is a hoax, she takes the elevator down to the lobby again. Nervously mindful in case the man is still in the hotel, Therese picks up the envelope. It has her name, Therese Liu, scribbled on it. Still standing by the reception desk, her heart palpitating, she rips open the envelope and takes out a piece of folded single-lined paper. One sentence in a stringy scrawl is written on it:

> I can be a great help to you in your research for your story. Miseng anak Rigop

Miseng anak Rigop. What kind of a name is this? What kind of a joke is this? Other than her grandfather, who in Kuching would know she is looking for material for a story? Therese tries to dismiss the matter from her mind, but she stays awake for a long time, wondering if the man she saw reading the sign about The Astana and again in the hotel lobby is Miseng anak Rigop.

Therese receives a call from the reception desk the next morning, saying another note has been left for her:

> I can really help you. Meet me at the front entrance of the State Legislative Building tomorrow at 10 a.m. Miseng

The same stringy handwriting on single-lined paper. He's now on first name terms with her. Who is Miseng? The hotel receptionists have no idea who has left the message. They rarely take note of people coming in and out of the lobby, unless their behaviour gives reason for concern.

Why is she being targeted? She knows nobody in Kuching except her grandfather. She has never set foot in Sarawak until now. Someone is trying to reach out to her. Therese is curious. She knows there are always bad individuals who stalk single females in a strange country, lure them to some isolated spot, rape and kill them, or sell them to brothels in a faraway land. But what if the sender of those notes comes in good faith? Therese's curiosity gets the better of her. She should probe further. After all, what could he do to her in broad daylight in one of the most prominent and busiest spots in town with hundreds of passers-by around? Therese has to get to the bottom of it all otherwise it is going to bother her for the rest of her stay. Grandpa Liu has told her never to go with strangers. A cautionary cliché, but there should be no harm in meeting the author of those notes at ten in the morning. She won't tell her grandfather though, lest he insist on her staying with him for the duration of her visit.

4

At nine-thirty the next morning, Therese walks to a jetty on the riverbank near the Courthouse. Across the river is the new imposing State Legislative Building looking like a huge golden pagoda. Perched unobtrusively on a low hill to its right is a relatively small white structure, Fort Margherita. Therese has read that it was a sentry post built in 1879 to guard the tidal stream as it enters Kuching. And further to the left of the State Legislative Building is The Astana.

Therese takes a tambang across the river to the landing closest to the State Legislative Building. Situated between The Astana and Fort Margherita, and dwarfing its two historically notable neighbours, the building looks all the more imposing and awe-inspiring close-up with its golden circular frame some nine floors high ending in an umbrella-shaped pinnacle. It has become the landmark of Kuching, visible from a good distance in all directions.

As she climbs up from the riverbank, Therese begins to feel self-conscious and apprehensive. She knows someone may be watching her, the stranger she's about to meet, the one about whom she has allowed herself to entertain a lot of curiosity. She feels a sudden rush of adrenalin. Perhaps she's on the brink of discovering something exciting, a ground-breaking story that would make a good feature article for her creative journalism course. Or her blog, at least!

At ten in the morning, many people are bustling in and out of the State Legislative Building, and a group of tourists, mostly Asian, converge outside listening to their guide's story about the grand building that was completed in 2009. Therese stands in the shade by the massive wooden door with its shiny brass embossments, watching everyone coming up to the entrance, studying particularly the faces of young men with darker complexions. Suddenly, close behind her, Therese hears a male voice.

"Hello!"

Therese feels goose bumps and immediately turns around to face a man in his mid- to late twenties, of medium build and height, with a lean and well-defined face, glossy black hair, which is short and spiky, brown skin, and wearing faded blue jeans and a black T-shirt with white lettering that says *Mau San Tourist Association*. On his feet are brown open-toe sandals. And he is wearing sunglasses… No doubt, he is the man in the *I love New York* T-shirt she saw at The Astana and whom she passed in the lobby of the Santubong that night. He is Miseng anak Rigop.

"Hi," Therese returns the salutation tersely, her wariness sounding in her tight voice.

"Thereese?" the young fellow asks, his thin lips curving into a disarming smile.

She winces at his excessively long "e". "The name is pronounced *Thérèse*. It's French." She sounds curt.

"My mistake, Therese," he corrects. "I'm Miseng. A pleasure to meet you." His English is not bad, spoken with an unidentifiable accent. He removes his sunglasses, revealing deep-set eyes that carry a somewhat wistful gaze. He offers his hand to Therese, who takes it rather reluctantly and gives it a quick shake. At least, his hand is not clammy, though it is a bit rough.

Therese remains guarded, giving the stranger a cold, disinterested glance. "Did you write those notes?"

"Yes. I wanted to meet you."

"How did you know my name?" Therese sounds almost hostile.

"Well, I had heard about your grandfather from both my father and grandfather, even though we've never had the opportunity to meet him. My folks said he had a granddaughter living in Canada. With what information I had, I hit your blog on the internet. You wrote that you were studying to be a writer or journalist and were visiting your grandfather in Kuching."

"Oh, a cyberspace stalker!"

Miseng betrays a hurt expression, as though he has been slapped in the face. He recovers almost immediately and then says in a defensive tone,

"Your blog is an open book, isn't it? Surely you want people to read it. Otherwise you wouldn't be posting it."

Therese looks annoyed. "I don't post things in my blog for people to stalk me."

"That's not my intention."

"And how do you know where I'm staying?"

"I knew from your blog that you'd be arriving some time on the 31st of July. I got your grandfather's address from the phone book, waited outside his house and followed his taxi to the airport on my motorcycle. I saw him meet you there. I recognized you from the photos online. Then I followed you to your hotel."

"You'd better have a good reason to go to all that trouble to contact me."

"I do." A moment of awkward silence. "If you don't mind, shall we walk while I explain everything?"

Therese is silent, which Miseng takes for consent. They proceed towards the open ground between the river and the State Legislative Building, where there is a constant flow of human traffic. Miseng looks back and points to the State Legislative Building. "This building is in the shape of a *baruk*, a Bidayuh headhouse. The Bidayuhs are the dominant native tribe around here. The Sarawak government honours us in constructing this building in the design of a baruk."

"Us? So are you Bidayuh?"

"Yes," he says assertively. "Do you know about the Bidayuhs?"

"I've read that the Bidayuhs are the Land Dayaks of Borneo who live in longhouses on slopes further inland, as opposed to the Ibans who are called Sea Dayaks because they live in longhouses near the rivers and coasts."

"You've done your homework!"

"So what is it you want from me?"

"Please do not be offended by what I am about to tell you because I have come with sincerity; my intentions are good and honourable. You see, you and I came from the same ancestors. We are cousins."

"How can you claim to be related to me? I'm Chinese!"

"You are Chinese with a little Bidayuh blood, and I'm Bidayuh with a bit of Chinese blood in me."

"I beg your pardon?"

"You and I are descendants of a Bidayuh woman and a Chinese man who married a hundred and fifty years ago. Later, the two sides of our family went different ways as a result of a terrible accident. Since then, we've had nothing to do with each other. Sad, isn't it?"

"I've never heard of this before from my father or grandfather. It's news to me that I have a Bidayuh ancestor. I'm not taking your word for it." Therese purses her lips.

Therese meets Miseng's eyes for the first time. There seems to be a transparency in them that bespeaks sincerity. But mastermind villains are good at that camouflage. She cannot trust him. She must not trust him.

"I can tell you what they say happened to cause the split," Miseng says. "It was something awful, but a long time ago, when your grandfather was very young."

Therese interrupts before he can go on. "OK, don't give me bullshit. I don't believe a word of what you say anyway. Just tell me what you want."

"I want the two sides of our family to reconcile. We were none of us involved then, and after all these years it's time to make peace and forgive."

"Why didn't you contact my grandfather yourself?"

"The tragedy resulted in so much bitterness between the two families that your great-grandfather vowed neither he nor his descendants would have anything to do with our side anymore. His son, who is your grandfather, grew up not having any contact with us at all. To avoid rejection and embarrassment, my folks have never tried to approach him. But I have a feeling that you can bring us together. We will be grateful if you will help us. Our ancestors will be grateful."

"I don't believe we share the same ancestors," Therese emphasizes. With a sceptical laugh, she adds, "You talk like your ancestors – not mine – could hear you."

"They can. I believe in their spirits. Our ancestors are our ghosts from the past. They are our beloved dead who protect us from harm." Miseng looks over to Therese. His eyes rest upon a green trinket hanging from a gold chain around her neck. "This that you are wearing, where did you get it?" He points to it with his eyes.

"The jade Buddha? It belonged to my Hakka ancestor who came from China. It was passed on to my father who gave it to me."

"There is a bark painting of my great-great-great grandmother in my longhouse. She was the one who married the Chinese immigrant back in the mid-nineteenth century. In that painting, she is wearing a gold chain with a jade Buddha, just like yours!" Miseng cannot hide the excitement in his voice.

"Very interesting. These objects have been around for centuries. It doesn't prove we are related, if that's your drift." Conscious that she has been terse, to the extent of being rude, which is not like her usual self, and curious about the stranger who has accosted her, Therese changes the subject, saying, "What do you do and where's your family now?"

"I am taking some computer courses at ICATS here in Kuching. It's a community college specializing in hi-tech studies. It's the internet that got me interested in tracing the Chinese side of our family. As for my family here, my father was chief assistant to the Pemanca in Bau – that's the head guy in Bau – until he retired a couple of years ago. My parents have a house in Bau. I have a sister who works in Bau and lives with my parents."

"Just how far is Bau from here?"

"Twenty-two miles through the Batu Kitang Bridge. No big deal to go there and back in a day. But in my grandfather's time, it'd take half a day to drive from Kuching to Bau, and at some point the car had to be rowed across the river on a raft."

I suppose going upriver into back country and visiting one of the Dayak longhouses would be quite an experience, muses Therese, letting down her defences.

"If you'd allow me, I can take you to my longhouse kampong," continues Miseng, as if reading her thoughts, "and you can see how my people live – their lifestyle hasn't changed from the way my ancestors lived – maybe with a few modern extras, like electric generators, better outhouses and cars. This will be great material for your writing. In fact, my parents and sister are back there this week to see my grandparents. My grandfather is ninety."

Therese looks at Miseng, betraying a glint of interest in her eyes. Miseng must have caught the weakness in her guard, for he goes on, "My longhouse is one of the oldest Bidayuh longhouses around here. The headhouse is quite impressive and was built over two hundred years ago. You can still see the original skulls from headhunting days. We've always been a peace-loving tribe. Our people killed only in self-defence."

"And chopped off the enemies' heads?"

"They were the trophies to prove one's manhood and bravery in the old days. Don't worry. We're civilized. Many Bidayuhs have moved to the cities to live and work. If someone wrongs us these days, we take him to court, not cut off his head! My father was chief assistant to the Pemanca in Bau, remember? And the Pemanca is Bidayuh too."

They have reached the riverbank, near the jetty where Therese alighted earlier from the tambang. The sun is very hot, the humidity extremely high. Beads of sweat trickle down Therese's forehead. Her blouse is sticking to her skin, trapping the circulation of air. Her mind wanders to the cooling sensation of a nice shower at the hotel.

"How often do you go back to your longhouse?" Therese asks, coming back to the reality of the fellow beside her.

"A few times a year. I rent a place in Kuching from a Chinese family during term, but over holidays I go back to my parents' house in Bau, and sometimes we all return to the longhouse, for sure during Gawai, our harvest festival."

They stand by the jetty and look out to the water traffic in the river, motorized boats chugging upriver, tambangs being rowed across.

"So peaceful, it seems nothing ever happens here," Therese observes.

"A lot of changes have taken place from the time of the White Rajahs," says Miseng. "We have a lot of history, but unfortunately the outside world doesn't know much about us. By 'we', I don't mean just us Dayaks, but Sarawakians as a whole, Chinese, Indians, Malays, as well as Dayaks and all the indigenous people in Sarawak."

"That's very true. Some of my friends back home didn't even know where Borneo was, let alone Sarawak."

"I would be very happy to show you my longhouse. I can really be of help to you in your research." Perhaps Miseng reiterates his offer once too often, for his words seem to have brought Therese back to the present.

"If I sounded rude, I'm sorry. But I don't believe you and your family to be my relations. You may have good intentions, but I'm not your cousin," she says decisively. "I will be busy with my grandfather while I'm here. I don't think I'll have time to see your longhouse. But thanks for your offer anyway." Looking at her watch, she adds, "I'd better go now."

Miseng twitches his lips, looking forlorn. Before they part, he hands Therese a small piece of paper. "I won't write you any more notes," he says, his voice lacking the gusto from before, "but here's my mobile phone number in case you change your mind."

5

Back in her hotel later that evening, Therese takes the manuscript her grandfather has given her from the desk drawer where she had placed it for safe keeping. She looks again at the title: *The Life and Times of Liu Hon Min by Mary Ann Warrick, as told to her by Liu Nan Sun*, turns a few of its pages, then goes back to the beginning and starts to read.

Liu Hon Min's ancestors migrated from Jiangxi Province to Guangdong in southern China in about the year 1278, when the Mongols chased the last Song emperor into the region, and settled in the village of Cheong Cuan in Dongguan County. They were known as Hakka, the term meaning guests, having moved to live in southern China from the north. They were farmers, growing mostly subsistence crops of rice, sweet potato and leaf vegetables. Some five hundred and fifty years later, Liu Hon Min's father and mother still continued the livelihood passed on to them.

The mid-nineteenth century was a time of civil strife, land shortages and increasing poverty in the rural regions of China. The Manchu Dynasty was in disarray and could do nothing to help the poor. In spite of the hardship in Hon Min's family, his father sent him to the village school until he was thirteen. Knowing how to read and write might become useful in later life, his father said. As he grew into adolescence, Hon Min, familiarly called Ah Min by all who knew him, worked on the family farm with his father. The yield was poor. They barely had enough to feed their household of six, which included Ah Min's three younger siblings, two brothers and a sister.

Their mother reared two pigs and some chickens to bring in more income.

Ah Min's best friend in the village was Lo Tai. His proper name was Liu An San, but because he was a year older Ah Min had always called him Lo Tai, an old friend and big brother.

"Ah Min, d'you want to get rich?" Lo Tai asked one day, when they were young men of nineteen and twenty.

"Of course, but how?"

"Some people were talking in the village hall about this place in Nanyang called Sarawak, on Borneo island. Lots of work in pepper plantations there. What's more, the place has gold mines. We could work for a few years there and earn enough money to come home rich."

"But where do you find the money to go?" Ah Min asked.

"There are brokers who contract workers to go and work as labourers. They pay for your passage, and you pay them back from your earnings with interest. And when you're off the hook and you've made your fortune, you can come home." Lo Tai paused a moment, and continued, "I want to pay for my own passage though, so I don't owe anybody anything, and I can come home any time. My pa said he could pay for my outward journey with his savings. I will pay him back, and more, when I come home. My folks won't have to work anymore when I am rich."

"We wouldn't have the money to pay for my passage. You are lucky to be able to go." Ah Min hesitated, and then asked, "But what about Ah Lan?"

At the mention of Ah Lan, Lo Tai nodded and said, "She's the one I'd hate to leave most, but I'm only twenty. I will come back in a few years and marry her."

For days, Ah Min thought a lot of what Lo Tai had said. If he went to Nanyang to work for some years, he could make a fortune and come back to a better life for himself and his family. If he stayed where he was, he would have no chance to improve his lot, or anyone else's. With so much poverty in the land, there was not much hope for them in Guangdong. However, if he were to go, it would have to be as a contract worker as he had no money to finance the trip. Ah Min voiced his thoughts to his father and mother. They were not happy with the idea of him being contracted to someone else, like a piglet sold in a market, they said, and so Ah Min did not bring up the subject again.

Then one day soon after, Ah Min's father said to him, "We have decided to send you to Nanyang as a free worker. We have the money to pay for your passage. Just work hard and when you have made your fortune, come home." When Ah Min saw the pigs missing, he knew his father and mother had sold them that he might go to Sarawak, a free man.

Liu Hon Min was nineteen when he left China in 1849 in search of fortune in Nanyang, the generic name for all the strange and exotic places of Southeast Asia at the time: Singapore, the Malay Peninsula, the island of Borneo and all the neighbouring islands of the South China Sea.

Before he set sail, his father handed him a large cloth pouch, saying, "Take this with you. The spirits of our ancestors will protect you on your way."

Ah Min opened the pouch and found inside three jars, one containing soil from his village, another a few small bones, which his father said belonged to an ancestor, and the third containing pebbles from the village stream. There was also a set of peasants' two-piece work clothes that had belonged to Ah Min's grandfather.

"When you arrive at your destination, dig a grave and bury these items in it. Mark it as the Liu Family Grave. It will remind you of your ancestral home in Tang Shan." Tang Shan was what everyone then called China, a name with an emotional overtone, full of patriotism and longing for the motherland.

Ah Min noticed the furrows on his father's face, deeply etched by the scorching sun under which he had sweated and toiled all his life. He bit his lip, and said to his father and his mother who was standing by, "I will come back, Pa and Ma, in a few years. Then we'll have a big ceremony at the temple to give thanks to my ancestors, and there will be stage performances to celebrate my homecoming. Firecrackers will be heard from afar and I will give a banquet for all our clansmen. I'll build a large house for you both and hire workers to work in the fields, so you will not have to toil anymore." Ah Min's father nodded, looking pleased.

Ah Min's mother took from her apron pocket a jade pendant in the shape of a Buddha on a gold chain and clasped it around his neck.

"Wear this all the time. Jade is good for the body, and the Buddha will protect and guide you on your way," she said, her voice on the point of breaking.

"I will always treasure it, Ma."

She then held out her broad-brimmed peasant hat, the kind with a black skirt at the back to protect the neck and nape and a hole at the top to fit the head.

"Take this with you too, my son," she said, crying. She then embraced Ah Min, holding on for the longest time.

"Don't get upset, I will come home in a few years and get married and give you a good daughter-in-law to wait on you and lots of grandchildren to hold." His mother smiled and cried all the more. She looked older than her years, her hair greying prematurely. Her hands felt rough and the heels of her unbound feet were heavily cracked. Ah Min's heart ached very much for her.

Ah Min's father and mother and his two younger brothers, Hon Yan and Hon Yee, and sister, Siu Chun, went with him to the wharf to send him off. His luggage consisted of a metal trunk secured with jute ropes and a canvas bag. His brothers helped lift the trunk onto his shoulder, while the bag hung across his chest to one side. He stepped carefully onto the wooden plank and walked to the moored river junk, turned slowly and smiled to his family. The heaviness in his heart was much greater than the weight of the trunk on his shoulder.

Ah Min saw Lo Tai saying farewell to his folks and to Ah Lan, his childhood sweetheart. Her eyes were swollen from crying. At least, Ah Min did not have that extra bond to make his departure all the harder. Lo Tai soon joined him on the deck. They waved relentlessly to the dear ones they were leaving behind on the shore until their images became too distant to make out. The junk meanwhile, with its sails spread, slowly meandered down the Pearl River to Hong Kong on the first leg of their voyage to Sarawak.

6

After five days of anxious waiting in Hong Kong, Ah Min and Lo Tai finally boarded the *Nam Wah*, bound for Singapore. It was a big three-masted junk with a large eye painted on each side of the bow, "the better to see her way", Lo Tai said. It was called a fish-eye boat, for good reason. The boat was packed with two hundred passengers, most of them ending their journey in Singapore, though a small number were also continuing on to Kuching, the big river town and capital of Sarawak.

They set sail from Hong Kong on March 3rd, 1849. March was the time of the north-east monsoon, which promised a favourable wind as they headed south-west on the South China Sea, past Hainan, Vietnam and on to Singapore. Their journey could last twenty to thirty days, or longer, depending on their luck with the weather gods. The first week, they had good weather, the azure sky matching the sapphire blue of the sea. Without contest, their boat cut a smooth path in the water, as it glided full sail in a running wind. They were never too far from land, they were told, in case they encountered a storm. Ah Min and Lo Tai slept on the deck, as deck space cost less than the cabin below, which was a big room for a lot of people. The decks were crowded too, but at least in the open space they had the salty air and sea breeze to disperse some of the stench of body odour and sweat, and the smell of vomit should it get rough.

They ate salted fish, salted egg and sun-dried vegetables with rice, which they cooked on the deck. Their only fresh vegetables were bean sprouts, germinated from the mung beans they had brought on board with them.

The bean sprouts provided nutrients to help prevent beriberi and scurvy, two of sailors' worst-feared curses.

"How long do you intend to stay in Sarawak?" Ah Min asked Lo Tai one evening at the bow, gazing into the dark unknown ahead. He had not probed that question to Lo Tai before, knowing there was really no definite answer. That night, however, he brought up the subject for he was suddenly struck with a desperate feeling of homesickness and needed some comfort, no matter how uncertain.

"Five years," answered Lo Tai, without hesitation. "In five years, I should have saved up enough to come home, marry Ah Lan, buy a farm and live comfortably off it. I'll only be twenty-five, still young." The finality of his answer was reassuring.

Ah Min had always admired Lo Tai's confidence. Lo Tai was a man of action, ready to take on risks. One time, when they were about twelve and thirteen, while walking from their village to a neighbouring Hakka village, they met three strange boys of about their age. Ah Min could tell they were Punti, locals from inland Guangdong, as they were not talking Hakka. These so-called Punti had lived in Guangdong for a long time, before the Hakka people had migrated from north and central China to the region. The Punti didn't like the Hakka, for they considered them usurpers of their land. That afternoon, the three local boys stopped Ah Min and Lo Tai at a plank bridge over a stream and refused to budge. Ah Min was ready to turn back, but Lo Tai straddled his legs in a fighting position, rolled up his sleeves, made fists with his hands, tossed his head, swinging his pigtail, and shouted, "Come, if you dare. We can handle all of you and more!"

Ah Min could not leave his friend there on his own, so he assumed a fighting stance as well. Two against three. Perhaps Lo Tai's brawny physique and confident bluff gave the somewhat scrawny local boys second thoughts, for they grudgingly stood to one side of the plank to let Lo Tai and Ah Min pass, both parties facing each other with threatening glares as their paths crossed.

Lo Tai's good build, with his rough country-boy features and tanned complexion, made him attractive to the girls of their village. But from his early teens, he had singled out Ah Lan and sworn secretly to Ah Min that he would take her as his wife some day. Knowing him, Ah Min was confident he would make good in Nanyang, come home in five years, as he had said, and marry her.

"We'll come home together," Ah Min rejoined.

Lo Tai gave him a gentle slap on the back. "For sure, we will. I won't leave you alone over there, ol' pal!"

Above their heads, the lantern swayed from the foremast, somewhat too vigorously for Ah Min's comfort, as the *Nam Wah* continued forward into the dark, unfamiliar void.

The next morning, the sky was a strange vermilion red. They were told a storm was brewing in the west, heading their way. Ah Min had no idea what to expect and could only hope for the best, while dreading the worst.

That same afternoon, the sun disappeared behind low, dark clouds. The sails were lowered. Then the rain started, and became heavier by the minute until the sound of it beating on the wood deck drowned all noise, except for the thunder that followed every streak of lightning. The boat was tossing from side to side as it plunged into the storm.

The waves were so high they came crashing down on the bow like a raging rapid. The deck was flooded and slippery, and people were slithering everywhere. The boat swayed so violently that Ah Min and Lo Tai tied themselves to a beam with the ropes from their trunks to prevent being tossed into the angry waters.

"Bet the folks in the cabin are glad they are down there," Ah Min said to Lo Tai during a momentary break between two plunging waves.

"I'd still opt for the deck no matter what," said Lo Tai. "I'd rather confront the storm this close, instead of waiting it out in a damp, stuffy cabin crammed with a lot of people, not knowing what's going on. If the boat capsizes, we will all go down, no matter where we are."

The rising and plummeting motion of the boat made Ah Min very sick. He was thankful to be on the deck, as his vomit was easily washed away by the pelting rain. After a while, all he expelled was a bitter green fluid. Lo Tai wasn't spared the ordeal either. His face was as white as the billows riding on the punishing waves.

The morning after the storm had struck, the winds gradually subsided, as did the swell. Naturally, nobody could cook during the storm, but Ah Min and Lo Tai couldn't have kept food down anyway. If any good came out of it, the rain gave them a much-needed bath, and they felt and smelled better after that. They also replenished a great part of their fresh water supply from the downpour. A couple of smaller storms lay in wait for them before they reached Singapore, but they had none of the ferocity of the first. In contrast, there were some days when there was not a breath of wind; the sails looked limp and lifeless, the boat was going nowhere. They prayed to the wind god to fill the canvas again.

They were thirty-seven days at sea before they reached Singapore and during this time there were two deaths on board, an old man and a young child who'd had a very high fever. They were lucky that no epidemic had broken out; the death count could then have been unimaginable. Still, many passengers fell ill during the passage, which given the privation was not unexpected.

By the time they reached Kuching, Ah Min and Lo Tai had been on the *Nam Wah* for forty-one days, including two days in port in Singapore.

7

As the *Nam Wah* sailed up the delta of the Sarawak River into Kuching waters, Ah Min stood on deck eager to take in all the sights, sounds and smells that confronted his senses. A couple of other seafaring junks were anchored in the deeper parts of the river downstream of Kuching; beyond these vessels the river narrowed and as the *Nam Wah* entered town, Ah Min could see quite clearly the buildings on both banks.

On the south bank were two-storey houses that appeared to be built mainly of wood, their upper floors extending over the wide walkways in front, shielding pedestrians from the tropical sun. They all had thatched roofing, which a deck hand said was made of *atap*, thatched nipah palm leaves. Below the south embankment, small boats used to transport passengers and goods between the anchored junks and Kuching town were moored on muddy shores.

Across the Sarawak River on the north bank, Ah Min noticed huts on stilts, some rooted in the land, others in the water; the same deck hand told him this was a Malay kampong. He then also pointed out to Ah Min a big house encircled by a wide verandah and stately pillars; it was shaded with palm trees and set apart on a mound from the kampong. This was The Grove, residence of James Brooke, the White Rajah, the English ruler of Sarawak, a spot from where he would have an excellent view of what was happening on the river. At that moment, the waterway was alive with sampans being propelled up- and downstream, and one vessel could be seen edging its way up from the delta to the anchorage below Kuching.

This then was the town Ah Min and Lo Tai had come to. Its oppressive tropical humidity and intense heat made their hot and sticky summers in southern China seem like a cool paradise. From the *Nam Wah*, Ah Min and Lo Tai took a sampan ashore to the waterfront, which was lined with a row of two-storey shophouses facing the river and referred to by the locals as the Main Bazaar. The smell of rotting fish and fruit, and stale human sweat, assailed their nostrils as they stepped onto the jetty. After so many weeks at sea the stench was almost overpowering. Leaving Ah Min to watch their belongings by the pier, Lo Tai went off on swaying legs to ask for work. There was no mistaking; Ah Min was a *sinkeh* fresh off the boat, a newly arrived Chinese labourer. As he stood there in his black farmer's jacket and pants, and farmer's hat, and with the metal trunks and bags beside him, he attracted many probing stares.

It seemed that most of the occupants of the Main Bazaar were Chinese. A few well-groomed men using the covered walkway across the street were attired in the businessmen's two-piece samfu, a collared jacket buttoned in front and loose-fitting pants. Most of the men working on the riverfront, however, were bare-chested, wearing wide-brimmed straw hats and rolled-up kung fu pants, while the women wore the peasants' black samfu, like the ones back home. There were some darker-skinned people, whom Ah Min later knew to be Malays, and a few bare-chested men scantily clad in loincloths, the local native Dayaks whose traditional homes he was told were in the forests inland, the towering rainforests of Borneo. A couple of these men had intricate tattoos the length of their arms, and all of them wore colourful, woven headbands or turbans. Vendors were selling a large, greenish aromatic spiky fruit and bunches of small bananas from big baskets at the pier. Coolies shouldering huge gunny sacks, some with one on each shoulder, made their way up from the moored boats to the shophouses, all the while giving loud and rhythmic heaving outbursts to ward off any thoughtless soul who might be standing in their way and thus break their momentum. Expressions of hardship and misery were etched on the faces of the labourers and their skin was dark from years of being in the unrelenting sun. If it were not for their facial features, and the pigtails the men wore, Ah Min would have mistaken them for the native people from the rainforests.

It was at least an hour before Lo Tai returned.

"The shopkeepers were not too friendly; I guess because I'm Hakka. They are mostly Hokkien and Teochew merchants. At least they can talk Hakka. I finally met one decent fellow outside his shop who gave me a bit more information. There's apparently plenty of work in rubber and pepper plantations not far from Kuching."

"What about the gold mines?"

"The mining town is called Mau San, about twenty miles from here. The miners are Hakka, mostly from Kalimantan, the Dutch side of Borneo." Lo Tai paused for a moment, looking intently at Ah Min. "You know. I want to try my luck at the mines. Besides, we'll be with our own kind."

"I'll go with you. We stick together," Ah Min said.

"That's what I want to hear, brother," Lo Tai said, slapping Ah Min on his back. "I also inquired about getting to Mau San. Apparently, we can't reach it by land, but need to take a boat upstream and get off at a riverside bazaar. Because we have luggage, I'm afraid from there we will need to get a horse and cart to take us on to Mau San."

"You're the leader, Lo Tai. Let's make our fortune and go home in five years."

"In five years!" Lo Tai replied, his face broadening into a grin.

They hired a boatman at the water's edge nearby to take them upstream in his tambang for the price of a salted fish left over from their sea journey; they had no money to pay him. The boatman happened to be a Hakka and said he was called Ah Choy. The tambang soon left Kuching behind and entered jungle country where rainforest lined both banks. The bare-chested Ah Choy, a tall, lean man in his forties or early fifties, was skilled in avoiding any debris that had fallen into the water as he stood in the stern of his boat and paddled against the current. Where the river narrowed, the trees overhanging the water gave them a little shade from the burning sun. In the shallows, Ah Choy used a long pole to push the boat along, but the water level was still quite high, as the rainy season had only recently ended.

Ah Min told the boatman they were from Dongguan, Guangdong, and were going to Mau San to find work in the gold mines.

"Gold mining is profitable but very hard work. I'm contented paddling my boat up and down river," Ah Choy said. "What I earn is just enough for three meals a day. No money to go back to Tang Shan."

"Have you sent news to your family in Tang Shan, or heard from them?" Lo Tai asked.

"In the first few years after I left, I sent a letter home every year, with a little money. It's not easy to send letters back and forth. I need to get someone to write them for me since I can't read or write. Then to post them I have to go to one of the shops in town that arrange for mail every few weeks to go to Tang Shan. I haven't sent a letter home in the last five years. I've only heard from my sister twice in the ten years I've been here. The first time was after she received my first letter with the money I'd sent home. The second time was when our ma died." Ah Choy was very quiet after that.

The tambang cut a smooth path through the meandering river. All the way upstream, fallen branches and the occasional dead trunk lay partially immersed in the shadowy water by the shoreline. Ah Min was enthralled by the densely layered leafy surroundings and the quietude of the rainforest broken only by the sound of the oar entering the water, the creaking of the boat and the barking of frogs on the banks, nothing that he had ever experienced in Tang Shan. He liked best the places where the river narrowed and the foliage almost touched above him forming a canopy. Then the river widened again exposing the blue sky, a few clouds and the scorching reality of the midday sun.

Five hours of paddling brought Ah Min and Lo Tai to the 16-mile bazaar. Ah Choy told them they were now in Hakka country, and they felt much more at ease. Tying up at the wooden jetty, he helped them ashore and shouldered one of the trunks, while Ah Min and Lo Tai carried the other and their bags between them as they walked up the slope towards the village. The 16-mile bazaar, with its strategic location on the river, was very busy. It had one main street lined with a row of some ten shophouses on each side. Ah Choy took them to the closest teahouse to inquire about transportation to Mau San and introduced them to a middle-aged man at the counter, a Mr Yong, the teahouse owner, who invited them to sit down and then called to an attendant to get the boatman some food. Ah Choy would spend the night in the 16-mile bazaar and return to Kuching the next day with a boatload of local produce for the town's traders.

"I can get a horse and cart to take you on to Mau San; that is easy," Mr Yong said. "But first, have something to eat here, for you must be hungry coming from Kuching."

"We have no local money," Ah Min said. "What do you accept for payment?" Ah Min could eat a cow, not having had anything since their morning meal of congee and salted egg on the *Nam Wah*.

"No need to pay. Any Hakka from Tang Shan is one of our own. I'm from Hoppu, Guangdong. I've been here for twelve years. I'll ask our cook to bring out some of our *kolo mee*. When in Sarawak, you must eat like the locals." That was their introduction to the tastiest noodles piled with a generous portion of spicy vegetables and pork.

"So you want to go to Mau San to work in the mines?" Mr Yong said, while they were waiting for the food. "Do you know anything about our mines?"

"We only know being a miner is hard but profitable work," Lo Tai said.

Mr Yong looked at them closely and asked in a slow, deliberate manner, "Have you heard the name Liu Shan Bang?"

Ah Min and Lo Tai shook their heads in unison.

"Liu Shan Bang is the headman of the miners' association in Mau San, called Twelve Kongsi. He's a very dynamic man, tall, strong, full of energy, and has good kung fu. He commands attention and respect wherever he goes. When you get to Mau San, ask for him. He will give you work, especially since you are his clansmen, same surname!"

By the time they'd finished their meal, Mr Yong had arranged for his son, Ah Keung, to take them to the mining town. They thanked their host and promised they would see him again the next time they passed by the 16-mile bazaar.

As Ah Keung urged the old and drawn brown horse in the direction of the mining town, Mr Yong called after them, "Remember the name, Liu Shan Bang!"

8

To Ah Min, Mau San was a dream town after having spent his life until then in his poor Dongguan village. Mau San Street, the main street, was lined with rows of wooden shophouses, as many as a hundred of them. Most were two storeys high and had thick atap roofs. Signs for teahouses and shops selling sundry goods hung from the front of the buildings and there were even a couple of inns for the wayfarer. At one end of the main street was a small temple, Tian Sze Lung Kung a plaque said. Not far from the temple stood a flagpole with a tall rectangular wooden base; a flag with the characters "Mau San Twelve Kongsi" was fluttering slowly, but high and proud, from its top in an almost imperceptible breeze. And in the background was Mau San, the mountain shaped like a flat-topped hat from which the mining town got its name.

Ah Min and Lo Tai arrived in the dimming daylight, but the town was still bustling with people. Men with pigtails, bare-chested, some in kung fu pants, some wearing only loincloths, walked about without shoes. There were very few women in sight. Perhaps night-time was when the men had fun and relaxed around town after a hard day's work at the mines, leaving the women folk to do domestic chores and mind the children at home.

Ah Min and Lo Tai checked in at the Mau San Inn for the night; there was not much else they could do at that hour. Again, they asked the innkeeper about payment, and again they received what they were beginning to perceive as customary Hakka hospitality in these parts. Upon learning they were

Hakka and recently arrived from Guangdong looking for work in Mau San, the innkeeper, a bespectacled greying man, bare-chested and wearing white shopkeeper's trousers with a wide belt, immediately told them they needn't pay until they had received their first wages. As he padded off in his black fabric kung fu shoes to show them a room, Ah Min started to wonder how far their Hakka ancestry could take them without costing them a cent. Such kindness was humbling.

Leaving their luggage in the room, Ah Min and Lo Tai stepped out of the inn to take in some of the local colour of Mau San before turning in for the night. After all, this was going to be *their* town for the next five years. The air had cooled a little and seemed less humid with the setting sun. The atmosphere was actually quite pleasant. Lo Tai had taken off his jacket and went shirtless and barefoot to be like the rest of the men in town. All he needed now was to replace his work pants with a loincloth, which no doubt he would do as soon as he could lay his hands on one. Ah Min kept his samfu and peasants' sandals on, which attracted a number of stares. As for wearing a loincloth, he thought it would take him a while, if ever, before he might feel comfortable in one.

They had walked just about ten steps from the inn entrance when a man called to them from behind. They turned and waited for him to approach.

"Where are you fellows from?" the young man, about their age, asked as he caught up with them.

"Guangdong Dongguan," Ah Min said, voicing his province and county in one breath.

"I'm Chee Ted Fook, from Guangdong Hoppu, like many of us here. Just call me Ah Fook – most people do," he said, his friendly disposition immediately setting Ah Min at ease. He was a tall man for someone from southern China, with a broad chest and muscular arms, probably acquired from working in the mines although he seemed generally of better build than the other men Ah Min had seen so far in town. He too was wearing a loincloth.

They walked down Mau San Street together that night, Ah Fook pointing out the different buildings to them. At the other end of Mau San Street from the temple, between two small but steep hills, was a big two-storey wooden house. It commanded a good view of the entire main street and all the activities taking place there.

"This is our *kongsi* house. See how hard this wood is?" Ah Fook tapped on the external wall of the clan house. "It's belian. We call it ironwood and it's very durable. Even the roof is made of belian shingles. Those of us without wives sleep inside the kongsi house. The married ones live in separate huts nearby."

"Are there many married miners?" Lo Tai asked.

"Most are not. Some left their wives back in Tang Shan. There are no brothels here either. Not allowed by the Kongsi. It's a pretty lonely life, with no women to keep our feet warm at night." Ah Fook chuckled. "A few ended up marrying native girls. They're not bad. In fact, some are quite comely."

"We want to meet your headman, Liu Shan Bang," Ah Min said, recalling what Mr Yong, the teahouse owner in the 16-mile bazaar, had told them.

"Tai Ko? Sure, you'll see him in the morning. He lives in the kongsi house too. He goes to bed very early, gets up at four."

"We heard he's a good leader and a big, strong man," Lo Tai said.

"He's fair, but his laws are very strict. And yes, he's strong. He practises his kung fu before he goes to the mines every day."

They had come to a big hut brightly lit on the outside with lanterns hanging from wooden beams. Light shone from open windows and the loud chatter of excitement, occasional guffaws and clattering of tiles could be heard coming from inside. Ah Min and Lo Tai peered in. There were two rectangular tables around which some men sat while others stood, but all eyes were intent on the small tiles, each the length of an index finger, spread out upon the tables.

"*Pai gow*," said Ah Fook. "Gambling."

"Do all the miners here gamble?" Ah Min asked.

"Just about, and they smoke opium. What else is there to do for entertainment and excitement when there are so few women around?"

"Do you? Gamble and smoke opium?" Ah Min pursued.

"I do a bit of this and a bit of that. We've got to, to be a part of the group and keep us from going crazy. I'll take you to all the joints, once you are properly settled."

"I'd like to try my luck at gambling," said Lo Tai, looking interested. "Who knows, Ah Min, we may end up making a bigger fortune and going back to Tang Shan sooner than we think!"

Ah Min looked unsure.

By then they had walked the length of Mau San Street and were back at the inn.

"I'll meet you here at four tomorrow morning and take you to see Tai Ko," Ah Fook said.

9

They saw him in the pre-dawn grey hours, brandishing a Chinese sword in exercise manoeuvres on the playground behind the temple, his long queue swishing left and right, back and forth like a weapon. He was a man of imposing stature, over six feet in height and of a handsome build. It was too dark to see his face, but his movements radiated strength and vitality. This, then, was the respected headman, Liu Shan Bang.

The three of them, Ah Fook, Lo Tai and Ah Min, stood in the dark shadows beneath a palm tree, unwilling, and afraid, to disturb him. When he finally ended his morning routine, they emerged under the lightening sky, led by Ah Fook, and approached. Ah Fook introduced Lo Tai and Ah Min.

"Welcome to Twelve Kongsi," Liu Shang Bang said. Once he started talking, he did not seem as intimidating as he had at first looked. There was a sincerity and spontaneity in his manner that put them all at ease. "Now that you are here, you are part of our family, for we are all Hakka, no matter whether we are of the same clan, from the same village, county or city. We look out for one another. You'll be initiated into Twelve Kongsi in the kongsi house. Have you seen the kongsi house?"

"Only from the outside," Ah Min said.

Liu Shan Bang walked back the length of the main street with them. When they reached the entrance of the house, he told Ah Fook to show them the inside and to make sure they had their morning meal before going to the mines.

The interior of the clan house was as spacious as it looked from the outside. In the centre was an altar, its front facing the main entrance. The chief deity honoured was Tai Pak Kung, the patron saint of Chinese pioneers. Plaques with names of pioneers were hung around the altar.

"This is where you'll be initiated into Twelve Kongsi," said Ah Fook, pointing to the altar.

On either side of the altar was a big room filled with bunks, each with a curtain around it.

"And I suppose this is where we sleep," said Lo Tai.

"Yes, and smoke opium too," added Ah Fook.

"What's on the upper floor?" Ah Min was curious, as it was obvious from the outside that the house was on two levels.

"Storage," Ah Fook replied. "Weapons."

"Weapons?"

"Yes. For our protection. You never know."

In the days following, Ah Min and Lo Tai joined other miners in digging ditches in the valleys of the hilly terrain. Wearing only loincloths, with the burning sun on their bare skin, their bodies drenched in sweat, they engaged themselves in the back-breaking toil of digging and shovelling, carving out gulleys which they flooded with water from reservoirs formed by a series of dams built across the valleys. Gates had been built into the dams to let the water out. The water brought with it the soil that contained the gold ore. As the earthy slurry moved down the gulleys, the gold sank to the bottom. Every three months, the miners cleaned out the ditches, removing the soil with its dirt and gravel, leaving the heavier gold at the bottom. The first time Ah Min and Lo Tai took part in collecting the sunken gold from the base of these channels, all the hardship they had borne since being at the mines was forgotten.

"At this rate, we'll strike our fortune in no time!" said Lo Tai with excitement, staring at the gold collected.

"We may be able to go home sooner than we think," Ah Min said, beaming eagerly.

No doubt, it was excruciatingly painful labour, building dams and gates, and digging ditches, but the reward was great. The camaraderie and cooperation among members of Twelve Kongsi made the hardship easier to bear, and the high earnings they shared from the sale of the gold, which Twelve Kongsi conducted directly with Sambas in Kalimantan, made it all worthwhile.

After a hard day's work, Ah Min and Lo Tai relaxed with the other miners in an outdoor shed by the kongsi house; this was also where they ate their meals. Mau San was self-sufficient. Some of the inhabitants grew rice and vegetables as cash crops, and some raised pigs and chickens; there was little they needed from elsewhere. Ah Min was one of the early sleepers, staying away from gambling and opium. He had moments when he felt the itch to take a puff at that wondrous pipe, or try his luck at pai gow, the game which could make or break a family fortune, a game which depended on luck, skill and instinct. But then when he thought of his father and mother back in Tang Shan selling the family pigs to raise money for his passage to Nanyang, the impulse passed and he was able to climb through his curtains and fall asleep.

Lo Tai regularly indulged in pai gow. In the beginning, he had some luck, which spurred him on to higher stakes. Most nights, he would come back to the kongsi house in the company of Ah Fook long after Ah Min had turned in. As time went by, Ah Min could sense that Lo Tai was more often than not now losing, as he sulked and refused to answer when Ah Min asked about his luck. Yet, he continued to gamble, confident it would provide a shortcut to fortune and a fast passage home to Tang Shan.

Soon after they settled in Mau San, remembering his father's bidding, Ah Min, with the help of Lo Tai, found a small clearing in the forest at the foot of a limestone hill where they could dig a deep hole. In it he placed the pouch his father gave him before he left Tang Shan containing the pebbles from their village stream, the soil from their field, the bones of their ancestors and the clothing that had been his grandfather's. To this, Lo Tai added pieces from the bamboos that grew behind his farmhouse in their village and a tin containing the dried pits of longan fruit from his family's trees. Ah Min had never seen that softer side to Lo Tai's temperament before, the importance he placed in the yield of his home soil, the earth of his ancestors. Neither did he know he had the items in his luggage. They covered the hole again with earth and erected a temporary wooden sign which read, "Liu Family Grave". In time, Ah Min had a proper gravestone cut, with the designated words engraved on it. And every year they were in Mau San, Ah Min and Lo Tai paid their respects at the grave, remembering their ancestors in Tang Shan. They burned incense and paper money, and placed fruit on the ground during the Ching Ming Festival in the spring and the Ghost Festival in the seventh month.

By the end of 1849, Ah Min had saved up a good sum of money to send home. For a sizable fee, a trader passing through Mau San took the money and a letter Ah Min had written to a shop in Kuching which acted as a forwarding agency for mail to China. The wait for a boat leaving Kuching for Singapore could be as long as a month and the onward sea journey from Singapore to China could take another two. In all, it might be three months for a letter from Nanyang to reach its destination. Ah Min was grateful that his father had sent him to school for several years, for he could write his own letters and didn't need someone else to do so for him, as was the case with many of the Mau San miners. He smiled to himself as he imagined his father and mother eagerly opening his letter with his brothers and sister watching, and finding money inside. Then one of his brothers – for they too had gone to school in their early years and like him were literate – would read its contents to his anxiously waiting parents.

10

Every morning as dawn broke, Ah Min and Lo Tai would leave the kongsi house after a meal of rice with meat and vegetables prepared by some of the women at Mau San. It was a good twenty-minute walk to the quarry from the town on a small dirt road. One of the frequent companions on their walk to work was a Bidayuh native called Joto. The Bidayuhs were Land Dayaks and were distinguishable from the Ibans, who were Sea Dayaks, because they lived further inland on hill slopes away from the river. Joto was a year younger than Ah Min, about eighteen when they first met. Surprisingly, he spoke decent Hakka. He said he learned it from his contact with Hakka migrants from an early age. In fact, he said his whole family understood and some spoke fairly good Hakka. His longhouse was on a hill about sixteen miles from Mau San in the rainforest on the north side of the river, too far to travel from daily, so he stayed with the miners in the kongsi house and only went home when he had a few days' rest from work.

"Come with me on one of my trips home. My mother and sisters will like meeting you," Joto said once when they were walking back to Mau San from the mines at the end of the day.

"I'd like very much to see your longhouse and meet your family," Ah Min said politely. However, ever since he had met Joto, something had been bothering him at the back of his mind. "Joto, does the Bidayuh tribe head hunt?" He had heard from other miners that headhunting was a practice with the Dayaks.

"The Ibans still indulge in headhunting," said Joto. "But headhunting is no longer practised among my people, except if we are attacked and then we might do it in self-defence. Don't you worry about that," Joto laughed. "Your head is safe with us! I'd like you to come to my longhouse and experience Bidayuh hospitality."

Ah Min promised he would.

Sometimes, Joto's sisters, Enti and Jinot, travelled from their longhouse to Mau San and brought their brother fresh produce from the jungle and food prepared the Bidayuh way, which he missed in Mau San. His sisters usually stayed overnight with one of the married Bidayuh miners' families. Quite a few times, Ah Min and Lo Tai were invited by Joto to share the food his sisters brought. They never declined. Ah Min particularly liked the chicken cooked in bamboo. Once, Enti and Jinot brought a fermented pork dish called *tekesom*. Its smell was awful, but the taste was delicious.

Joto was the oldest of the family's children; Enti was seventeen and Jinot just fifteen. The girls both wore what they called a *jomuh*, a black cloth wrapped around the body, reaching to the calf, and tucked above the chest below the underarm. Their long hair was tied up at the back into a tidy bun. There was a mature disposition in Enti's beauty, the well-defined features of her face expressing determination and confidence. Though a year younger than Joto, she acted like a big sister, pampering and caring for her two siblings. Jinot was sweet and cheerful, with dark, round eyes, dimpled cheeks and a captivating, demure smile. Her shyness and reserve were perhaps due to her being still so young. Lo Tai said if it were not for Ah Lan, he would be chasing after one of them. They spoke Hakka, though not as well as Joto. In appreciation for the food they brought Joto, which Lo Tai and Ah Min had been able to share, Ah Min gave Enti and Jinot each a little Chinese ceramic teacup he had brought with him from Guangdong. Dayaks loved Chinese ceramics, Ah Min had been told, and Bidayuhs, being Land Dayaks, were no exception. Enti and Jinot were delighted to receive the gifts. Jinot studied the mountain and river scenery on her teacup with great interest.

"China?" she asked, pointing to the design.

"Yes, the mountains and rivers in China are very beautiful, like in the picture," Ah Min said. She looked impressed.

Later, when they were alone, Lo Tai said to Ah Min, "Don't tell me you are sowing seeds. Hoping for a good harvest?"

"An act of thoughtfulness does not need a hidden motive," Ah Min defended himself, sounding cross with his old friend.

11

"I stayed up till very late last night, Grandpa, to read about the life of your great-grandfather – well, my great-great-great grandfather, and I'm still far from the end," says Therese.

"I see my guerrilla story will have competition," replies Grandpa Liu, smiling. "Good thing I found the manuscript and took it with me to Kuching. You'll have to tell me all about it when you finish."

"I promise I will read it to you, Grandpa. But first I want to hear your story. Just so I don't miss anything, I'll let you speak into my recorder with as little interruption as possible. You can pretend you are talking to a bigger audience. Let's begin," says Therese. She settles on a sofa beside her grandfather and puts her mini tape recorder on the coffee table. "So what made you join the communists, Grandpa?"

Looking self-conscious at the sight of the recording device, Liu Ka Ming clears his throat, and begins. "I first learned about communism in the Chinese secondary school I attended in Kuching. It was the Fifties, the decade after the civil war in China that ended in the communist victory and establishment of the People's Republic of China. I entered Nanyang University in Singapore in 1959. The three years I was there did a lot to mould and firm up my sympathy for the communist cause in Sarawak. The third and last White Rajah, Charles Vyner Brooke, had handed Sarawak to Britain after the Japanese surrendered at the end of the Second World War. Sarawak became a British crown colony in 1946.

"At Nanyang University, I went to secret meetings of students and teachers, usually held in someone's attic. We expounded our views on a social order built on communist ideals, and discussed ways and means to promote and spread communist thoughts and ideology in Singapore, Malaya, Sarawak, North Borneo and Brunei. For the students from Sarawak who attended those meetings, our political cry was to achieve independence for Sarawak from British sovereignty, to establish a democratic society based on socialist principles and eventually to make Sarawak into a communist independent state."

"How did you end up being a communist guerrilla?"

"To answer that question, I have to tell you about my friend Bong Lip Ngan. I met Bong, a second-year economics student, at one of the secret meetings. He had a girlfriend who also attended the meetings. Her name was Lai Fong Li, a pretty, quiet young woman who seemed to be following Bong everywhere, whether out of insecurity and shyness or just plain attachment to him I wasn't sure. Bong and Li, as she liked to be called, graduated in 1961, a year before me, and returned to Sarawak.

"The day before they left for Kuching, we met at a Chinese restaurant in Singapore's Chinatown for a farewell dinner. But it turned out to be more than that. The afternoon newspaper arrived, and the news was devastating: Tunku Abdul Rahman, the Prime Minister of Malaya, had proposed the formation of Malaysia, to be made up of Malaya, Brunei, North Borneo, Sarawak and Singapore. If such a federation were to materialize, our dream of an independent communist state of Sarawak would be crushed completely.

"I saw Bong and Li a couple of times in Kuching when I went home to Buso in November that year for my father's birthday. At Bong's urging, I joined him and some four thousand others at a rally in Kuching against the colonial government's passing of a law which gave the government the authority to exile anyone considered a threat to the security of the colony. We all knew the British imperialists were actually targeting the communists, trying to deport anyone who had a part in propagating communism. My father was upset when he learned that I was at the rally. At the time, I assured him that I'd been dragged there by a friend. He was relieved when I returned to Singapore to finish my studies. I graduated in the spring of 1962 and came home. By then, I had secretly joined the SCO, the Sarawak Communist Organization, the official voice for communists in Sarawak.

My father didn't know. It was a matter of time before I would do my part to fight for the cause of communism in Sarawak.

"In Kuching, I got a teaching position at Ling Tao Middle School, my old secondary school, and rented a place in the city, since my home in Buso was too far to commute from every day. School was in recess in November for two months and would reopen on the 2nd of January 1963. But a month earlier, on the 8th of December, the rebel force in Brunei that was opposed to the formation of Malaysia staged a coup against the Sultan of Brunei. The coup had the support of insurgents from Kalimantan, the Indonesian side of Borneo. Indonesia was strongly opposed to the formation of Malaysia, for a Malaysian Federation would reduce Indonesian influence in the region. The coup was crushed within days, defeated by the combined forces of British troops deployed from Singapore and the band of local native recruits who supported the colonial government.

"To prevent any communist insurrection within Sarawak after the Brunei uprising, the colonial government arrested members of the SCO who were considered to be a threat to the political stability of the colony. Within a month of the Brunei coup, a hundred people accused of communist activities in Sarawak had been locked up.

"On Christmas Day 1962, Bong met me at a *kopitiam* in Kuching's Main Bazaar. We sat in the far corner of the old coffee shop by the back door. He looked tense, not like his usual confident, cheery self.

"'The situation looks bad for anyone black-marked as a commy activist,' he said to me. 'I know I'm one, for I was a noisy protestor at the rally last November. And I have recently taken up the post of assistant editor of the *Sun Wah Pao*. The government has already banned a few commy papers, so it's just a matter of time before they close this one. This is what colonial democracy is all about. Many members of our Party have gone underground to avoid arrest. They have actually crossed into Kalimantan. The time of trying to reach our goal of turning Sarawak into an independent communist state by peaceful, constitutional means is gone. We have to resort to arms.' The next thing Bong said was to turn my world completely around. 'I've arranged for an Indonesian guide to take me across the border near Serikin, New Year's Eve.'

"'Has it come to this?' I asked, with great agitation.

"'And one more confession,' Bong said, ignoring my question. 'Li and I were secretly married two days ago. We decided to marry in a hurry because it would be difficult for her to come with me unless she were my wife.' He laid a hand on my arm, and said, 'Come with us, and fight for our cause.'

"I was silent for an eternity. My nerves were on edge with the idea of placing myself in harm's way; the thought of the danger I might face in armed combat frightened me. But what kind of a man would I be if I were to shrink from personal sacrifice in defence of my ideology for the common good? Finally I said to Bong, 'I've actually been waiting to take on a more active role in our struggle. I should act on it. Better now than never. Here's to freedom and equality in Sarawak!'

"'Meet me at the 7th Mile petrol station, next to the Chinese temple, on the 31st,' Bong said, very pleased. 'Be there at 6 p.m. and a car will take us to Serikin. We'll cross the border together.'"

12

"I went home to Buso for the Christmas holidays, but returned to town the morning of New Year's Eve. I had told my parents earlier that I would be celebrating it with friends near 3rd Mile and needed to make a head start in case the river traffic got busy. I stole a last glance at my mother, who was busy opening up a durian on an old newspaper on the kitchen floor, while my father was watering potted plants by the kitchen window.

"'Want some durian before you go?' she asked, without looking up.

"'I'm fine, Ma. See you soon,' I said.

"'Be careful, son. Don't drink too much,' she said.

"'I'll be careful. Happy New Year, Pa, Ma,' I said. Looking from my father to my mother, I added quickly, 'You two are the best,' and left the house without saying more. Another moment and I would betray myself.

"I took a tambang downriver from Buso to Lorong Dock at the Kuching waterfront. I walked to my rented room in the Main Bazaar to retrieve a backpack in which I had left some clothing and essentials, including a pair of hiking boots and rain gear. I was early for my meeting with Bong and Li, and I was hungry, so I stopped at a kopitiam across from the bus terminal for some *kuey teow*. It might be a long time before I could taste these noodles again, if ever. That was my mindset for what I was about to embark on; the revolution, a time to live in the service of my people, my homeland of Sarawak, and a time to die if I had to in defence of my political beliefs. At twenty minutes past five, I took a taxi to the 7th Mile Chinese temple. I then walked over to the petrol station, staying back from the road so as not to be seen by motorists. Bong and Li were not there yet. It was now a quarter to six and still daylight. Sunset would not be for another hour. I waited behind the garage building.

"A little after six, a small black car drove up. Bong got out. I immediately emerged from my cover to greet him. He opened the rear car door and motioned to me to get in. He took the front passenger's seat. Li was in the back, beside me. The driver was a Chinese man, early thirtyish. We did not say much as the car sped in the direction of Serikin and eventually came to a riverbank. The driver got out and walked over to a small hut by the dock. A man appeared and after some negotiation indicated that we should get the car onto the raft which was tied to the dock. It was by then about six forty-five. We soon crossed the river and continued on towards Serikin. The traffic was light, it being New Year's Eve; most people were getting ready to ring in 1963. The sun would be setting soon. Our little black Austin was doing forty miles an hour on the unpaved road.

"We passed Siniawan, but did not stop, and carried on towards Bau, bypassing it shortly after seven. When we came to the intersection where the road to Serikin cut a side road to Lundu, our driver stopped and let us out to relieve ourselves. I had no idea how much he knew of our plan, but it was obvious he was on our side. After this break, Li offered us some pork buns, which we ate while we bumped our way along the packed earth. I was thankful for them, for I was hungry. We finally reached Serikin shortly before eight. By now, it was dark and we got out of the car with our backpacks on the outskirts of the town. The driver at once turned round and drove back the way he had come. We were alone at the edge of a forest, the lights of Serikin were ahead, and just about a mile beyond the town was the border with Indonesia's Kalimantan."

13

Therese turns off the recording device. "You have such a good memory, Grandpa, recollecting so much detail and what was actually said. I don't know how you could remember all this."

"When they are important events that change your life forever, you remember them. I can't recall the conversations word for word, but the essence is there."

Seeing signs of fatigue around his eyes, Therese says, "Shall we call it a day?"

"Just a little more." It seems once Grandpa Liu starts reminiscing, the memories feed on each other and he becomes more articulate, as though he is dictating a memoir.

"That night, a skinny, bearded Indonesian met us in a shophouse near the far end of Serikin and took us across the border, following small tracks through the jungle to avoid the checkpoints and barbed wire fencing on the Sarawakian side. Crossing the stretch of no-man's land before reaching the Indonesian side was nerve-wracking. Once we had left Serikin behind, we were in the darkness of the forest, relying on our guide ahead to lead the way. Moonlight shone through where the trees thinned overhead and lit up the occasional muddy puddle on the path. The jungle was creepy at night, lots of eerie animal sounds, and we constantly feared being detected by the Sarawakian border patrol. It made the trek seem much longer. A jeep was waiting for us just beyond the Kalimantan border and we clambered gratefully aboard. The

Indonesian driver set off for Singkawang on the edge of the South China Sea, seventy miles to the south-west on more bumpy unpaved roads.

"Singkawang was a small town populated mostly by Hakka. It was one of the main locations used to train members of the SCO for armed insurgence against the British colonial government and, later, the Malaysian. There were about fifty of us from Sarawak when we first joined the camp. We were in our prime, none of us older than thirty, and this was to be our home for the next few months while we were trained in the use of arms and learned communist dogma. Wearing our jungle green uniforms, we proudly swore an oath of allegiance to the SCO, pledging unconditionally to fight for the freedom of Sarawak. We pledged never to yield under any danger, threat or torture, and never to betray the Organization or the communist cause, to the point of death. We studied the thoughts of Mao Zedong so that we could spread its ideology; to me, communism was the only way to democracy and equality for the people. I was ready to sacrifice my life for the communist ideals. The intensity of my fervour was not to be abated.

"At our first training session, the commandant, a member of the SCO, a Hakka from Lundu, addressed us new arrivals with stern but rallying words. 'You are joining the guerrillas in the armed struggle against the establishment of Malaysia, and ultimately to form an independent communist-controlled Sarawak,' he said. 'Life as a guerrilla is very harsh. You will be living in the jungle, where it's hot, wet, muddy, and full of insects and diseases. Food will be short, sometimes there'll be none. Our connection to the outside will be very limited. You will be cut off from your family and friends.' I remember him pausing and looking at us before he continued, 'You will confront the enemy. There will be casualties and you will witness your comrades being injured and killed. Most of the time you won't be able to help them, even though you may want to try. Injury or death often occurs unexpectedly. If and when death does come to you, it will most likely be agonizing. Know what you are in for, the commitment and sacrifice you are making. But the end will justify the means. We will eventually be victorious, and we will establish communism as the basis of an independent Sarawak, for ourselves and for future generations. In striving to attain your goal, you will have reached the ultimate level of humanity.'

"Life was very harsh in the camp. The jungle was a breeding ground for various diseases, and in the first months after our arrival there were several cases of scrub typhus, the victims bitten by infected mites. The equatorial temperatures coupled with the humidity made daily living almost unbearable, especially since we were outdoors most of the time. We were constantly soaked in sweat, a round-the-clock steam bath, and were always picking off leeches. Sunstroke, heat exhaustion and muscle cramps were common. The risk of heatstroke was ever present because of the long periods we spent in the sun and the exertion of our training. The danger of heatstroke hit home two weeks after we'd been at the camp when one of our comrades, a twenty-two-year-old from Serian, collapsed one afternoon marching in the sun; he was in a coma and never regained consciousness. He died that evening, and we buried him in a plot at the camp.

"We slept in three wooden houses fitted with tiers of bunk beds. There were only five women in the camp, two of whom were married. Li was one. The three single women slept at the end of one of the houses, their bunks separated from the men's by the married couples' section. The married couples had the privacy of a partitioned double-width bunk. In spite of the hard life, Li seemed happy to be where Bong was. In addition to her military training and indoctrination she readily accepted her duties in the communal kitchen, helping to prepare the meals for everyone in the camp. In those early days, while food was never abundant, it was nutritious. We had rice with vegetables from our own gardens, tapioca and sweet potato, wild ferns from the jungle and occasionally fish from the coast. The water from the nearby streams carried parasites and was not drinkable, so we relied on rainwater mainly and collected it in a big cistern at the camp. Still, there were times when it came down to a choice of heatstroke from dehydration or dysentery from unclean stream water. There were several cases of dysentery at the camp during those training months; most survived but it left them weakened. I do remember one comrade dying while at Singkawang.

"'This is not much of a honeymoon for you two,' I said to Bong and Li one evening when we were sitting outside our quarters.

"'I'm happy to be with Bong, and his place is here, preparing for the revolution,' Li said.

"'We are fighting for a better society for ourselves and for future generations,' Bong added. 'Li thinks like I do. That's why she married me.'

"'Your children will have a good life because of your sacrifice,'" I said.

"More comrades joined us in Singkawang in the first quarter of 1963," Grandpa Liu continues. "Some crossed the border at Tebedu into Entikong in Kalimantan. Others came by the sea route, sailing from the coast north-west of Lundu to Tamajok, in West Kalimantan. Not all who tried to cross into Kalimantan were successful; some were caught and arrested before reaching the border. In May 1963, Indonesian military personnel took over our training, teaching us the use of weaponry, tactics and the strategy of guerrilla warfare. By then, we were about a hundred and fifty strong, mostly men, with a handful of women, mainly from the SCO. Our region of operation was to be along the border of the First Division in Sarawak.

"In July, recruits who had been in Singkawang for six months or more were moved to other camps. Bong, Li and I were among those transferred to Asu Ansang, near the northern tip of West Kalimantan, close to the border with Sarawak and only about sixteen miles from Lundu. The camp was at the foot of Mount Asu Ansang in a region of rainforest laced with winding rivers.

"By the time the Federation of Malaysia was formed in September 1963, we were ready for action. The aim of the combat wing of the SCO was to establish centres for guerrilla operations in Sarawak from which to expand territorial control. Our role was at first mainly to propagate communist ideology and recruit more guerrillas, and to carry equipment and act as guides in border raids conducted by Indonesian-led anti-Malaysian forces. Even though we were not initially active in the raids, our roles were still dangerous and we were always on the alert for a possible ambush by the enemy: the joint Malaysian and British defence force. Since the formation of the Malaysian Federation, the Commonwealth forces in Sarawak consisted mainly of Gurkhas, with some Malaysian troops from the Peninsula. The defence force also had a lot of support from the native population.

"Before our first real incursion into Sarawak, I took part in border crossings to talk to locals at border settlements and distribute propaganda material. We had cut a track through the jungle from Bukit Lomit on the

Indonesian side across the border three miles to the east of Lundu. Most of the border communities spoke Hakka. The locals were very hospitable to us, regarding us as their own kind, and offered us food to take back to camp. We never accepted anything without payment, a strict protocol among us Chinese communists. We always paid the villagers and were grateful for what we were given. Food was always a concern in the jungle. Speaking to the villagers to convince them of the good days ahead under a communist government was important, and we targeted their young people as possible guerrilla recruits.

"On a few occasions, we were tipped off by local youths acting as lookouts for us and we'd disappear back into the jungle to cross into Kalimantan ahead of any approaching Malaysian and British troops. Once, we were almost ambushed. A farmer we met soon after we'd got into Sarawak recognized us as having been at his bazaar earlier, where we'd left propaganda leaflets and bought a number of provisions. He told us he'd seen about twenty Malaysian soldiers just a mile ahead, a quarter mile from his bazaar; they'd left their jeeps and set off eastwards into the jungle with weaponry, including a machine gun. We'd be walking into their line of fire. We wasted no time in making our way back across the border.

"From September 1963 to March 1964, the Chinese guerrillas continued to provide support to the Indonesian forces. We had little weaponry of our own and relied on the Indonesian military for a minimal supply of guns and ammunition. The situation changed in April 1964, when we were moved again, this time to a camp of some sixty guerrillas near Entikong in the rainforest which straddled the border into Sarawak, close to Tebedu.

"We were ready for our first real armed insurgence."

14

Ah Min and Lo Tai had been in Mau San for a year when there was a big migration of Hakka miners from Kalimantan. They came with their families to escape the kongsi war with the Dutch south of the border. They asked Liu Shan Bang for asylum and for work in the mines. Liu Shan Bang never forgot his own migration from Kalimantan twenty years earlier, in 1830, when he led his fellow workers across the border into the Mau San area when they too had been driven north because of kongsi rivalries. He welcomed these newcomers and invited them to stay and work in the mines of Mau San. By the end of 1850, the population had grown to about four thousand and more women were seen about town.

One of the miners lately arrived from Kalimantan whom Ah Min and Lo Tai befriended was a Hakka from Guangdong Hoppu called Lai Kee Chok. In his mid-thirties, he was older than Ah Min and Lo Tai and lived in one of the atap-roofed timber huts that were built to accommodate newcomers, most of whom had brought their families with them. He invited Ah Min and Lo Tai several times to his home for supper, cooked by his young wife, Ah Moi. They especially enjoyed her *lui cha*, a savoury soup made of pounded tea leaves, roasted peanuts, diced green vegetables, seeds and grains, and her stewed pork with vegetables; this was Hakka food they hadn't had in a long time.

"You're lucky to have a wife who's such a fine cook," Lo Tai said.

"Yes, I'm very lucky," echoed Lai Kee Chok, looking at his wife, who was about ten years his junior. "I arrived in Sambas five years ago. Ah Moi and her father had arrived two years earlier from Guangdong. When I saw her, I wanted her for my wife, and her father approved. Many of the men married native women, but I got a Hakka wife who can cook!"

A couple of times, they brought their friend Ah Fook with them to Lai Kee Chok's house for supper. The older man didn't seem to mind.

"The more the merrier," he said. "We are all our own kind. We are lucky we are welcomed here after the trouble in Kalimantan."

"We are lucky we enjoy such freedom here, even though the White Rajah is in Kuching keeping a watchful eye on us and on our gold," Lo Tai said.

"He's twenty miles downriver. He'll leave us alone," said Ah Min.

"He'd better not mess with Liu Shan Bang. Tai Ko will not let him take away our rights. The Mau San miners were here long before James Brooke became White Rajah," Ah Fook said. "We must not give in to his demands. If he gains an inch, he'll take a mile."

"Come, Ah Moi, bring us more *samshu*," Lai Kee Chok beckoned to his wife, who had been listening to their conversation, her eyes darting from one speaker to another. "Let's drink to our health and wealth!"

Ah Moi filled their glasses with the rice spirit.

"And long live Liu Shan Bang and Twelve Kongsi!" Ah Min said, as they raised their glasses.

15

Ah Min visited Joto's longhouse in the spring of 1851. The mines were closed for three days for the Lunar New Year and as Joto was returning home Ah Min took the opportunity to go with him. Lo Tai did not accompany them, viewing the Lunar New Year as a chance to play pai gow.

"Give my regards to Joto's sisters," he said, his eyes squinting mischievously, as if to say, "I'd flirt with them if I went along."

"I sure will pass on your regards," Ah Min said with a straight face. Then he added, "Good luck, and don't gamble till you lose your pants."

"And don't lose yours," Lo Tai yelled back, "to the ladies!"

To get to Kampong Tikuan, Joto's longhouse village, the two friends hiked four miles on a dirt path from Mau San to the 18-mile bazaar, a one-street small bazaar on the Sarawak River, and then crossed the river by sampan. Another twelve miles of jungle trekking north of the river took them to Joto's home.

"I want you to meet my mother," said Joto. "She's a remarkable lady. My father was killed years ago in a battle with Ibans who attacked our kampong. My mother raised me and my two sisters. She's also the longhouse *bedan*, and has delivered many babies."

"I look forward to meeting her, and seeing your sisters again," said Ah Min.

The kampong was situated on a gentle slope. The first building they came to was round with bamboo walls and a cone-like atap roof with a pointed top. It was raised on high poles made of belian about six feet from the ground and they had to climb some steps to enter. "This is our most important building," Joto explained. "It's the baruk, the headhouse."

"You mean this is where the head of your village lives?" Ah Min asked.

Looking at Ah Min with an amused grin, Joto said, "No. It's called a headhouse because this is where we keep our enemies' heads."

"Are you bluffing?" Ah Min said, with a slight tremor in his voice. "You said headhunting was a thing of the past."

"Headhunting is something of the past with my tribe. And it was only practised in defence against attacking enemies anyway." Taking Ah Min to the centre of the baruk, where a fire was burning in a fireplace, he told him to look all the way up to the apex. Hanging there was a basket of skulls, which Joto said were heads of enemies chopped off by warriors of his kampong a long time ago. The skulls were there to keep the kampong from harm. The baruk was considered the most important building and it was where single men of the kampong traditionally slept. There they kept a lookout for intruders and assembled before battle in times of attacks. It was also there their medicine man performed rituals.

"Impressive building," Ah Min said, keeping his eyes away from the basket of skulls above him. Gongs hung all around on the walls and a big long drum, about twenty feet in length, was suspended high across the hall.

"Our war drum," Joto said, pointing to the long drum. "We use it to send signals to other longhouses in times of enemy attacks. But come, let's see the real longhouse."

They exited the baruk by a doorway opposite and what greeted Ah Min at the end of a bamboo walkway was indeed a longhouse. Constructed largely of bamboo with a roof of nipah palm, it was about three hundred feet in length, fifty feet wide and stood on even taller stilts, "to better guard against enemies, from a height," Joto said.

"Welcome to Tikuan, our kampong-under-one-roof!"

"How many people live in your kampong?"

"About one hundred and eighty at the moment, but on the increase with the addition of babies all the time. This is a very fertile longhouse!" laughed Joto. "We have more births than deaths."

Many villagers came up to greet Ah Min, men in loincloths, women wearing the jomuh, the one-piece cloth garments that Enti and Jinot wore, secured above the chest. Others also wore them tucked at the waist, exposing the breasts. At the sight of these women, Ah Min felt embarrassed and secretly shocked. He was careful to avert his eyes from them as he followed Joto through the long covered public hallway, the *awah* he was told, while Joto greeted everybody, including the bare-breasted, without batting an eye. Some of the women wore brass rings, encircling their ankles and calves. Others wore them on their arms, from the wrist to as high as the elbow. How they could be comfortable Ah Min could not imagine. Joto said they were worn as ornaments, for beauty's sake. He introduced Ah Min to an elderly aunt of his who was weaving a rattan basket, a *juah*, on the open verandah. She was wearing a jomuh fixed at the waist, her sagging breasts almost touching her belly. Ah Min was flustered. He had trouble looking her in the face, and just mumbled a greeting while keeping his eyes on the ground.

"Why's your face so red, Ah Min?" Joto asked, after they left the aunt to her weaving.

"To be honest, Joto, I've never seen anyone, I mean, a woman, not wearing upper garments."

Joto broke into a peal of laughter, making Ah Min feel all the more embarrassed. "This is Dayak culture, Ah Min! You embarrassed seeing breasts? You'll get used to them, and then you won't think anything of them."

"It's just that in China, women cover themselves up from neck to foot. I guess we just have very different customs." Ah Min shook his head, still feeling the heat in his face.

Joto took Ah Min on a tour of the longhouse. The interior had a row of living units, or *asuok*, twenty-two in all, each with its own door opening into the awah. On the other side of the awah, along the front and stretching the whole length of the longhouse was the spacious open-air verandah, the *tanju*. The floors of the longhouse and the verandah were constructed of smooth, semi-flattened split bamboo pieces tied together with rattan over supporting bamboo joists beneath. The young men were mostly kept busy working in the fields, or in building additions to the existing longhouse. A number of women and older men sat along the awah making handicrafts, some weaving mats with rattan and beaten bark, some chiselling at pieces of bamboo, carving intricate designs into cylindrical containers of various sizes, some making necklaces with beads, wild boars' tusks and teeth. A couple of young mothers were gently swinging rattan-woven baskets that hung low from a beam in the awah ceiling and in which their babies slept.

"We are very much oriented to nature. We respect the spirits of the forests and make best use of what nature provides us; we don't waste anything," Joto explained. They passed two women making headbands in red or black. "Our headgear is made from bark. The colours we use, like these, are natural vegetable dyes. And see that old man? He's cutting a vest with material stripped from the inner bark of a tree; not bad, soft enough."

Joto's sisters, Enti and Jinot, came up to greet them. Thank goodness they were always dressed decently, their black jomuh tied above their breasts. And they never wore the disfiguring brass rings. Ah Min was happy to see them and felt at ease almost immediately. Joto wanted to show Ah Min their asuok, one of the twenty-two in the longhouse. Above all, he wanted him to meet his mother. While Enti and Jinot both lived with their mother, Joto, when he was home, would spend a lot of time with them, but at night slept in the baruk like all the other single young men of the kampong.

Their asuok was very spacious, over thirty feet from front to back. The split bamboo floor was covered with a large woven straw mat, which they sat and ate on during the day. Another stood rolled-up against a corner and was used for sleeping at night. The asuok also had a kitchen and an indoor toilet, the latter opening through the floor boards to the ground below. A wooden ladder carved out of a small tree trunk led to a loft for storage.

Joto's mother, Udet, was a tall, matronly woman in her mid-fifties. She had moderately high cheekbones, strict thin lips and dark, deep-set eyes, commanding and intense. To Ah Min's relief, she wore a black jomuh tucked above her breasts. He could cope with the brass rings on her lower legs! In her youth, she could have been a beauty. Perhaps Enti had some of her features, only softer. Behind the stern face, however, was a welcoming smile for Ah Min.

"Welcome to our longhouse," Udet spoke in comprehensible Hakka. "Joto's friend is our friend."

"Thank you for your kindness. I feel very honoured," said Ah Min, taking from his pouch a slim eight-inch Chinese ceramic blue and white vase with scenery of mountains and a river, not unlike the pattern on the teacups he'd given Enti and Jinot. He presented it to Udet, who smiled once more and was very happy. Like most Dayaks, she loved Chinese ceramics. Ah Min was to receive more attention from her during his short stay than her own son.

Chinese and Bidayuhs got along well, Ah Min was told by people at Mau San. They were right. Everywhere he walked at Kampong Tikuan, he was greeted with warm and courteous looks. The two days he was there, he was fed like a stuffed duck. He enjoyed particularly the soup Udet made with chicken, lemon grass and ginger, and her smoked wild boar meat. Udet made great tekesom too. Enti and Jinot must have learned all their cooking from her. Ah Min indulged in the fruit fresh from their trees. The papaya and small bananas were sweet and succulent. But it was the durian that he enjoyed most. Lo Tai had never developed a liking for the large spiky fruit with big pits, each segment encased in white pulpy flesh. He called it cat's droppings. Ah Min was offended by the term, as he had cultivated a keen taste for it. To him, the smell was sweet and exotic, and the flavour exquisitely rich. And to top it all, Udet offered him the best *tuak*, a home-fermented sweet rice wine, and a fragrant fruit wine made from sugarcane and local *tampui*.

"Your mother is very nice, and she's a good cook," Ah Min said to Joto, as they walked from the longhouse to the baruk for the night.

"She's able and efficient, a very strong and tough woman, partly because my father died young and she was left widowed with three small children," said Joto. "But we don't want to oppose her!"

"I'm very sorry about your father. It must have been hard on your mother. I can see why she needs to be so tough."

"I was too young to remember how she took my father's death. We grew up having her as both parents. She loves us, sometimes to the point of being possessive and controlling."

"Mothers tend to be like that," Ah Min said. He thought of his all-giving mother who was different, how she sold her pigs in order to pay for his passage to Nanyang. Not many mothers were like her. His heart ached when he thought of her love and sacrifice, and his eyes began to water. Luckily it was dark and Joto could not see his tears.

Joto continued, "Mother could have remarried, but she dedicated her life to raising us. She's a loyal woman, to her children and to our traditions. She would have nothing to do with the Christian missionaries who came by from Kuching. She believes firmly in spirits, which are everywhere: in the elements, the mountains and rivers, in the fields and the earth, in plants and animals, even rocks. And she's strict with my sisters. Enti has had several young men interested in her, but so far everyone who's visited in the evenings Mother has turned away. Luckily, Enti's picky herself when it comes to choosing a husband. She's not keen on marrying just yet."

The two evenings he spent at the longhouse, Ah Min sat with Joto and his family after supper in the awah. It was a happy communal time for the residents of the kampong, as they socialized over fragrant, sweet tuak and home-distilled *arak*, a strong Dayak liquor. Old men reclined, smoking a water pipe made from carved bamboo, young men sat telling jokes, punctuated with wild guffaws, women gathered in groups chatting and gesticulating with their hands while their children ran happily on the middle bamboo floor, the haunting melody of a flute floating occasionally down the awah, often drowned by the din of the gathering. When it was time to turn in for the night, Ah Min went with Joto to sleep in the baruk.

On the second day of Ah Min's visit, Joto, Enti and Jinot took him on a jungle trek to look for edible ferns and interesting pitcher plants, a route which involved crossing several streams. To Ah Min, the Bidayuh bamboo bridge was a very smart invention, but nerve-racking to use. It was built of bamboo poles which crossed each other diagonally the whole length of the bridge. Where the poles intersected, a narrow walkway about ten inches wide was constructed out of more bamboo poles running the entire span of the bridge. The bamboos were secured with rattan. Joto, Enti and Jinot were amused at the look of dismay that must have appeared on Ah Min's face as they were about to confront one such structure above a small stream.

"Jinot's agile as a monkey when it comes to crossing bridges. Jinot, why don't you lead the way for Ah Min?" suggested Enti.

Jinot began to cross the wobbling bridge, beckoning to Ah Min to follow. He walked behind her, his hands gripping the poles that served as a rail on either side, the toe of one foot touching the heel of the other every step forward, while the bridge shook beneath their weight. The creaking of the bamboos made Ah Min very nervous. Jinot looked back occasionally and smiled reassuringly. She was obviously having a good time. Suddenly, Ah Min stumbled and plunged forward, making Jinot lose her balance as well. They both fell on the narrow walkway, him on her back. He was too embarrassed to fear for his safety, and scrambled up, apologizing. Jinot's youthful face was as red as a beetroot, and she dared not look Ah Min in the eye. They continued crossing in silence. Ah Min was lucky that Lo Tai was not around.

The visit to Joto's longhouse was one of Ah Min's most pleasant memories of Nanyang, a time of sunshine before the looming darkness that was to come. And by the end of his visit, he had grown accustomed to seeing bare-breasted ladies puttering barefooted about the longhouse.

16

In the late spring of 1851, Ah Min received a letter from his brother Hon Yan. It had taken several months in its long journey from Guangdong across the South China Sea to Singapore and then on to Kuching. From there it had come in a mail pouch upriver to the 16-mile bazaar, finally arriving at the doorstep of the kongsi house. It was the first of two letters he received from home. Anxiously, he read it by the light of the setting sun.

Dear Elder Brother,

    I hope you are in good health and doing well in Nanyang. Pa and Ma and all of us at home miss you very much, but we know that you are working hard in a faraway strange land for the sake of a better life for us all. We received your letter with a nice sum of money last year and were very excited and happy to learn about your life in Nanyang. Pa and Ma asked me to read your letter to them many times, each time listening with such interest as though it were the first.

    Since you left, life at home has become harder. The farmers are suffering more and more from poor harvests and the incapable and corrupt government of the Manchus. I see the end of the Qing Dynasty coming. It is a matter of how it will end and who will lead us out of the mess we are in. A wise and enlightened man by the name of Hong Xiuquan has risen in Guangxi Province and fought successfully against the oppression of the Manchus. He is calling for followers from Guangdong. Ah Yee and I have found his teachings of equality among men and women, and equal distribution of land and property among all the people, very wise and enlightening. His goal is to put an end to the vices of the Manchus and bring peace and prosperity back to our land. Ah Yee and I believe there is hope for China under his leadership. For this reason, we have decided to leave home and follow him in his march to Nanjing. There will be sacrifices, including the loss of many lives. We will fight in his army against the Manchus, under his flag, Tai Ping Tian Kuo.

Pa and Ma too want the best for our country. They said there could be no improvement to our lives without sacrifice. So they are willing to let us go. Siu Chun will help them on the farm and look after them in their advancing years. We also know you will come home some day.

Farewell, Elder Brother. We wish you well. I do not know what holds for us in the future. If we do not meet again in this life, we will see each other again in the next.

Younger Brother,
Yan

Hon Yan's letter was most disturbing to Ah Min. He worried about his father and mother, how they would manage without their sons, and he worried about his brothers joining an army of rebels, of which he had little knowledge, against the Manchus. But there was nothing he could do from thousands of miles away across the sea.

Ah Min stayed on, for to leave everything and go home then would mean giving up all that he had left home for. By the close of 1853, he had been in Sarawak for four years. He had no idea how his brothers were faring, in fact if they were dead or alive as they fought their way to Nanjing under the leadership of Hong Xiuquan. Since Hon Yan's letter, his father had commissioned a letter-writer to send him another letter in which he said life was hard but they were still managing in the village. He had not heard from Hon Yan and Hon Yee and he feared for them, but the ancestors would look after them, he said. He asked Ah Min to work hard in Nanyang. He did not ask when he would be returning. But Ah Min was counting the days and months when he would get on one of the boats at Kuching's waterfront bound for Singapore. He had saved up enough money to cover his passage and still have a decent sum, though not exactly as much of a fortune as he had hoped, to take back. He could accumulate more with time, but he was very anxious to return to Tang Shan. Every time he brought up the subject, Lo Tai was evasive and reluctant to talk. Finally, Lo Tai laid it bare to Ah Min.

"I can't go home until I've saved up enough. Remember the fortune we're going to make? I don't have it yet."

"How much do you have?"

"I have been losing a lot at the gambling hall. But I'll make good. I'll go home with enough money to marry Ah Lan and give my folks a good life. Just give me a bit more time." But Ah Min knew better; he knew that his friend had lost everything he'd earned in the years they'd been there.

"Next year will be our fifth year. I want to go home to Tang Shan after that, but I don't want to leave you here," Ah Min said.

"Look who's talking! I was the one who said I wouldn't leave you alone out here!" Lo Tai laughed, but it was a bitter laugh.

"I won't desert you. We will go home together," Ah Min said quietly but firmly.

17

On the eve of the following Lunar New Year, 1854, Twelve Kongsi had a big banquet in the open field by the kongsi house for all members of Twelve Kongsi and their families, as had been the tradition for several years. Gold output was high. Twelve Kongsi was doing good business. Mau San was self-sufficient and flourishing, with the population count at four thousand. And although Rajah Brooke was always trying to put a foot into their affairs, he had till then left them to conduct their economy independent of Kuching. It was a good time for Mau San with much to celebrate.

That night, a lot of alcohol was consumed. Four pigs were roasted and there was chicken cooked in rice wine. The Bidayuhs among them provided tekesom and chicken and rice cooked in bamboo, which Ah Min loved, and fruits including miniature bananas, guavas, pineapple and jackfruit. Joto's sisters, Enti and Jinot, were there and Ah Min was happy to see them. Ever since his visit to their longhouse, he had felt a comfortable familiarity towards them. As usual, they stayed over with one of the Bidayuh families.

Later that evening, leaving the party of men, women and children, Ah Min took a walk along the dirt road leading from the town to the mines, past some palm plantations and clumps of banana trees. The alcohol was getting to his head and he needed a little quiet time and fresh air. As he passed an old abandoned hut, he heard a shuffling noise inside. Instinctively, he stood in the shadow of a tree. Shortly afterwards, he saw a woman emerge from the hut and hurry down the dirt road in the direction of the town. Under the moonlight, the woman looked like Lai Kee Chok's wife, Ah Moi. Minutes later, a man appeared out of the hut, adjusting his kung fu pants. In shock and disbelief, Ah Min froze. The man was his friend Ah Fook.

For days, Ah Min kept the discovery to himself. Should he confide in Lo Tai? What good would it do if Lo Tai knew? Ah Min continued to torture himself with the knowledge of the illicit affair, a crime punishable by death under the law of Twelve Kongsi.

Finally, he decided to confront Ah Fook, to shake him up and put some sense into him. He caught him alone one evening after supper.

"Fook, I know what you've been up to," Ah Min began. "You are doing something very wrong, and very dangerous."

Ah Fook was quiet, no questions asked, no attempt at self-defence.

"You've got to put an end to this, Fook," Ah Min continued, "before you're found out. You know what the punishment is, don't you?"

"No one can know, unless she tells them herself, and she's smart enough not to."

"Fook, I beg you for your own good, please stay away from her."

"Don't you worry, Ah Min. I'll be very careful. I want her so much."

About two weeks after Ah Min and Ah Fook had talked in private there was a big commotion outside the kongsi house one morning before the start of the workday. Ah Min went out and saw Lai Kee Chok clasping a battered and weeping Ah Moi by the wrist and talking urgently to none other than Liu Shan Bang.

Lai Kee Chok had suspected Ah Moi of infidelity for a while, as she had become cold and distant towards him. That one fateful night, Ah Moi, not knowing her husband was only pretending to be asleep, quietly slipped out to meet her lover, as she had done many times before. Lai Kee Chok quietly followed Ah Moi to the hut where Ah Min had seen her and Ah Fook together on the eve of the Lunar New Year. That night, however, Ah Fook was late getting there. As he neared the hut, knowing Ah Moi would be waiting for him, he glimpsed someone in the trees nearby. He stopped immediately and ran back the way he'd come, disappearing into the jungle. But Lai Kee Chok had seen Ah Fook's back, alerted by the sound of his feet as he made his escape, although he had not seen the man's face. He decided it was unwise to make chase in the dark and instead took Ah Moi home and beat her to make her confess to the identity of her lover. Unable to withstand the pain longer, Ah Moi finally muttered Ah Fook's name.

The events leading to Ah Fook's arrest were told by Lai Kee Chok at his trial. Ah Fook was convicted of adultery, and under the law of Twelve Kongsi the male co-respondent in the affair was to be punished by death. There was no leniency, no second chance. Ah Min was completely shaken. Ah Fook was sentenced to die by the *keris*.

The night before his execution, Lo Tai and Ah Min visited him in his cell. It seemed he had aged twenty years in the few days since he had been convicted and sentenced.

"I'm scared," he cried, falling on his knees and clinging to his friends. "Help me. Plead with Tai Ko for me!" But Lo Tai and Ah Min knew they had no hope of obtaining any leniency.

They had brought Ah Fook the strongest arak they could find. He drank it all. Lo Tai and Ah Min were allowed to stay with him in his cell through the night and took turns holding him as though he were a young child, even as he lay succumbed to the excess of spirit. All too soon, the cockerel announced the break of day.

As the guards came for him, he held on to Ah Min and Lo Tai like one deranged. He was bare-chested as usual, wearing only his workman's pants, which he had soiled. He struggled as they tied his hands behind his back and took him out of the cell, screaming as one who had lost his reason. He was taken by cart down the main street, Ah Min and Lo Tai walking alongside before stopping at the flagpole not far from Tian Sze Lung Kung Temple.

A small crowd had gathered, but most of Mau San preferred to stay indoors, not to watch one of their own die, no matter how deserving they might think he was of such a grim punishment. Guards helped him out of the cart and Ah Min went up and embraced him, whispering, "This will be quick. It'll all be over in a blink. I'll see you in the next life, my friend." Lo Tai went up and said his farewell too, though there was no telling if Ah Fook heard either of them. He had stopped crying and just looked delirious, glassy-eyed, shaking violently. He was given a strong drink to dull his senses and made to kneel at the foot of the flagpole. Too weak to resist, or perhaps the draught had taken away his awareness, he remained a wretched sight. The hooded executioner appeared as if from nowhere and stood holding his keris with its long, straight blade. Ah Min hadn't intended to watch, but his eyes seemed glued to the instrument of death, against his will. The executioner raised the sword and took aim at Ah Fook's right collarbone. With one forceful blow he thrust the blade right into his shoulder and through to Ah Fook's heart. It all happened within seconds. Blood spurted profusely as the blade was pulled out. Ah Fook slumped. It was over in an instant.

Soon after Ah Fook's execution, Lai Kee Chok sent the distraught and shamed Ah Moi away, back to her father in Kalimantan. For weeks after Ah Fook's death, Ah Min could not pass by the flagpole. When he finally went there, the ground at its foot was still stained with Ah Fook's blood. Even the lowest segments of the flagpole were tainted red.

18

Ah Min let another year go by. And another. It was now 1856. Lo Tai finally said he was ready to go home, although he wished he had more of a fortune. They made plans to leave for Tang Shan that September.

Meanwhile, the winds of change were blowing from downriver where the White Rajah, James Brooke, had been keeping a scrutinizing eye on Mau San and Twelve Kongsi. News came in the late spring of 1856 from Kuching that Rajah Brooke had enlisted the Borneo Company to control all trading in Sarawak, including the export of gold. Until then, Twelve Kongsi had enjoyed a high profit in selling the gold mined in Mau San directly to merchants in Sambas, in Dutch Borneo, bypassing Kuching. The presence of the Borneo Company would be a big setback to the economy of Mau San. Now all trading had to be conducted through the capital.

To add oil to fire, the Rajah wanted a headcount of the population of Mau San for the purpose of taxing Twelve Kongsi for the consumption of opium, regardless of the actual number of men smoking it. Ah Min had joked that they should send in the headcount minus one, for he had abstained all the years he'd been there. In the event, Twelve Kongsi reported a much reduced census figure to avoid paying a hefty tax. With the population of Mau San close on four thousand following the influx of refugees from Kalimantan in 1850, the Rajah would be a fool to believe the headcount reported. James Brooke accused Twelve Kongsi of smuggling opium across the border from Kalimantan. Security was reinforced at the border to catch smugglers and the relationship between Twelve Kongsi and the Rajah became perilously tense.

"If we leave now, we'll be deserting our brothers at a time when they need our support most," Lo Tai said to Ah Min just a month before they were due to get on a boat bound for Singapore.

Ah Min hesitated and said, "I suppose our staying another month or two is not going to make a big difference. We may as well see how the trouble resolves before we leave." They stayed on in the mines through the rest of the year.

In January 1857, a Hakka from Mau San was caught smuggling opium into Sarawak by the Rajah's men and fined heavily. In addition, a member of Twelve Kongsi who was caught in an adulterous relationship escaped to Kuching and asked James Brooke for asylum. The Rajah took him in and refused to surrender the man when Liu Shan Bang paid a visit demanding he be brought back to Mau San for execution. The Rajah was seen as meddling in the internal legal affairs of Twelve Kongsi.

Liu Shan Bang decided that if nothing could be resolved peacefully, a resort to arms would be the only solution. The people of Mau San wanted to return to the way of life they'd enjoyed before the White Rajah imposed his will on them. The smell of an armed rebellion was in the air.

For Ah Min and Lo Tai, the choice was clear-cut: they could desert their brothers in trouble or fight by their sides. They both chose to stay.

The date for the miners' uprising was set for February 18th, 1857, twenty-four days after the Lunar New Year. The evening before, Ah Min sat with Lo Tai outside the kongsi house long after everyone had gone to sleep. There was so much on their minds. Even though they expected the uprising to be short and successful, with Rajah Brooke giving in to their terms without much bloodshed, they could not be certain of the outcome. And here they were, trapped by their loyalty to Twelve Kongsi. To turn their backs on their fellow miners and set sail for Tang Shan in their moment of crisis would be cowardly.

They were made of finer steel.

"Ah Min, to tell you the truth, although I now have enough money to go home, the fortune I promised my folks does not exist. All because of my gambling. I cannot even afford to marry Ah Lan."

Since coming to Nanyang, Lo Tai had sent a letter home every year to Ah Lan. He might have an irresistible itch for gambling, but his loyalty to his sweetheart was undiminished.

"We should go home regardless," Ah Min said. "I can help you pay for the wedding, a frugal one, but I don't think Ah Lan or her parents would mind in these troubled times."

"I am forever indebted to you. I'll try very hard to repay you. I've disappointed my family and Ah Lan. She had said before I left that she would wait for me, no matter how long."

"Let's not keep her waiting anymore. After the uprising, we'll go home," Ah Min said.

"May the deities protect us and give us victory."

"Lo Tai, it may not be lucky to say this, but just in case something happens to me, you will bring the news home to my pa and ma, won't you? Take what you need from what I've saved up for your wedding, and give the rest to my family."

"You're right; I don't like this kind of talk. The uprising will succeed, and we'll go home together."

19

As her stay progresses, Therese begins to find that she is becoming more and more interested in the history of Sarawak. She spends most of her time with her grandfather by day, when he reminisces about his experiences as a communist guerrilla, or wanders in the older parts of town soaking in its past, and at night she lives the adventures and perils, romance and intrigue of an exotic wild country on the edge of the world by the light of her reading lamp.

"Your first real armed insurgence, Grandpa," Therese prompts, on the fourth day of her visit.

There is an expression of youthful vigour on Grandpa's face, as his mind wanders back. "We had a map showing the way to our target, a defence position near Bukit Langdu, east of Tebedu, where we were to search for weapons and ammunition. It was a night raid and we used a track in the jungle hacked out a year earlier by Chinese communists who had crossed to Kalimantan to escape arrest and for guerrilla training. Now we were making our way in reverse into Sarawak. There were twenty-five in our unit, including Bong and myself, and we were led by Koo Ming Bok, a Hakka from Bau.

"We waited on the Indonesian side of the border till an hour prior to sunset before setting off through the rainforest. Each of us carried a shotgun, given to us after we had arrived in our new camp near Entikong, and Koo, Bong and a few others also had knives. We kept a lookout for jungle patrols, which had increased after the recent incursions by Indonesians and communist guerrillas into the Lundu area of the First Division and the Lubok Antu area of the Second Division. The attacks had resulted in a number of deaths and injuries to Commonwealth troops, although the casualties suffered by the insurgents were also high, in fact greater. We learned from an intelligence source that the Sarawak government was considering resettling rural Chinese families who lived in border communities of the First Division to a controlled area, as they were suspected of supplying information and food to the Chinese guerrillas. Forced encampment of the Chinese had been the strategy used by the British in Malaya during the last guerrilla war fought between British Commonwealth forces and the Malayan communists in the Fifties, putting an end to any hope of communist domination of the Malay Peninsula. That could be the death of us too.

"For a moment, I had a deep sense of sadness to be returning to my own homeland as an invader. I was acutely conscious of the danger my comrades and I were in. Every step I took could be my last. My life as a guerrilla was a living death, but such I considered true living, when I could commit myself to fight and die for an ideology I saw as the basis of all social good.

"It was already quite dark in the forest, our path lit only by waning daylight filtering through the cover of the leaves high above. At least, it was the dry season, relatively speaking. There had been no rain all day, although the weather had remained oppressive. It was more tolerable now the sun was going down. We walked in silence, the only sounds accompanying us were the scrunching of our boots on the forest floor and the call of barking frogs and the chirping of crickets – jungle sounds. As we would be returning to the border with Kalimantan in complete darkness after the raid along the same track, we tied strips of white cloth on a low branch about every thirty yards we advanced on the trail; with two ribbons each time we made a right turn and three at every left.

"'Don't forget, when we come back tonight, it will be two markers for the left and three for the right!' Common sense, but an important caution from one of our comrades, especially when we'd be in a frantic hurry to cross back into Kalimantan.

"We had acquired intelligence about the defence's position from a couple of our scouts. They had spoken to locals and made sketches of the site a few days earlier. An hour's trek took us to within fifty yards of the target. It was a good-sized post, manned by ten Malay soldiers and five Gurkhas. Our scouts heard that the post was shortly to be reinforced with more men. At the time, it consisted of a large, one-level whitewashed building, about two-thirds the length of a soccer field, with a separate wooden lookout tower, probably added when the place was turned into a defence position. One soldier could be seen on the watchtower. Our scouts had told us the guards changed shift every two hours, on the hour. The building was protected by a barbed wire fence, which we would have to cut. Our plan was to surprise and restrain the relief sentry as he emerged to go up the watchtower. Then one of us would go up in his place. The sentry up there would think it was his relief until our man got to the top and restrained him also. We would then have the two soldiers take us to the weapons store with the least disturbance. The best scenario was that the troops inside the building would sleep through the raid. If they didn't, we would shoot our way in and out.

"The sun had already set, but we waited in the forest until it was really dark and the lights in the building had been turned off. By ten-thirty we were ready to move; it was quite black except for a small porch light at each of the entrances. A little less than half of our unit, ten of us, including our leader, Koo, Bong and myself, crawled flat on our bellies to the barbed wire fencing at the side of the building closest to our exit route. We managed to reach the fence without being detected and, still in a prone position, clipped the wire from the ground so we'd have sufficient room to crawl out with the captured weapons. Within fifteen minutes, we were under the fence and inside the perimeter. The rest of the unit was to act as lookouts and lay down covering fire for us if necessary as we made our escape. They would also help carry the captured guns.

"We made our way without disturbance to within ten yards of the base of the lookout tower and waited behind a wooden shack for the relief sentry to come out of the building. It was by then ten-fifty. The minutes went by slowly. Then just before eleven, a Malay soldier, not a Gurkha, who would be easily identified from his hat, emerged from the side door closest to the lookout tower. From the light of the porch, I could see he had a pistol at his belt and was holding a rifle. He took a few steps in the direction of the lookout tower, but Bong and I were on him from behind and took him down in seconds. Bong covered his mouth and held him at knifepoint while Koo and I disarmed him of his weapons, gagged him and tied his hands. Koo immediately proceeded up the steps to the lookout tower, while Bong and I remained with our prisoner among the scaffolding below so that we would not be seen. The other seven who'd come in with us stayed out of sight behind the shack. We heard a slight commotion at the top, but not enough to wake the soldiers in their sleeping quarters. A couple of minutes later, Koo came down without the sentry. He indicated he was dead and later told us he had slit his throat as the soldier, another Malay, had put up a fight and he could not afford to let him wake the whole station.

"The Malay whom we had bound and gagged took all ten of us into the building through a side door at the far end from the tower. This was very convenient as the door was close to the hole we'd cut in the barbed wire fence. Urged along at knifepoint, the sentry led us to the weapons store. It was locked, but under pressure he pointed with his head to a box on a shelf nearby which held the storeroom key. At first glance, I estimated there were at least twenty guns in the room and a lot of ammunition. Six of us quickly started removing it all and formed a relay line from the building's side door to the severed fence. One comrade took the sentry, still bound and gagged, as far away as possible from the building and tied him to a fence pole. We knew he would not try to alert his fellow soldiers as we would simply kill him. The remaining three men who had crept into the camp with us were guarding the sleeping quarters at the other end of the building, ready to shoot and kill the entire defence unit should anyone wake. Within ten minutes, we had cleaned out the weapons room, taking every last gun and piece of ammunition, and passed most of it to our cover team on the other side of the fence. We couldn't believe our luck. The soldiers had slept through it all! Once the storeroom was empty, those of us left in the building made a quick exit through the side door.

"We had all reached the hole in the fence when we heard a noise. We looked back to see the lights go on in the building, followed by much shouting. The last of our raiders had just crawled under the wire when a few soldiers began shooting at us. Our cover team returned fire. We ran as best we could into the refuge of the jungle, carrying what we had looted in addition to our own weapons. None of us had been hit and we would be safe in the jungle as long as it remained dark. The enemy wouldn't yet know we had emptied their weapons store, but we couldn't stop because as soon as they did and dawn broke they'd be after us.

"Koo led the way, looking out for the white markers, making left and right turns as their numbers indicated. Even in the night, they were visible. In fact, they stood out like ghosts flitting in the dark, the sounds made by the small creatures of the swampy forest adding to the eeriness. We made slow progress, weighted down with the guns and ammunition, but each followed the man in front at a distance in single file. I was the fifth in line, my sense of security depending entirely on the footsteps and faint image of my comrade ahead; I kept close enough so I could just make him out. Every time we passed a white marker, the last man would untie it, keeping it in his pocket. We would leave no trail for our enemy.

"By the time we reached the border, it was still dark. It had taken us just over an hour to cover the distance to the defence position unencumbered before sunset, but it had inevitably taken much longer on the return. However, what mattered was that we had not got lost and that we'd made it back before dawn. We knew the Commonwealth troops would waste no time in pursuing us once it was light, even over the the border into Kalimantan, so we kept going at the border and continued back to basecamp.

"On that night raid near Tebedu, May 30th, 1964, we captured twelve rifles, eight shotguns, a couple of pistols, two light machine guns and four thousand rounds of ammunition. An amazing haul. As for casualties, the sentry in the watchtower was dead, and others might have fallen when our cover team returned fire. Miraculously, none of our unit was hurt.

"It was the day following our return from this first armed incursion that Li told Bong, who immediately shared the news with me, that she was pregnant. Their baby would be born in early January 1965."

20

February 18th, 1857 | *Day 1*

Liu Shan Bang assembled the men of Twelve Kongsi in front of the Tian Sze Lung Kung Temple. Incense was burned at the altar of Master Zhang Tian Shi, one of the Taoist deities, while the flag of Twelve Kongsi flew high on the flagpole nearby.

They were six hundred strong, equipped with swords, clubs, shotguns, rifles, and torches, which they would ignite when they neared James Brooke's residence, The Grove. They would walk on dirt paths from Mau San to the closest bank of a tributary that flowed into the Sarawak River, about a mile from the mining town, where longboats would be waiting to take them downriver to Kuching. On reaching Kuching, they would divide into two camps: Liu Shan Bang leading half of the men to attack The Grove on the north bank, while his lieutenant, Bong Gap, would lead the other half to ransack the government buildings and stem any resistance on the south. Lo Tai and Ah Min were with Liu Shan Bang. A few of the Bidayuh miners decided to fight with the Hakka, among them Joto, who was with Bong Gap's group. Many of the miners who had migrated from Kalimantan in 1850 were married and had children. It was especially hard for them to say goodbye to their families, although they expected the separation to be short.

They got to the riverbank in half an hour and boarded some thirty longboats. It took them two hours of paddling downriver to reach the riverside bazaar of Tondong. As it was still light, they stopped there until sunset before continuing to Kuching.

They waited two hours at Tondong, and had done their best to sleep, but the sun had now begun to set and the men dipped their paddles in the water once more. It would be at least another six hours before they reached Kuching. They were very quiet and all that could be heard on the river was the sound of oars entering the water and the croaking of frogs on the banks. They met little traffic on the river. One small craft was being paddled downstream by a Malay, who said he was returning home to the 16-mile bazaar a little further down as his wife was about to have a baby; the rest were trader boats going upstream. Liu Shan Bang made the Malay swear to secrecy about the hundreds of miners in their longboats who would be following in his wake, before allowing him continue.

Shortly after midnight, Kuching was in sight.

Ah Min and Lo Tai landed with Liu Shang Bang's group on the north shore of the river, near a Malay kampong west of The Grove. They made as little noise as possible. Nonetheless, the inhabitants of the kampong probably heard them, but they were too shocked and scared to come out of their riverside homes. The miners marched with Liu Shan Bang in the direction of The Grove, lighting their torches as they neared the Rajah's residence. Shots were fired at them from the direction of The Grove, hitting two of the miners. The men were immediately helped while the rest of the group broke into a run, heading for the gates. The firing had stopped by the time the group reached the gates and they smashed the chains with a hatchet. Once inside the compound, some of the men furtively circled the house while others broke down the heavy wooden front doors. They went from room to room, but the place was deserted, no one was in sight. James Brooke and his men must have fled when they saw the size of the advancing force. They searched for Brooke both inside The Grove and in the grounds, but he was nowhere to be found. At Liu Shan Bang's orders, they collected anything they thought might be valuable and took it to the vacated guardhouse by the bank, leaving two of their men on guard, before setting fire to the house.

Across the river, the miners under the leadership of Liu Shan Bang's right-hand man, Bong Gap, were doing the same to several government buildings. A sampan carrying a handful of men, shouting loudly, was being rowed across from the south bank. It didn't take long for the boat to dock at the jetty, where the men excitedly jumped out.

"James Brooke is killed! James Brooke is dead! Long live Twelve Kongsi!" they continued shouting.

"Didn't think it was going to be quite so easy," Lo Tai said to Ah Min, on hearing the news.

"I'm just shocked that he was killed. I was hoping we could avoid bloodshed," Ah Min said.

"You think the problem could be resolved without bloodshed? Don't be so naïve, Ah Min. At least, we killed the head. The rest should be easy," said Lo Tai.

Liu Shan Bang crossed the river to the south shore in the sampan that had brought the jubilant miners over. He had ordered most of the group who were with him, including Lo Tai and Ah Min, to follow him in their longboats, leaving a dozen of the men on the north bank to keep watch by the burning residence. The river and night sky were red with the reflection of the fire. The whole town seemed aglow, although only a few buildings were actually in flames. Liu Shan Bang ordered the head of James Brooke to be hung on a high pole just outside the Court House, a big wooden building on the south bank not far from a wooden riverside fort.

Ah Min had seen James Brooke once before when Brooke had visited Mau San a few years earlier at a time when relations between the Rajah and Twelve Kongsi were already strained but not beyond repair. He remembered him as a tall, middle-aged white man with dark curly hair. He looked quite different to Ah Min in death, a horrid gruesome spectre, his hair matted and blood still oozing from where the neck had been severed from his trunk.

It looked as if the uprising against James Brooke might be over in one night. The revolt had been successful! Without James Brooke, Twelve Kongsi would enjoy again all the freedom its members had enjoyed long before he came to Sarawak. Five white people lost their lives that night at the hands of the rebels. When Ah Min heard that two of them were children, he was shocked and angry. But under the circumstances, he could only keep his feelings to himself. The miners, on the other hand, lost no one, although a few men had received gunshot wounds from the little resistance put up. On Liu Shan Bang's orders, their injured were brought to the bishop's house not far from the waterfront. Bishop Francis McDougall, a tall, bearded Englishman, was also a doctor and he was asked to tend to them. This he did. He had no choice.

The fires on both sides of the river continued to burn through the night, long after the attack was ended. By dawn, the burning had subsided, leaving Kuching an ash-coloured town with smoke still rising here and there from buildings that continued to smoulder. The townsfolk, mostly Teochew and Hokkien Chinese, and Malay, stayed in their houses, afraid to show themselves. The Europeans had taken refuge in the bishop's house. Liu ordered that they be left alone, as the miners had no issues with them, only with James Brooke.

21

February 19th, 1857 | *Day 2*

The miners had taken all the weapons that they could find from The Grove and the buildings on Kuching's south bank. James Brooke's impressive library was torched, and cash and an assortment of valuables were taken from the government buildings before these also had been set on fire. But Liu Shan Bang ordered that no shops or homes of the people be touched.

The miners took shifts to guard the town, especially keeping an eye out for any traffic on the river. Some patrolled the open areas by the riverbank and others combed the streets. But the streets were now practically deserted, so different from the day Ah Min and Lo Tai had arrived eight years earlier and the few times when Ah Min had revisited the town in the years he was at Mau San. All the shophouses were now boarded up. The Hokkien and Teochew Chinese in Kuching had never trusted or liked the Hakka miners from Mau San. In fact, they had befriended James Brooke and given him support from the moment he'd set foot on Sarawak soil. The rebellion against the White Rajah, and his unexpected death, must have increased the antagonism these Chinese townsfolk now felt towards those from Mau San.

That afternoon, Liu Shan Bang and his chief assistants met at the Court House with the high officials of Kuching. Among these were Bishop McDougall, an Englishman who managed the Borneo Company and the Malay *datu*. When Liu Shan Bang finally came out of the lengthy meeting, he spoke to his men in the open square outside the Court House beneath the bloodied head of James Brooke.

"My fellow members of Twelve Kongsi, I congratulate you all on the success of our mission to regain our autonomy, so that we can once again enjoy life in Mau San as we have done for the last twenty-seven years. Now Rajah Brooke is dead. We, Twelve Kongsi, rule in Kuching as we do in Mau San. But because of the distance by river between the two places, we will delegate some of the responsibility for the administration of parts of Kuching to local leaders. All, however, will be under the jurisdiction of Twelve Kongsi. We will stay in Kuching till order is fully resumed and the authority of Twelve Kongsi is firmly established. Remember, no looting of shops or homes while you are here. Take only what belonged to the White Rajah, not for your own gains but for the treasury of Twelve Kongsi."

February 20th, 1857 | *Day 3*

There was now nothing left of The Grove but smouldering timber and blackened, broken walls. To these, Lo Tai and Ah Min returned on the third day of the uprising, while most of the Hakka miners were on the south bank eating and drinking in local teahouses kept open for them, some even venturing into gambling halls and opium dens. The rebels still took turns patrolling the streets and keeping a lookout on the river, but their vigilance had slackened as there was no sign of resistance from any quarter in the city or from the river. Order seemed to have returned.

Lo Tai was anxious to go back to the ruins of The Grove with Ah Min. He was secretive when Ah Min asked him why. They walked a good distance east along the south bank till the main part of town was out of sight before hiring a tambang manned by a local Malay man to take them across. Lo Tai was careful not to be seen by fellow miners guarding the riverfront. He dismissed the tambang when they reached the opposite bank, and then walked back along the bank through forest and a collection of palm groves to reach what had been James Brooke's residence. No one was in sight. All the miners were now on the south bank, patrolling or enjoying themselves. Only a few dogs remained to sniff among the rubble. The guardhouse, where the rebels had been told to leave the valuables looted from The Grove and the highly prized weapons, was empty; everything had been loaded into longboats docked on the south bank and secured under a tarpaulin. A better watch could be kept on it there. Lo Tai and Ah Min were alone among The Grove's ruins.

Leading Ah Min to the back of where the house had stood, making sure they were still out of sight of anyone across the river, Lo Tai stopped at a well in the rear garden, not far from what had been the kitchen, a few blackened pots still hanging over the charred wood of an extinguished fire beneath an exposed grate. Lo Tai pulled at a long rope that hung into the well, at the end of which was a metal bucket that scraped against the well's sides as he drew it to the surface. Draining the water onto the ground, he revealed a small tarpaulin-wrapped package. Lo Tai removed the tarpaulin and handed Ah Min a brown leather pouch. Surprised by its weight, Ah Min quickly loosened the drawstring and looked inside. He gasped at what he saw. It was full of gold coins!

"These are worth a fortune," Lo Tai said, just above a whisper.

"Where did you find them?" Ah Min whispered back, his hands shaking.

"In one of the rooms, inside a chest, the night we burned the place down."

"You'll be in deep trouble if Tai Ko or anyone finds out you are hiding them."

"They are worth the risk. You and I will take these coins with us to Tang Shan. We will share them. Our families back home will benefit a lot from them. This is our fortune, Ah Min, yours and mine. Think about it."

The treasure could change their lives. Lo Tai would be able to afford an expensive wedding. He and Ah Min would have money to better their lives and those of their families. The temptation to keep the coins for themselves was too great to resist. On the other hand, if discovered, they could face dire punishment under the law of Twelve Kongsi, most likely death.

"How can we keep this a secret?" Ah Min asked hoarsely, bypassing any objection his conscience or fear of discovery might have.

"We cannot go to the south bank with them, least of all back to Mau San. We need to bury them in a safe place where no one will find them," Lo Tai said.

Returning to where the kitchen had been, Lo Tai found a small shovel near the fuel bin. He took it with him while Ah Min carried the bag of coins wrapped again in the piece of tarpaulin. They continued on foot in the direction from which they had come earlier until they arrived at a forested slope some distance from the river. At the base of a huge belian tree, they used the shovel to dig a deep hole. Dropping the bag of coins into the hole, they quickly replaced all the soil and scattered some dry leaves and twigs over the surface. Lo Tai carried the shovel as they made their way down to the riverbank, where, out of sight, on a completely deserted part of the shore, he threw it into the river. They'd had no time to count the coins, but there must have been at least fifty of them, the face of James Brooke impressed on each. They were a fortune in solid gold.

"We'll come back for them, before we leave for Tang Shan," Lo Tai said.

Back on the south bank, after walking the rest of the way to the landing on the opposite shore and hiring another tambang to take them across the river, they rejoined their fellow miners. Lo Tai did not gamble that night. Perhaps their deep secret had changed his outlook and he realized that he no longer had to take chances at making a fortune. He and Ah Min had found one.

22

February 21st–22nd, 1857 | *Day 4 and Day 5 morning*

"We are leaving Kuching, going back to Mau San!" The order came in the early morning of February 21st, sent out by Liu Shan Bang. It rang loud and clear, delivered by messengers walking the streets of the town to get word to the miners wherever they were billeted. By mid-morning, every one of them had gathered in the public square in front of the Court House to hear what Liu Shan Bang had to say.

"I have been warned by the bishop that James Brooke's nephew, Charles Brooke, is in Simanggang, seventy miles east of here, and may lead the bunch of Iban Dayaks loyal to him to avenge the death of his uncle. I have asked the bishop to convey the message to Charles Brooke that I have no quarrel with him. We mean Charles Brooke no harm, as long as he leaves us alone. He can rule the Dayaks in Simanggang for all he wants. But not only has he better and bigger guns than we have, we will be outnumbered by the Ibans, who are fierce headhunters, if Charles Brooke is not reasonable and cooperative but chooses to turn them on us. For this reason, we will return to Mau San. I have secured an oath of allegiance and signed documents sealed by the blood of a white cock from the representatives of the foreign and Malay communities here, and from the bishop, stating that no one will pursue or attack us on our way back to Mau San. Let us now board our longboats and go home!"

By noon, the miners were well on their way upriver towards the 16-mile bazaar. Paddling their longboats, they took with them all the weapons and ammunition they had found, as well as other items of value, such as pottery, paintings and anything made of gold. The longboats carrying the looted goods were in the middle of the flotilla going upstream, and were well guarded from the front and back.

Two hours after leaving Kuching, a loud commotion erupted.

"Enemy coming from behind! We're being attacked!"

Ah Min was in the fifth longboat from the front. Liu Shan Bang, who was two boats behind, passed an order down to the longboats that rounded up the rear to open fire to fend off the pursuers. After a brief exchange of gunfire, messages were relayed to the front saying the enemy had turned back. They had been identified as Malays. The datu had broken his promise to Liu Shan Bang and gone after the miners. For that, Liu Shan Bang resolved the Malays had to be punished as an example to others that their oath of allegiance to him and Twelve Kongsi had to be observed. But first, he decided to get reinforcements.

After two more hours of upstream paddling, they reached the 16-mile bazaar. It was four in the afternoon when they tied up the boats and sought somewhere to rest. They were once more in friendly Hakka territory. Liu Shang Bang ordered the miners in the boats containing the guns and other valuables to leave all the weapons with him, take the valuables to Mau San by horse and cart and return with another hundred men to the 16-mile bazaar, where the rest of the miners would be waiting. The plan was to return to Kuching and wreak havoc upon the Malay kampongs.

Their reinforcements arrived shortly after eight in the evening. Liu ordered everyone to rest at the bazaar for the night and to be ready to set out for Kuching at three the next morning. Most of the men just lay in the shelter of the five-foot ways of the shophouses waiting to be called to duty. Paddling downstream at this early hour was relatively effortless and they were back in Kuching before seven. The town was still sleeping, little expecting Liu and his men to return. At Liu's orders, they docked near the Malay kampongs on the north bank, to the west of the ruins of The Grove. The occupants of the kampongs must have heard, or seen them, for they fled from their homes. Liu ordered that no shot be fired, but they set fire to the kampongs and many houses were destroyed.

23

February 22nd, 1857 | *Day 5*

That morning, while the kampongs were still burning, the rebels were shaken by news brought by one of their river guards. A ship flying the English flag had been seen working its way up the river from the delta, but what was most disturbing was the news that James Brooke was on board!

"It might be a phantom ship with the ghost of James Brooke on it!" Lo Tai blurted out.

But they all knew better. They too soon saw the ship coming up the Sarawak River into Kuching waters. Without binoculars, Ah Min could not tell for sure who exactly was on the ship, but the messenger was probably right. No wonder Ah Min had not recognized the severed head on the post! He thought then that it bore little resemblance to the James Brooke he recalled once seeing alive. He looked over to Liu Shan Bang who was standing on the riverbank in front of the Court House. The Twelve Kongsi leader's face was like one carved in stone: grey, grave, expressionless. The Malay kampongs on the north bank were still burning in places, and Liu Shan Bang gave orders for the wooden fort situated not far from the Court House to be set alight. The sight of these flames and the vast number of rebels assembled on the banks must have given James Brooke second thoughts about proceeding further, for the ship turned around and began to make its way downstream again towards the mouth of the river. The miners were safe, for the moment.

But now they were faced with a dilemma. If they retreated back to Mau San as planned, James Brooke would return as the White Rajah and they would lose all that they had gained in the last few days. Liu Shan Bang, his lieutenant Bong Gap and other top assistants in the rebellion were determined to remain in Kuching.

February 23rd, 1857 | *Day 6*

Well before noon, a steamer was heard chugging into Kuching waters from downriver. It was identified as the SS *Sir James Brooke*, belonging to the Borneo Company. On deck were James Brooke and a large gun positioned to fire on Kuching town. Charles Brooke had also arrived with his Iban warriors in another boat, which had sailed up behind the *Sir James Brooke*. Shortly after their arrival, the Ibans came ashore in small rowboats and wasted no time in setting about destroying the miners' longboats moored near the town.

Liu Shan Bang immediately called a retreat to Mau San. There were not enough boats left for all the miners to return by river, so some were obliged to make their getaway on foot through the interior and were pursued by the Ibans. Fifteen longboats had been left further upstream, away from the town, against such an eventuality, and, led by Liu Shan Bang, Ah Min and Lo Tai made their way there. Packing themselves into a longboat with twenty other miners they paddled for their lives, as did all the miners in the other longboats. In five hours they had reached the 16-mile bazaar and went ashore. Confronting their pursuers on land would give them a better advantage than on the river, so they disembarked, following Liu Shan Bang to Jugan, a hilly area less than a mile outside the main bazaar. There they set up their defence position, waiting for James Brooke's men who would surely land at the 16-mile bazaar once they'd seen their boats.

Ah Min was relieved to spot Joto among the miners who had landed at the bazaar. They stood a better chance against the enemy there than those who had fled into the jungle outside Kuching. No one was more adept at moving through jungle territory than the Dayaks, be they Iban or Bidayuh, and Ibans brandishing their *parangs* in hot pursuit of the miners was something Ah Min cared not to think about. The rebels at the 16-mile bazaar had the additional good fortune of the leadership of Liu Shan Bang and Bong Gap. Their presence, especially that of Liu Shan Bang, boosted general morale. Their plan was to fend off James Brooke's men, English, Malay or Iban, at the bazaar, return to Mau San and then defend it. James Brooke needed to know they were a formidable opposition and not to be beaten. Then he would sit down with Liu Shan Bang and other leaders of Twelve Kongsi and talk terms. There was hope still.

As expected, James Brooke's men came ashore at the 16-mile bazaar and marched on to Jugan. The miners saw them coming and at once opened fire from their positions on the hill. The miners were dispersed among dense vegetation on the slope and had the advantage over Brooke's men, who had little cover below and would be easy targets. It didn't take long for them to realize this and retreat back through the 16-mile bazaar to the river and set off again downstream.

That night, Liu Shan Bang ordered the miners to stay at the bazaar in case Brooke's men returned. They would head back to Mau San by land in the morning.

The shophouses at the bazaar, which had been boarded up when the trouble had started earlier, opened up that night for the miners. Ah Min went to Mr Yong's teahouse. The kindly Hakka was shaken by the events of the day, but was pleased to see him.

"I wish you and Lo Tai a safe return to Tang Shan," he said, when Ah Min told him their plan of going back to China after the uprising was over.

"I hope that something good will come of this," Ah Min said. "Lives have been lost, and many have been injured."

"Liu Shan Bang is a dynamic leader. He will bring autonomy back to Mau San. You mark my words!" Mr Yong said emphatically.

They heard the thudding of feet outside and left the teahouse to investigate. Four of James Brooke's men, Malay by the look of them, were waving a white flag and carrying two large barrels slung between poles. They had clambered up from a longboat docked at the riverbank, and on seeing the men at the teahouse had asked to see Liu Shan Bang. The barrels were filled with arak, the finest available they said, and they were a token of peace. They also had a message to deliver from James Brooke: he would sit down with Liu Shan Bang in a few days to discuss terms of settlement between them.

"I told you we're going to win," Lo Tai said to Ah Min. "James Brooke will give in to our terms. He'd better, now that he knows we are invincible."

"I'm just glad we decided to stay to give our fellows support before leaving for Tang Shan," Ah Min said, a look of relief on his face.

"And don't forget the fortune we have hidden in Kuching," said Lo Tai quietly. "If we had left before the uprising, we wouldn't have found the gold."

"We'd better dig it up before anyone else finds it. What if James Brooke decides to build on that land?"

"Don't worry. We'll get to it soon," said Lo Tai, looking gleeful and confident as usual. "I can't wait to see Ah Lan!"

Liu Shan Bang asked the messengers to thank James Brooke for the arak and to send word to the Rajah that he expected nothing short of complete autonomy for Mau San. The messengers soon left the bazaar in their longboat.

As the sun went down an atmosphere of mild jubilation settled on those in the 16-mile bazaar, the arak adding to the mood. The miners indulged heavily in the alcohol, confident now that the fighting was over and they would be going home to their wives and children, and that peace would return.

The revelry continued until many were so intoxicated that they were obliged to lie down in front of the shophouses on the main street of the bazaar and there fell asleep, lost to oblivion. All was peaceful until some time after midnight a single shot rang out in the dark, then another, and another. Within fifteen minutes, more than fifty miners lay dead on the main street of the 16-mile bazaar.

The arak had been a Trojan Horse. They should have suspected something of this nature from the White Rajah; he was not the sort of man to loosen his hold on power without a fight. When the shooting began, Ah Min was chatting with Joto and Mr Yong inside the latter's teahouse. Mr Yong had boarded up his shop, leaving just one panel unplaced. The three of them peered out through the narrow doorway and saw Brooke's men, Malay and English, firing at the miners on the main street where they lay, and the Ibans with their parangs, thrusting the long, sharp blades into those who had managed to get to their feet and were running away. Miners were falling everywhere. Within minutes, the scene on the main street of the 16-mile bazaar was one of rampant and bloody slaughter. Those who had somehow been able to escape the sudden onslaught of knives and guns ran in confusion in the direction of Jugan, where they had formed a stronghold earlier in the day, but Brooke's men were at their heels, killing without remorse.

In all the confusion on the street, Ah Min suddenly caught sight of Lo Tai running to take cover in a shophouse not far from where he and Joto were sheltering in Mr Yong's teahouse. The next moment, a shot rang out and Lo Tai plunged forward and fell. Frantically, Ah Min made as to dash to where Lo Tai lay, but Joto forcefully held him back.

"I must get to Lo Tai!"

"You'll only get yourself killed too," Joto said. "Wait till they are gone."

Ah Min could see Lo Tai writhing on the wooden platform where he'd fallen. He waited until the gunfire on the main street had subsided and the attackers had left the bazaar in pursuit of any surviving rebels who'd made it to Jugan. Unarmed, Ah Min crept out into the darkness of the main street to where Lo Tai lay. His friend was unconscious and bleeding from the back of his head. Joto joined him and together they carried Lo Tai into Mr Yong's teahouse. Mr Yong and his son made enough space for Ah Min and Joto to be able to lay Lo Tai down on the floor at the back of the shop.

"Lo Tai, you'll be okay. You won't die, Lo Tai," Ah Min was crying like a baby, his tears cascading onto Lo Tai's face. "Please don't die! Don't die, Lo Tai!"

Mr Yong gave Ah Min towels to mop up the blood and ripped up a tablecloth to bandage Lo Tai's head, but the wound kept bleeding. Ah Min held Lo Tai's icy, clammy hand, squeezing it.

"Lo Tai, think of Ah Lan, think of us going back to Tang Shan for your wedding. We will go back together. I can't go back without you. I can't do without you!"

But Lo Tai did not open his eyes. His hand lay limp in Ah Min's. His face was white as a sheet, his lips blue. His breathing was faint. Ah Min held him close, nestled his bloody head on his lap and gently rocked him like a baby until he finally expired in his arms.

"Ah Min, you and your friend must leave. You can't stay here, for they will return and search all the shophouses. We will all die if they find you here," Mr Yong said pleadingly, looking from Ah Min to Joto.

"Mr Yong, can you please hide Lo Tai's body? If I survive this, I'll come back to bury him. But if you don't see me back in a day or two, please bury him for me."

Mr Yong thought for a moment, and said, "I'll hide him in the attic for now. But I can't keep him up there for long in this heat. I'll have to bury him soon in the field behind the shophouses. Don't come back till the storm is over, and don't go in the direction of Jugan. Go out through the back door and make your way back to Mau San by following the river, but stay clear of the bank where their boats are. You'll come to the 18-mile bazaar two miles from here. Then take the dirt road left of the bazaar for another four miles, and you'll be back at Mau San."

"Thank you, Mr Yong," Ah Min said, his eyes showing deep gratitude. Turning to Joto, he said, "We need to go now." With one last look at Lo Tai, Ah Min left with Joto by the back door of the teahouse and they made their way towards the 18-mile bazaar, steering clear of Jugan from where they could hear the chilling sounds of gunfire.

24

February 24th, 1857 | *Day 7*

Joto and Ah Min made their way in the darkness along a path that ran parallel to the river but was largely hidden from it by trees and undergrowth. They reached the 18-mile bazaar in forty minutes. Ah Min had been there with Joto before, on the way from Mau San to Joto's longhouse several years earlier. It was a one-street bazaar of some ten shophouses, much smaller than the 16-mile bazaar. They were not the only ones who had arrived there running from Brooke's men. Some of the miners who'd survived the slaughter in the 16-mile bazaar and Jugan were also in the street, clearly fearful, and shouting, "Liu Shan Bang is dead! They shot him in Jugan!"

The villagers had boarded up their shops and were staying indoors, refusing to open up to anyone. Predominantly Hakka, they would have wanted to help the miners, but under the circumstances, harbouring them would mean certain death.

The main street of the 18-mile bazaar soon became a scene of utter confusion and carnage. Brooke's men had caught up with the rebels and began spraying volleys of bullets at them. In the chaos of the gunfire, Ah Min and Joto became separated, each trying to duck as best he could behind any column, tree or shed. Then Ah Min saw Joto fall, hit by a bullet only about twenty yards from him as he struggled to find shelter. Ah Min knew he could not go to him: to do so would cost him his life, from a bullet or the blade of an Iban parang.

Ah Min was beyond tears. Beyond hope of rescuing Joto, his survival instinct taking control, and without a weapon to defend himself, he followed the dirt road left of the bazaar and ran as fast as he could together with a handful of surviving miners in the direction of Mau San. Brooke's men were still engaged in slaughtering rebels at the bazaar, so Ah Min and his companions managed to put some distance between themselves and their adversaries. Another forty minutes of breathless running and they were back in Mau San. The men with families hurriedly made for their huts, and gathering up their women and children they ushered them, without pausing, into the jungle south of Mau San and towards the border with Kalimantan.

But many women and children were left alone; there were now no husbands or fathers to come for them. Afraid to escape into the jungle on their own, but realizing their predicament, they began to cry for help. It wasn't long before Mau San reverberated with their frantic screams and the women, knowing that they couldn't run far, were grabbing their children and making for the path that led to the mines. Ah Min could have headed for the border with the other men and their families, but he caught up with a woman clutching her newborn to her breast with one arm, her two older children, a little boy, just a toddler, and a girl of about three or four, clinging to her and impeding their progress. Ah Min quickly lifted the two children into his arms and hastened with the woman and the rest of the crowd in the direction of the mines.

Near the mines was a small shrub-covered hill and as every miner's family in Mau San knew, at the foot of the hill was an opening into a cave. The region's limestone rocks were peppered with caverns, but this one was large and was Mau San's closest. When they eventually reached it, one by one everyone scrambled inside; there were hundreds of women and children. Ah Min made his way in also, the two children still in his arms, their mother beside him with her baby.

Through a dim, narrow passageway they filed into the depths of the cave. As they got further from the entrance, it became darker and darker until they could barely see and they had to grope their way. They tried to keep quiet, but the babies and children could not be silenced. Water was dripping from the ceiling, hitting pools that had already collected on the ground. There were eerie moaning sounds of an underground draught and the flapping of the wings of bats. Echoes and the near blackness added to the scariness of where they were. Perhaps the cave had another exit. But what if it had no opening except the one through which they had come? Would Brooke's men be there, waiting to kill everyone who emerged? Perhaps James Brooke had a heart and would not allow the slaughter of women and children. Ah Min began to wonder if he was the only man in the cave. He had not intended to hide there and would not have done so but for the helpless mother and her terrified offspring. They finally came to the end of the narrow passageway and found themselves in what seemed to be a big chamber. They were still not in total darkness, a faint light followed them from the direction in which they had come, and they could feel round the walls of the void. However, there appeared to be no way out. There they all waited in the dampness of the cave, their feet sodden and their bodies dripping with sweat. They were totally exhausted from fear and effort, the children all crying in terror.

Ah Min had no idea how long they remained there. It felt like an eternity. Surely, Brooke's men must have heard the children's cries and been alerted to their hideout. The silence outside and lack of action were unnerving. Then, Ah Min became aware, slowly at first, of a smell of burning, and gradually the atmosphere inside the chamber became acrid and stuffy. Something was definitely burning, but not inside the cave or it would have created light; it was coming from elsewhere. At once the awful truth was clear: Brooke's men were lighting a fire at the cave's entrance and filling it with smoke. There was no way out except through that entrance. People were gasping and suffocating inside the cave, trampling on one another as they succumbed to the smoke and fell. It was utter pandemonium. Ah Min heard shots fired from the direction of the entrance. He knew some must have tried to escape. Death was a certainty, whether they stayed or fled.

Was this how Ah Min's life was going to end, deep in the dark bowels of the earth, suffocated by a bonfire? The children he had helped carry into the cave had already collapsed. Ah Min could see them lying limp on the floor beside him. There was no hope for anyone. He could not even help himself. Weak from lack of air, he dropped on all fours and crawled away from where he knew most of the women and children were gathered.

Perhaps if he was on his own he'd find better air. Slowly feeling his way, he touched a cold pillar rising from the ground. A stalagmite. Crawling past, he continued until eventually he could go no further. His way was blocked. This was presumably the far end of the cave. Leaning against the wall, he closed his eyes and waited for the end to come. The smell of smoke was still there, but despite this he was filled with a strange tranquility. His breathing became slow and shallow, and then as he began to feel very faint he sensed the slightest wisp of a phantom breeze.

This must be the wind from the underworld. Years spent in Mau San, where many miners were Taoists, had taught him that when a ghost entered a domain, one was supposed to feel a wind from the spirit world. Likewise, when someone departed to the underworld, he would be accompanied by that same wind of death. Then Ah Min drifted into unconsciousness. Darkness was all.

25

"Let's skip dinner tonight, Grandpa, and just have something here. I want to hear more of your guerrilla stories, but after that, I want to go back to the hotel and continue reading about Liu Hon Min. I've got to the point where he was facing death with the failure of the Chinese Rebellion. I must know what happened!"

"It seems you are living two past lives here, that of a guerrilla by day and a rebel by night. I'll be surprised if you don't soon turn into a radical yourself!" Grandpa chuckles to himself. "Now, where was I yesterday?"

"You ended on a high note, with the success of your first raid on an enemy defence position, and the news of Li expecting a baby."

"Yes, after we'd got back from the raid with the cache of arms and Bong heard he was going to be a father, he was walking on air for days.

"'Your baby will be a lucky child, with the good life his parents are fighting to build for him,' I said, my spirit genuinely uplifted for the first time since I'd joined the combat force in the jungle.

"'Why do you think it's going to be a boy, Ka Ming?' Li asked, smiling. 'I want a girl!'

"'I don't care if it's a boy or girl, but if Li wants a girl, a girl it will be,' Bong said, enjoying the euphoria of the moment.

"'Born in the Borneo jungle, to guerrilla parents! What unique attributes our child will have. We are lucky that there's a doctor in our midst,' said Li, referring to a young medic from Kuching who had recently arrived at our camp.

"'What did Koo have to say when you told him?' I asked Li.

"'He's obviously not excited about it. I'll not be in combat for a while, but I can do everything else. What can he do? He can't ask me not to have the baby. I would rather die,' Li said.

"'That's the craziest paradox I've ever heard! You have to live, Li, in order to keep the baby!' I was laughing."

"Throughout the rest of 1964, many raids were conducted on border settlements especially in the First Division of Sarawak, some by Indonesians, some by communist guerrillas and some by the combined forces of both. There were many casualties among the guerrillas." Grandpa Lui hesitates a moment. "From our camp of fifty, we lost eight Chinese comrades that year, killed in action. Many others were injured, some seriously. Not only were we in constant danger of ambushes during our incursions into Sarawak, we could also be targeted on the Kalimantan side of the border by Commonwealth troops who often infiltrated into Indonesian territory for a good mile or more from the border. The defenders had become the aggressors.

"Bong sustained a wound in his leg during a raid near Tebedu, and was lucky to have made it back across the border to camp. Li was hysterical on seeing so much blood. Her pregnancy had made her nervous and given to mood swings, her spirits escalating to new heights one moment and descending to the abyss of desperation the next.

"In the late summer of '64, the Malaysian government distributed leaflets in an attempt to persuade communist guerrillas from Sarawak who had been trained in Kalimantan to surrender. They said they would guarantee a new life to those who took up the offer, but no mercy would be shown to those who chose to remain in armed combat against the government. Soon after this news circulated in our camp, I heard Li shouting at Bong in a tantrum, the first time since I'd known them.

"'You have no right to ask me to leave without you! How dare you! You don't want us around, I know. We are a burden to you!'

"'I ask you to leave because I love you and our baby. This is for your safety and well-being, don't you see?' Bong tried to reason with her.

"'Why don't you leave with us? You want our baby to grow up without a father? You have no right to send us away when you are here getting yourself killed. You want to make a widow and an orphan of us! You hate us! You don't want us! We are a burden to you! You don't want us!' And she broke into a frenzy of weeping.

"'You know your accusations are unfair. You know I want you to go because I want you and our baby to be safe. You know I love you, and I love our baby. It's only if you go back to Kuching that you can give our baby a good life. Do you want our child to suffer? To be deprived? Go hungry?' Bong yelled back, losing his temper too.

"'If I go, you'll never see me again. I repeat. You will never see me again! And you will never see your child! Our child will grow up without a father.' More spasms of uncontrolled weeping followed. 'I hate you for telling me to leave without you!'"

At this, Therese laughs. "Grandpa, you'd make a good actor. You sound like someone with a split personality, one side of you arguing with the other."

"I'm not making it up. I remember their argument vividly, maybe not every word, but pretty close." Grandpa Liu takes a sip of his coffee and continues, "Li never left. She stayed with Bong, doing chores at the camp, cooking, washing, minding our food and medicine supplies, which were dwindling alarmingly. The Chinese farmers living near the border on the Sarawak side used to be a reliable source of food for us. But gradually, their help waned under severe threats from the government. Medicine was short and much needed, not just for the injured in action, but for those who suffered from diseases prevalent in the jungles of equatorial Borneo.

"Li gave birth to a son on the 18th of January 1965 in a tent used for the injured and infirm at our camp near Entikong. The young medic from Kuching attended her, helped by two of the women in our force. Luckily, no scheduled raid was planned at that time and so Bong was able to be there with her, to comfort and calm. They named their son Lin Sun, meaning born in the jungle.

"'Bong Lin Sun. I like it. He'll grow up proud of the circumstance of his birth,' I said to Li and Bong.

"'If something happens to me, you'll be the one to take care of him and Li, for me,' Bong said to me.

"'You and Li will survive this together, and give your son a good life,' I told them, trying hard to sound convincing."

"From 1965 on, Commonwealth troops intensified their aggression towards the guerrillas, both Indonesian and Chinese, especially since the Tunku had asked for more military aid from the Commonwealth following Indonesia's exit from the United Nations. Not only did they increase the distance of their cross-border pursuit of retreating guerrillas into Kalimantan territory, they also staged pre-emptive ambushes on guerrillas, both in Sarawak territory and as far as about five miles into Kalimantan. As a result, the guerrilla casualty count increased drastically. Our camp, hidden deep in the jungle three miles west of Entikong and off the main guerrilla and enemy beaten track, was not particularly threatened for the while, but the heightened aggression by Commonwealth troops rendered it very hard for us to secure food and medicine from sympathetic Hakka border communities in Sarawak." Grandpa Liu reaches for his coffee cup before continuing.

"Throughout the spring of 1965, we continued to make incursions into Sarawak, to ambush enemy troops searching the area. We had a few contacts during that time, taking down several enemy soldiers, including some Gurkhas. However, we were running low on ammunition as we'd been unable to mount any raids on enemy posts since the tightening of border control. Our casualty count was hurting too. I suffered a flesh wound during one sortie when we were ambushed on the Indonesian side by invading Commonwealth troops. During that skirmish, we lost two comrades from our camp; one was a woman, a good friend of Li's who had helped at Lin Sun's delivery.

"For a while, I noticed Bong saving some of his daily ration of rice and tapioca for Li; she needed as much sustenance as she could have while nursing the baby. In the first three months of his life little Lin Sun was thriving at his mother's breast, oblivious to the scarcity of food around him and the hardship his parents were suffering. His cheeks, and his arms and legs, were filling out, and he would smile and gurgle when talked to. It was amusing to see a fighter in jungle uniform clowning like an orangutan and making funny faces to entice the approval of Lin Sun.

"Not all at our camp were happy about the presence of a baby though, especially when life became harder by the day. But Commander Koo remained consistent in his earlier decision to let Bong and Li keep their child at the camp. Not that he encouraged relationships beyond friendship among the single men and women, although there was no law set down by the SCO forbidding it. In fact, permission to marry had been granted to one couple the first months we were there. Neither was there a rule against bearing a child in wedlock at the camp, although Lin Sun was the first and only baby born in the jungle to guerrilla parents in my time. If ever there was a pool of sunshine in the impenetrability of the rainforest – the dark, wet and torrid environment that was our camp – it was Lin Sun in the first few months of his life."

26

Ah Min was sure he had died and gone to heaven. This could not be hell, for he felt no fire or pain. He opened his eyes and saw beams of wood above him and a bamboo wall to one side. He was not in the presence of the god of death; instead, a beautiful fairy appeared in the light of a doorway, slowly coming towards him. She was not dressed in the traditional long flowing Chinese costumes fairies were depicted as wearing, but was wrapped in a black cloth from chest to calf, her neck and shoulders exposed. She was a barefooted goddess.

Touching Ah Min's forehead gently, she said in Hakka, "Don't talk. Just rest."

Ah Min lifted his head, trying to get up from his reclining position, but could not. His head was heavy and he felt nauseated.

"Where am I? I'm dead, no?"

"You are alive. You are in our kampong. You were near the air vent when Enti and I went into the cave after the massacre. You were breathing."

Ah Min recognized the voice. It was Joto's sister Jinot.

"You saved me? How?"

"There's a hidden exit from the cave, at the opposite end of the chamber from the entrance."

"What day is it today?" Ah Min's mind wandered.

"The 3rd of March. We got word yesterday that the Rajah's men had finally left Mau San. We decided to go there, hoping to find survivors, including Joto." Jinot could not go on, as tears streamed down her cheeks. Ah Min tried to say something, but no words would come. With great effort, Jinot continued, "We crossed the river at Tondong and hired a horse and cart to take us to Mau San. The place was deserted and we went on to the cave. There was no one alive at its entrance, or outside, only the rotting dead. The smell was overpowering and we decided to get in through the secret vent at the back.

"When we found you there we had hopes of there being others alive, but no one else had got that far. Further on in the main chamber it was just terrible, a scene of utter ghastliness… There were simply hundreds of dead; mothers lying with their babies in their arms, trying to protect them, children straddled on top, or scattered at their sides. Bodies were just everywhere." Jinot paused again, her sobbing renewed. "When we saw this," she continued, "we knew it was a miracle that you had survived. Fortunately, you had got close enough to the secret passage for the air from the vent to reach you. We tried to rouse you, but you were only semi-conscious. We had to drag and then lift you over the rocks of the passageway to get you out, and were thankful that you weren't bigger than you are. Eventually, we brought you back to our kampong the same way, crossing at Tondong and hiring another cart."

Ah Min held out his hand to take Jinot's, and said, "Your brother…"

"I already guessed." She let Ah Min hold her hand while she remained silent, her eyes closed, fresh tears welling on her eyelids, as though she was bottling up her thoughts of Joto – and her sorrow. After a while, she asked in a quiet, controlled voice, "Where did he die?"

"At the 18-mile bazaar. He fell about twenty yards from me. I couldn't get to him in the midst of all the bullets. I'm sorry."

"I understand. He died fighting for a cause he believed in. You couldn't have helped him, or you'd be dead too."

"I will go back to the bazaar to find him."

"Enti and I will go. You can't go. They'll kill you if they see you. They'd know you to be a rebel. I heard the villagers at the 16-mile bazaar found Liu Shan Bang's body and buried him in Jugan secretly. You have to stay here in our longhouse until things have settled. They spared no one, not even the babies. Mau San is wiped out."

"Why do I live, when my friends are gone? Lo Tai was killed in the 16-mile bazaar. And Joto gone too. Why didn't you let me die in the cave?" Ah Min was sobbing uncontrollably.

"There must be a reason that you stayed alive in the cave when everyone else died. Just because those you cared about are dead does not mean you have to die with them. The more reason you have to live, for yourself, for Joto and Lo Tai, for all of them." She broke off and let her tears fall on Ah Min's face as she wept over him. And he raised his arm to wipe her wet cheeks with his rough and blistered hand.

After a while, Ah Min asked, "How did you know about the back opening in the cave?"

"When I was a child, I followed Joto and Enti to the cave. We were playing in the area and found this very narrow split in the rock which then widens into a short, uneven passage leading to the big chamber. It's not visible from the back of the hill, as it's completely hidden by the trees. It's even harder to see the passageway from inside the chamber, even with a light; the entrance to the passageway is really just a narrow gap and is hidden in the folds of the wall. Unless you felt every nook and cranny in the wall, you would easily miss it. We never thought much about the cave or the secret way out as children. It was just another cave to us," Jinot said, resting her teary eyes on Ah Min.

The headman of Kampong Tikuan let Ah Min stay on at the longhouse. At first, Ah Min was in an asuok reserved for the sick. After a week, when he felt stronger, he moved in with the other single Bidayuh men to sleep in the baruk. But he had his meals with Enti, Jinot and their mother, Udet.

"In life, my son was your friend," Udet said in Hakka. "Now that he's gone, you are like a son to me. You are welcome to stay here for as long as you wish. I believe Joto brought you to us."

When Jinot and Enti first broke the news of their brother's death to their mother, Udet took it stoically, without much outward show of emotion.

"Bring back his body. I want to have my son back for cremation," she said firmly but quietly. Her ashen face betrayed little sorrow. It was impossible to tell the pain she felt in her heart.

Two days after Ah Min was rescued from the cave, Jinot and Enti went to the 18-mile bazaar accompanied by two young braves from their longhouse, looking for Joto's body. As they approached the bazaar from the riverbank, they began to retch, for the air was filled with the stench of decomposition. Corpses were everywhere. No one had attempted to remove them for burial. The bazaar was totally deserted, its inhabitants, mostly Hakka, having fled their shophouses after the massacre. In the unrelenting tropical heat and humidity, it didn't take long for bodies to rot, as well as to attract scavengers, animals and birds. It was a scene of utter horror.

There were no predators there the morning Jinot and Enti and their two escorts got to the bazaar; they mostly came at night. The four of them alighted from their cart and covering their noses with a cloth, walked down the street of the bazaar. Weaving their way among the corpses, they steeled themselves to look at every one in the hope of finding Joto. The faces of the dead were in such states of decomposition and mutilation that most were beyond recognition. They were about to lose hope when Jinot spotted a silver chain with a wild-boar-tusk pendant carved in the shape of a snake's head hanging round the neck of one of the corpses. It was Joto's chain and talisman which he wore all the time. His face was unrecognizable, but the proof was there; it was Joto. Tattered pieces of his loincloth were still attached to his bullet-ridden body. The smell of decaying flesh was brutal. The two Bidayuh men helped Jinot and Enti hurriedly wrap his body in a straw mat, carry it to the riverbank and once on the other side continue to Kampong Tikuan by horse and cart.

At Udet's request, Joto was cremated in a simple ritual presided over by the *pinanuh*, the man in charge of funeral rites at their kampong, and attended by all at Tikuan, including Ah Min.

27

In his first days at Kampong Tikuan, Ah Min wished indeed that he had died with the others. There was no hope, no future for him. The grief and emptiness that gnawed at his very being was beyond endurance. Was this all a nightmare that would end when he woke? Many times, in utter despair, or perhaps in the hope he would wake to the reality of an ordinary mining day in Mau San, he would knock his head against a wall, and once in complete desperation he slashed his arm with a knife. Jinot found him bleeding in the asuok reserved for the sick where they had first brought him. Shocked and flustered, she stemmed the flow with Dayak herbs, dressed his wound with a local ointment and carefully bandaged it.

Ah Min had to stay in hiding in Tikuan, among the Bidayuhs who, though kind, were not his own people. Tang Shan was the only place he wanted to be, but he had no way of getting there. The Bidayuhs from the kampong had brought news that James Brooke had sent his men out to hunt everywhere from Kuching to Mau San and its vicinity for rebels who might have survived and still be in the area. Luckily, Brooke's men would not venture into the Dayak longhouses.

Ah Min wanted to know if Lo Tai had had a proper burial. Enti and Jinot offered to go to the 16-mile bazaar to inquire of Mr Yong. They would be safe from Brooke's men, who wouldn't suspect anything of two young Bidayuh girls. Besides, James Brooke was smart enough not to antagonize the Bidayuhs. He knew better as he wanted to have the Dayaks, both Iban and Bidayuh, on his side. Three weeks after the uprising had ended,

Ghost Cave

Enti and Jinot journeyed to the 16-mile bazaar. They found Mr Yong in the teahouse.

"He told us the Hakka villagers buried the dead in a mass grave outside the 16-mile bazaar a few days after the massacre," Enti told Ah Min on returning to Kampong Tikuan after the mission.

"I never wanted Lo Tai buried in a mass grave!"

"Wait till you hear what I have to tell you, Ah Min," Enti said patiently. "Mr Yong and his son dug a grave at the foot of a small hill in Jugan, put Lo Tai in a coffin they'd bought from the local coffin-maker and buried him there, not in the mass grave, but in his own plot, about ten yards from where the villagers secretly buried Liu Shan Bang. They planted a few bamboo saplings beside it. Mr Yong said he would show you where Lo Tai was buried some day. But he said you must not go there now. Brooke's men are still about. Just two days ago, they found a miner hiding in a pepper plantation near the 18-mile bazaar, took him back to Kuching and summarily executed him."

"I wonder who that poor miner was. For sure, someone I knew at Mau San. The uprising is over. There's nothing the few of us left behind can do. Why does James Brooke still want us dead?" Ah Min's face was contorted with anger and pain.

"Sometimes, we cannot explain why certain tragedies happen, why there is so much injustice. But we have to overcome our sorrow, and live," Jinot said.

"Easier said than done. I've lost all my good friends in Sarawak," Ah Min replied rather curtly.

"We've lost a brother, but while we grieve for his death, and miss him very much, we have to live on and make the most of our lives without him," Jinot said.

Ah Min's face softened as he looked at Jinot, who was on the point of tears. "Forgive me for my thoughtless words. I know how you must feel about Joto's death."

Jinot touched Ah Min's shoulder gently. Ah Min took her hand and held it for a few moments before letting it go. Enti looked away. After a while, Ah Min said, half to himself, "I don't know how to begin again when I can't go home to Tang Shan."

"You'll go home some day. For now, stay with us at Tikuan. You are among friends. You'll be safe here. This is your home, no matter how temporary," said Enti.

"I can't thank you and your people enough," said Ah Min, looking from Enti to Jinot. "Some day, I'll repay you."

Udet, who was also present during the conversation, spoke up. "We're not looking for repayment. Now that I have lost Joto, you are like a son to me," she said. "He has sent you to me. From now on, you will take his place in our home."

There was a finality in her voice which Ah Min found disconcerting.

28

In early March, the rice stalks in the hill paddies of Tikuan were laden with yet-to-ripen grains. The rainy season had come to an end. There was not much to do now with the crops but to await their transformation to the colour of gold.

After the first few weeks of mourning and bemoaning, Ah Min made an effort to gather up strength in mind and body and be useful around the kampong. Whether it was building huts or collecting the myriad raw and natural endowments of the rainforest, at every chore he attempted he found himself to be a fresh apprentice, but he was learning and absorbing the Bidayuh way of life. He had his queue cut soon after Enti and Jinot took him back to Tikuan, and as a miner had long since grown accustomed to wearing a loincloth. With his deeply tanned skin, he blended in well with his Bidayuh companions, so that it was hard to tell he was not one of them. He worked hard, partly as a token of gratitude to his kind hosts, but also as a distraction from constant dark remembrance of the tragic events, the loss of his friends, the despairing thoughts of his grave situation and his homesickness.

Ah Min went on treks in the jungle with his friends at the kampong. He learned to identify and pick wild-grown tapioca, lemon grass and tea leaves, cut edible ferns such as midin and the equally tasty *paku*, and collect medicinal herbs that could cure and mend. He was also taught to avoid plants that were poisonous.

"Today I helped make bamboo roofing for the new shelter at the edge of the rice field," Ah Min told Udet and her daughters at supper in their asuok one evening. "Bidayuh people have to be the most innovative and resourceful. Who else could think of overlapping split bamboos, open sides facing each other, to form a roof! Perfectly sun- and rain-proof! Incredible!"

Udet looked pleased. "We make good use of what the spirits of nature give us. If we waste their gifts, we will anger them and not receive their endowments anymore."

"I guess we take some things for granted," said Jinot. "They are so much a part of our everyday life we just don't think they are that special."

"I'm glad you are taking an active part in our kampong life," Enti said. "You'll really be involved come harvest time."

"I was right in saying Joto sent you to us," said Udet. "You have to stay."

Ah Min soon learned that the process of rice cultivation on the hill slopes of Tikuan was quite different from that of Dongguan's wet paddy fields. Every year, in August and September, hill slopes were cleared of dead vegetation, which was left to dry and then burned for the ash that would enrich the soil. In October, rice seeds were planted into holes punched on the slopes and nurtured by rain during the wet season that followed. There was no transplanting of seedlings to flooded paddy fields. Rice plants sprouted from the seeds in the holes, bloomed and grew, and eventually bore grains. Every family had its own plot to farm.

During the planting season, until the year before the miners' uprising, Joto used to take a few days off from his work in the mines and return home to help. The womenfolk would take care of the weeding during the rains, as well as the back-breaking task of harvesting.

By late March, the rice stalks had grown to over three feet tall and the grains turned yellow. During the harvest, in that year of the uprising, Ah Min helped out in the paddies. As he cut the rice stalks burdened with ripened grain with a small knife, his mind wandered back to Tang Shan, and how as a young boy he'd helped his father and mother at home. Harvest was an exciting time, the labourers singing old country songs while they worked in the village fields, cutting rice stalks, threshing, gathering and binding the hay, and winnowing. He remembered his hunger at the end of the day and how at supper he would gobble down three bowls of rice with the vegetables his mother had cooked with a scrap of pork, often saving her own portion of meat for him. His hand involuntarily went to the little jade Buddha hanging at his chest. Without forewarning, tears suddenly ran down his face. Jinot who was working close by saw him crying and went over to him. She made him sit down in the field among the uncut rice stalks and put her arm around his shoulders. He turned to face her, a torrent of tears. She too broke into a paroxysm of weeping. Sitting among the yellowed stalks, they cried without reserve in each other's arms, finding solace in their physical closeness, while a late afternoon downpour added to the cathartic moment that was finally theirs.

29

Since their emotional outpouring in the rice field during harvest time, Jinot and Ah Min had become inseparable. They worked together to prepare the rice for storage. Occasional laughter, unheard for a long while in Jinot's home since Joto's death, rang out from where they were either threshing the cut stalks with their feet, or pounding the grains to remove the husk before winnowing. There was an unspoken bond between them, an understanding that was theirs alone. Enti, though actively involved in the harvest, began to feel out of place when the three were together. Often, she would move off to take on another task. As for Udet, little escaped her eagle eyes, but of Jinot's escalating friendship with Ah Min, she pretended not to take notice.

In mid-April, Gawai was held at Kampong Tikuan to celebrate the harvest. The rice spirit was thanked for a good year and petitions were made for a still better one in the next through the kampong's two mediums, the old shaman of the longhouse and the priestess, his female counterpart. She was a mousy little middle-aged woman who claimed also to be the healer of the sick. The festivities lasted for three days. There was food and more food, rice cooked in bamboo, sweetened tapioca wrapped in leaves, bamboo chicken and pork, and gallons and gallons of tuak. The mediums performed mystical dances to the haunting vibrations of multiple gongs. Their trance-like movements, though repetitive and stilted, were meant to bring pleasure to the rice spirit.

On the evening of the second day of Gawai, at Jinot's suggestion, Ah Min left the drinking and noisy socializing at the longhouse to walk with her to the edge of the rice field. A strong charred smell of newly burned vegetation filled the air, but it was very peaceful there. They climbed up into the shelter that Ah Min had helped build before the harvest to enjoy the sweet snacks of tapioca and a bottle of tuak Jinot had with her.

"You're very quiet tonight," Ah Min observed. "Do you always go off on your own at Gawai?"

"I don't like the noise. I like solitude, unlike Enti who loves to be with the crowd. But I've never wandered off on my own at night. I'm afraid of the dark, believe it or not, and I'm scared of spirits in the forest. I'm here tonight because you are with me. What about you? Do you believe in spirits?"

Ah Min nodded. "I do. I believe in the spirits of our ancestors, who protect us from harm and whose primary concern is our welfare. Mostly, they are not seen, only felt by the sensitive among us. And, very occasionally, when these spirits choose to manifest themselves to the human eye, for reasons that are important to them, we call them ghosts."

"Those are the spirits we are not afraid of," said Jinot. "But I also believe there are evil spirits who may be called upon by someone who wishes us harm to cast bad spells on us. Those are the ones I fear."

"You have nothing to be scared of with me here," assured Ah Min. "Let's change the subject and enjoy the moment."

"I am enjoying the moment. This atmosphere is so bewitching and mysterious, the darkness outside, the rustling of the trees in the forest behind us, and yet I feel safe because you are with me," said Jinot, moving closer to Ah Min, as she had tended to do oftentimes of late. Ah Min would usually put his arm around her shoulders, as a protective, brotherly gesture. It seemed to Ah Min that he was filling the void in her heart left by Joto's death. He saw her as a little sister.

"There's something I've meant to ask you for a while, rather personal. Perhaps this is a good time." Ah Min took a breath and continued, "Both you and Enti are such nice and… and wholesome young women. I'm just surprised you are both still unmarried."

Jinot looked down and was mute for a while, such that Ah Min began to worry that he might have offended her with his tactlessness. Finally, she said in a matter-of-fact manner, "My sister is a very independent woman.

She enjoys being single and free. She told me she would not get married until she found someone she was truly in love with. I hope she does one day, for she's not young, twenty-four, you know, and Mother needs a man to help in the paddies especially now that Joto is gone."

"And you?"

Jinot looked down again and just shook her head. This time, she remained silent, her fingers kneading one another incessantly. Ah Min sensed her nervousness, her agitation, and deeply regretted his bold insensitivity. He wanted to apologize, but was at a loss for words. Blame it on Jinot's feminine distress at his questioning, or the excessive tuak, along with the full moon on that Gawai night, he suddenly no longer saw the shy fifteen-year-old girl who visited her brother at the gold mines of Mau San and brought him home-cooked Bidayuh meals. Instead, he saw in Jinot a sensuous, vulnerable, desirable woman. In the moonlight, he noticed the penetrating softness of her large, round eyes, the lusciousness of her full lips, the taut curves on her jomuh that were her breasts, and he was excited by what he saw. Jinot's nearness to him, her body casually brushing against his, gave him a whole new sensation that she had not aroused in him before. He felt a shudder running through his entire being, a stirring in the groin, a moment of awakening. Impulsively he gathered her to him in a way he had not done previously, one hand groping the small of her back. She did not object to his actions. He let down her hair, which as always she wore in a bun, and it cascaded onto her shoulders. He kissed her forehead, the tip of her nose. His lips found hers and he kissed her long and hard. Nervously, with clumsy fingers, he untied her jomuh and let his hand wander to her small but firm breasts.

"I love you," Ah Min said hoarsely, anxiously caressing her.

"I've loved you from the first time I saw you," she whispered. She was crying.

"I'll make it up to you for my unforgivable blindness to such beauty. You saved me from death, and now you are giving me a new life."

30

With Ah Min's courtship of Jinot, there were no evening visits of boy to girl's home, which was Bidayuh custom. Ever since Ah Min took asylum at Kampong Tikuan, he had eaten almost every supper with Udet and her daughters in their asuok, and he would usually sit out on the tanju for a while afterwards in the company of Enti and Jinot before walking back to the baruk for the night. Udet would leave them alone while she visited with her friends of the longhouse, chatting in the awah and drinking tuak.

As their relationship took an intimate turn, Ah Min and Jinot could not hide their feelings for long from the inhabitants of the longhouse. The casual touching of hands, the tender gazes into each other's eyes, the eagerness to be in each other's company, whether at work or play, filled the pages of an open book and became the subject of eager gossip at Tikuan. Udet naturally was the first one to observe it all, but she turned a blind eye to it. The lovers took her silence as approval. Enti, too, went in search of her own friends after supper and left them to spend some quiet time on the tanju. Sometimes, Ah Min and Jinot would go for a walk in the deserted rice fields. After all, in 1857, Jinot was twenty-two. She needed no chaperone.

One evening as they strolled among the banana trees behind the longhouse, Ah Min stopped and said, "Jinot, I have two questions for you."

"Yes?"

"First, will you marry me?"

Jinot paused, and then said in a playful tone, "My answer to this depends on what your second question is."

"The second question is harder to ask. Will you go to Tang Shan with me as my wife?" Jinot took a few seconds to formulate her answers. This time, she sounded serious.

"I want to be nobody's wife but yours. As your wife, I would follow you to the ends of the earth. I have always been fascinated with China. I'd dearly like to go there with you some day, and greet your father and mother and serve them in their old age." Jinot looked forlorn. "But there's a problem. If we marry, my mother will want you to stay in the longhouse, especially now that Joto is gone. She is already looking on you as her son. She wants you to help with the farming, not just for one year, but the rest of your life. I don't blame her. Every household needs a man. She would not let us leave the longhouse."

"If we marry, I should stay here and help your mother. I will not think of going back to Tang Shan just yet. But there's a good chance we will be relieved of our obligations here. There is a way out," said Ah Min.

"What? How?"

"Enti is twenty-four and should be marrying soon. We need to get her a husband! Then there will be another man in the family and my presence will not be so important. After all, she's the elder daughter."

Jinot could not help smiling and responded by saying, "I hope Enti will meet someone she can fall in love with soon. But until then, will you stay with me here?"

"Yes, I will stay. I cannot live without you, Jinot. You are my new life, remember?"

"What will your father and mother say to your marrying a Bidayuh girl?" Jinot asked, looking at Ah Min questioningly.

"When they see how good, gentle and kind you are, they will like you very much and they will be happy to have you as their daughter-in-law."

"I hope so much I will see your China some day, the mountains, rivers and beautiful, fair and exquisite ladies in long flowing robes, not coarse and brown-skinned like me," Jinot said, looking into the distance.

"Skin colour is not a criterion to judge one's beauty. You are the most beautiful and exquisite woman in my eyes. Tomorrow, I will ask your mother to give me permission to marry you."

31

Ah Min was breaking all the rules in his courtship of Jinot. There was no go-between to present Udet with his proposal to marry her younger daughter. Instead, he personally asked her for Jinot's hand the next evening.

"As Jinot's husband, you'll be assuming the important role of the man in the family," Udet said in Hakka, in an authoritative yet positive tone of voice. "You will help in the paddies, in our pepper and cocoa plots, and in taking care of our fruit trees. You will look after our pigs and our chickens and roosters. You will defend our well-being, our lives and our honour, if and when enemies attack, to the point of killing our enemies and bringing back their heads. You will take an active part in the communal life of our longhouse, sharing in all the work our men do, be it building, farming, trekking or hunting. You will be a Bidayuh by marriage, though not by blood. If you agree to all these terms, you can marry Jinot."

"I do agree to take on all these responsibilities," Ah Min said, thus pledging his loyalty to Udet and to Kampong Tikuan.

As his engagement gift to Jinot, there was no gold ring, or black jomuh, as was the tribal custom. Instead, he gave her the jade Buddha his mother had given him before he set sail for Nanyang, which he had worn through all the hardships and trials, and in the crossfire of the uprising.

"This jade Buddha, I present to you, Jinot, as my engagement gift and a pledge of my love and fidelity. It is all that I have, my most precious possession given to me by my mother. It has protected me all the years I've been in Sarawak. May it protect you, always."

The Journal: 1857–1858

For the remaining months of 1857, Ah Min tended to Udet's pepper and cocoa plots, her durian, pineapple, papaya and banana trees, and subsistence crops of vegetables. He worked with other men in the village to build bamboo pipes that would carry water from a dammed mountain stream above the longhouse to the kampong for irrigation during the drier months of March to October. In September, he took part in clearing dead vegetation from the hill slopes and burning the remaining dried stems to prepare the rice fields for the following year's crops. And on a sunny and dry October day, Ah Min joined the men in the strenuous task of making the holes in the hill slopes with a sharp pointed pole into which the women would plant the seeds. Thus began another life cycle of rice planting in the hill paddies of Kampong Tikuan.

On March 1st, 1858, after a year had passed since the Chinese Rebellion and Joto's death, Ah Min married Jinot. Udet had invited everyone from Kampong Tikuan as well as relatives and close friends from neighbouring Bidayuh kampongs to the wedding. Decked in the native garments of a loincloth, a vest made of beaten tree bark, a decorated red headband and a necklace of bears' teeth, Ah Min made a young and handsome Bidayuh bridegroom. The bride was a radiant beauty in an ankle-length black skirt decorated along the edge with silver coins, a red blouse with silver trim and a finely beaded cap. The ceremony was held in the late afternoon on the tanju of the longhouse. The old shaman sprinkled the wedding couple with rice and beads and showered them with prayers. The priestess prayed over them while they were fed ceremonial delicacies by an aunt of Jinot's who had had a good and happy life that they might enjoy the same good fortune. Plenty of food was served, followed by dances performed to the music of the ever-haunting gongs. Marital advice was given to the wedding couple by those attending the wedding for a happy and lasting relationship.

Udet spoke in Bidayuh, which Enti translated to Ah Min in Hakka: "Tonight, I am very happy because I have gained a son. I welcome you to our family, Ah Min. I give you my daughter Jinot. Be good to her, care for her, treasure her. Jinot and Ah Min, be kind and faithful to each other, and be worthy of each other's trust and respect. Work hard at your responsibilities, in the fields and at the longhouse, that you may enjoy abundance and contentment. May you give me many grandchildren to be a comfort in my old age and who will continue our family, extend our kinship, for many years to come."

One of Jinot's cousins, Sibon, the son of a brother of Udet and a few years older than Jinot, was a talented artist who had painted portraits of many of his elders, including the chief of his longhouse. A free spirit, he was no warrior, and would have been a disappointment to his tribe but for the fact that he was such a good artist that he had become the visual record-keeper of his kampong and his extended family. His kampong was some five miles from Kampong Tikuan, and he was spending a few days at Tikuan to visit his relatives and friends there before attending the ceremony. On that wedding night, he presented a gift to Jinot and Ah Min. It was a waist-length portrait of Jinot, drawn on a piece of treated bark of about ten by eight inches, and painted with natural dyes from the forest. It depicted Jinot in the most complimenting light, set against a pale blue background, her dark hair cascading down her bare tanned shoulders to the top of her black jomuh. She was a picture of contentment, her deep brown, round eyes beaming with happiness, her red lips curved into a coy half smile, accentuating the dimples on her cheeks.

Jinot was elated at seeing the portrait, but questioned Sibon at length about how he'd managed to paint her without her formally sitting for him. He responded somewhat embarrassedly. Later, she explained to Ah Min that unbeknownst to her he'd discreetly sketched her during his first few days at Tikuan, capturing her movements and expressions, and had then composed and painted the portrait in private, applying the final touches just the morning of the wedding.

"What a great talent your cousin has!" said Ah Min, admiring the portrait. "I love it, but above all, I love the person it represents. We'll treasure it forever!"

And so, Ah Min became a Bidayuh by marriage. He moved in with Jinot, staying in Udet's asuok. Udet had cleared a former storage area in the loft and made it comfortable for the newlyweds. In time, when they had children, they would have their own asuok in the new longhouse being built nearby in the grounds of the kampong.

32

Ah Min and Jinot led the lives of happy and carefree newlyweds in the months following their marriage. Not that they slacked in their daily chores, for with the end of March came the rice harvest. Then there was the perennial care of the fruit trees and the pepper and cocoa plots, and the jungle treks in search of edible ferns and medicinal herbs. While Ah Min learned the art of bamboo carving, Jinot continued to produce exquisitely woven juah that were the envy of her peers. Their days went by quickly, for they were in love and life was good. And at night, when they finally retired to their little nest in the loft of Udet's asuok, they gave completely of themselves to each other. Ah Min was the nurturer, the life-spring, Jinot the nurtured mother earth. Ah Min was yang, Jinot yin. Together, they became complete, like the black and white circular symbol Ah Min grew up with in China.

"In Tang Shan, we keep mallard ducks in our ponds. We call them yin-yang, female and male. They are always in pairs, mated for life. You and I are like a pair of mallards," Ah Min said to Jinot one evening.

"Wouldn't mind living in the water with you. I'd love the freedom."

"Often, several baby ducklings will follow a pair of yin-yang in the pond."

"What are you thinking of?"

"We'll have many babies!"

Jinot lowered her eyes. "I'd like that."

"But you know what? The male mallard duck is more attractive than the female. She has plain brown feathers, but his are a lovely glossy emerald green!"

"I don't think I like that comparison then."

Living in the same asuok as Udet meant that cooked food was waiting for Jinot and Ah Min when they came home from the fields each evening. It was convenient, but Udet's domineering matriarchal presence was beginning to make Ah Min uncomfortable, though he did not voice his unease to Jinot. It was not that Udet was unkind to him; she was very considerate, serving him the best part of any meat, piling fried midin on his plate because he loved the wild jungle fern, and securing the outdoor shower for him at the end of the day ahead of the neighbours' boys. She wanted Ah Min to have all the comforts of longhouse living. It was clear she wanted him to stay.

"Ah Min, about going to China, I'm afraid of Mother," Jinot said one day when they were in the jungle near Tikuan. They could not discuss the matter in the asuok, or at night in the loft, for fear Udet might overhear.

"Don't worry about that. We won't go until Enti gets married and Udet has another son-in-law to help her. She won't mind us leaving then."

"You don't know my mother. There's no telling what she might do if we oppose her. Let's hope Enti will save us from her wrath by marrying someone she approves of." Pausing for a moment, Jinot continued with a sigh, "I also worry about how we'll get to China when all your savings were lost in Mau San."

"Jinot, I have a secret to tell you, but you are to tell no one. Lo Tai and I found some gold coins in James Brooke's residence during the uprising and hid them in the forest. We planned to take them back to Tang Shan with us and buried them not far from the ruins of the residence. Now that the area is safe, we should choose an appropriate moment and go and dig them up and hide them back here somewhere. They are worth a great deal. When the right time comes to leave, we'll be able to buy our passages back to Tang Shan and then give half of the gold to Lo Tai's folks and keep the rest for us and my family." Ah Min pursed his lips for a moment and added, "Perhaps, if it will please your mother, we could also offer her a few of the coins."

"No, Ah Min. If you found it, the gold is yours and Lo Tai's. Do not give any to my mother." Jinot hesitated, and continued, "Besides, and it hurts me to say this, she may want to keep all the gold – and us!"

Two months after their wedding, and shortly after Gawai, Ah Min and Jinot took a rest day on the pretext that Ah Min wanted to go to the 16-mile bazaar to find out where Lo Tai had been buried and to pay his respects. James Brooke's determination to seek out any surviving Mau San rebels had abated with the passage of a year. Their plan was to go to Kuching, dig up the gold and stop on their return trip at the 16-mile bazaar to visit Mr Yong and see Lo Tai's burial place. They would not tell Udet that they were going as far as Kuching in case they aroused her suspicion that they were witholding something from her.

Through a friend of Jinot's, they arranged for a Malay tambang boatman to meet them at the landing on the bank of the Sarawak River across from the 18-mile bazaar. He would take them to Kuching, wait for them while they did what they needed to there, and then bring them back to the 16-mile bazaar later the same day. They would spend the night in the 16-mile bazaar and visit Lo Tai's grave.

The trek from the longhouse to the landing opposite the 18-mile bazaar would take them at least four hours. So with a full day ahead of them, the couple set out in the small hours of the morning before any of the longhouse occupants stirred.

On their backs they each carried a juah. In Jinot's basket were swiflets' nests she had collected from nearby limestone caves. These were considered a great delicacy by the Chinese, who used them mainly to prepare soups. The Dayaks commonly collected them to barter for imported luxury items, such as ceramics, woven cloth and coloured beads. Ah Min and Jinot would use the nests as payment for their expenses. About a quarter of a mile into their trek, Ah Min retrieved a shovel which he had hidden the day before to avoid arousing the curiosity of anyone from their kampong should they be seen leaving with it. The shovel fitted well into his large juah and he covered the handle with a cloth.

They reached the landing across from the 18-mile bazaar at eight in the morning. The boatman, Awang, a gaunt fellow with a high-pitched voice, was waiting for them. Barefoot and wearing just his loincloth, he steered his tambang skilfully down the Sarawak River in the direction of Kuching, negotiating the frequent shallows and avoiding rocks. They were thankful for the cover the tambang provided, for by late morning it was swelteringly hot and it was not until after two that they reached Kuching. On the north shore, where The Grove had stood, James Brooke had built a new residence and had named it Government House. It was a much larger building than The Grove had been, whitewashed and worthy of being called a mansion. Two imposing towers faced the riverbank from where Brooke commanded a good view of the Chinese and Indian markets across the river, and the Malay kampongs further up- and downstream. A path led down to the riverbank to a bobbing pontoon, the private landing place for the Rajah's sampan. The tambang transporting Ah Min and Jinot pulled into a small wharf on the north side of the river, some distance past Government House. The two climbed ashore, instructing Awang to return to the jetty at half past four that afternoon.

The thirty-minute trek from the jetty to where Ah Min and Jinot were headed cut through thick undergrowth and towering forests of belian, tapang and betang trees. Though they were not far from the riverbank, they caught only the occasional fleeting glimpse of water through the vegetation. Eventually they came to the point where the dirt path began to climb. Ah Min led the way up the incline until they reached a majestic belian tree. Taking the shovel from his juah, he said to Jinot, "Well, this is it!" They smiled nervously at each other and Ah Min carefully began to dig at the foot of the belian's trunk on the side that faced away from the path. When he and Lo Tai had dug the hole over a year earlier they had had to negotiate the tree's roots and doing so again proved no easier a task. It was unlikely that anyone would have got there before him; he had left the spot on what was an infrequently used path well camouflaged and in a tropical forest new growth appeared quickly. Nonetheless Ah Min's heart beat hard within his chest as he removed more and more soil. Finally, as he reached down into the hole, his fingers touched what he knew to be the tarpaulin. With the help of a long, sturdy branch that lay nearby he eased up the well-wrapped brown leather pouch.

Jinot couldn't contain herself as she took the pouch in her hands, loosened the string and peeked inside. She gasped. Taking out a single gold coin, she exclaimed, "Ah Min, these must be worth a fortune!"

"With this, we will be able to return to Tang Shan and let my family and Lo Tai's live a good life."

Ah Min put the bag of coins into the bottom of his juah, filled up the hole at the foot of the tree again, returned the shovel to his basket and arranged the cloth on top. The sky had become overcast and rain threatened as they made their way back down the hill towards the river and the waiting Awang. The boat, with its excited but slightly uneasy passengers, slid noiselessly out of Kuching waters towards the 16-mile bazaar, an eerie greenish hue now colouring the heavily darkened sky. An afternoon downpour was soon upon them. The thunderous deluge was disquieting, but it failed to relieve the oppressive Borneo heat.

33

The 16-mile bazaar appeared to have completely recovered from the terrible events that had taken place there during the miners' uprising, at least from what Jinot and Ah Min could observe. At nine in the evening, it was still bustling with locals, some sitting and chatting with friends in teahouses, others enjoying the cooler though still humid night air in front of their shophouses. Ah Min led the way to Mr Yong's teahouse, and found him just getting ready to board up for the night. He was surprised and very happy to see Ah Min and his bride of two months. Mr Yong remembered Jinot from when she had arrived with her sister soon after the rebellion to find out what had become of Lo Tai's body.

"I got the feeling that you had a special relationship with one of the two pretty young women even back then," Mr Yong said to Ah Min when Jinot was out of hearing.

"You knew something about me that even I didn't know at the time!" Ah Min said, laughing.

Ah Min and Jinot had planned to spend the night at the local inn, but Mr Yong would not hear of it. "Never refuse Hakka hospitality. We are our own people," the teahouse owner said, nodding to Jinot. "We have a spare room upstairs for our guests. Rest well. In the morning, I will take you to Lo Tai's grave."

"I cannot thank you enough, Mr Yong. It meant a lot to me, what you did for Lo Tai. His body and spirit have a home because of you." For a moment, Ah Min was beset with emotion and could not go on. He recovered himself and continued, "It is good that this bazaar has survived the tragedy and returned to the way it was before."

"This is only as far as your eyes can see," Mr Yong said. "Nothing is quite the same anymore. How can we ever get over the killing of our people, right here on our street, and in Jugan? Even the great leader Liu Shan Bang fell here. Our residents regularly burn incense at his secret burial place, but how can his spirit be appeased when the entire Twelve Kongsi was exterminated and just about every man, woman and child in Mau San perished at the hands of the White Rajah and his men?" Mr Yong put his arm over Ah Min's shoulders, and continued, "But you, my friend, are very lucky to have survived, and now to have such a lovely wife at your side. The best you can do for Lo Tai, for Liu Shan Bang and all those who sacrificed their lives in this terrible conflict is to keep their memory alive, not just in our lifetime, but for future generations. It is for us to tell their story to our children and grandchildren."

"I will keep their story, and their memory, alive for all the generations to come," said Ah Min, looking over to Jinot, who kept her sad eyes downcast. She was surely thinking of her brother.

At the break of dawn, Mr Yong and his two assistants were already busy preparing food for the morning's customers. After satisfying Ah Min and Jinot with noodles, rice cakes and tea, Mr Yong left the teahouse to the care of his son, Ah Keung, and the three of them set off on the short trek to Jugan.

Liu Shan Bang's grave was marked by an inconspicuous little mound of earth with a few incense sticks planted upon it. No tombstone or plaque suggested the identity of its occupant for fear of exhumation by the Brooke regime. About ten yards from the leader's burial site was a small cluster of bamboos.

"This is Lo Tai's burial place," Mr Yong said. "Ah Keung dug up the earth and we placed his coffin in the ground. We didn't add a tombstone for it would only have drawn the attention of the Rajah's men to the spot and to wondering whose the nameless grave was close by. It was Ah Keung's idea to plant some bamboos beside Lo Tai's grave."

"That was so thoughtful. Lo Tai had bamboos growing around his house in Tang Shan."

Ah Min burned some incense at Lo Tai's grave and knelt mutely in front of it for a good while, sharing a little quiet time with his old friend. When he got up he walked over to Liu Shan Bang's grave, lit some joss sticks for him also and kowtowed three times to his Tai Ko.

Before Ah Min and Jinot left the bazaar later that morning, Ah Min gave Mr Yong two gold coins.

"Convert them to currency some day, but do not do so at the moment lest the Rajah gets to hear about them and wants to trace their source. I only hope they cover the cost of Lo Tai's funeral, with a little left for your hospitality. Better room and board we cannot find in all of Sarawak!" When Mr Yong protested, Ah Min simply said, "This is the least I can do. I am forever grateful for your kindness, Mr Yong."

"I thank you then, for your generosity. I will be discreet with these coins. I know a fellow in Kuching who will take them in exchange for today's currency. No questions asked, all done under the table," said the kindly teahouse owner, with a wink of his eye.

When Ah Min and Jinot had finally taken their leave of Mr Yong, the boatman, Awang, took them back upriver to the 18-mile bazaar. Ah Min wanted to stop at the bazaar and asked to be let off at the jetty on the south side of the river.

"Revisiting the 16-mile bazaar has helped me come to terms with the tragedy that took place there. For the same reason, I need to see the 18-mile bazaar again and confront it in the hope that perhaps my emotional wounds can start to heal," Ah Min said to Jinot.

The residents of the 18-mile bazaar who had hidden or fled the place had returned to their homes in the weeks following the massacre. They had cleared all the dead from the street and buried them in a mass grave outside the bazaar, about two miles to the west. More than fourteen months had passed since the massacre and on the day Ah Min and Jinot stopped there, the place was peaceful and quiet. The one street running through the bazaar looked clean and a new row of shophouses was being built adjacent to the original, at the end closer to the river. To someone seeing the street for the first time, it would be difficult to imagine an atrocity having taken place there.

Ah Min and Jinot took a brief rest at a grocery store run by a Hakka family from Kityang district in Guangdong Province. The owner, a Mr Wen, invited them to sit down at the back of the store, the family's living room, and served them tea.

"We have all been scarred by the cruel tragedy," Mr Wen said, referring to the uprising and subsequent massacre. "Our hands were tied at the time, so to speak. You could never imagine the agony we went through, hiding in our houses, unable to help our Hakka brothers while we listened to the shooting and blood-curdling cries outside."

"We understand," said Ah Min. "There was nothing any one of you could have done, unless you wanted to be killed too. They spared no one on the streets."

"Even after we came back and cleaned up the place, the smell of decomposition lingered in the bazaar for weeks. It was not until the heavy rains came that the air was cleared and the last traces of blood were washed off the gravel," Mr Wen said.

They soon said their goodbyes to the grocery store owner and walked back down to the riverfront where Awang was waiting to row them across to the north bank.

Back on their side of the river, they climbed out of the tambang and began the long twelve-mile trek through the jungle trails back to Kampong Tikuan. At the foot of a tall tapang tree about half a mile from the kampong, they dug a new hole and buried the bag of gold coins, rewrapped in its muddy tarpaulin. They then discarded the shovel in the depths of the forest before continuing home.

At supper that evening, Udet asked about their trip to the 16-mile bazaar. They had a lot to say about it, poignant and true. Udet listened attentively and looked impressed when she learned how kind the teashop owner and his son had been. Had she known that they had gone there by way of Kuching, she would definitely have wanted to know why.

34

About a month after their trip to Kuching, as part of Ah Min's continuing painful journey of healing, he took Jinot with him to Mau San, where he was confronted with a distressing experience. For a start, the town had been renamed and was now called Bau, a Malay word meaning bad smell, indisputably referring to the decomposing bodies that had lain strewn on the streets after the miners' uprising. The thoroughfare was no more. Tian Sze Lung Kung, which had stood at one end of the main street, was gone. Only a broken wooden sign with its name in Chinese characters remained, half buried in the rubble where the temple had once been. Nearby, all that was left of the Twelve Kongsi flagpole was its damaged stubs still planted in the ground, about eight feet high, burned and blackened, a bit of red paint still visible here and there. The kongsi house at the opposite end of the street, a symbol of authority and unity of Twelve Kongsi, was torched past recognition. Most of the atap shophouses had either been demolished by the Rajah's men, or were charred beyond possibility of habitation. A handful of the end houses still stood intact, and those were where the few families who had returned to Mau San a year after the uprising were living.

Ah Min and Jinot made their way to the gold mines, which had been shut down after the rebellion. The entire area was deserted; it was nothing more than an eerie ghost town. The dams, the ditches and the reservoir had been left untouched for more than a year; they were disintegrating and derelict. The occasional mongrel roamed, lean and hungry, scratching at mangy patches and sniffing at anything that might pass for food. There was no human in sight. The land in and around the mines had become the ground of the damned.

And in the heart of it all was the cave where hundreds of helpless women and children had been shot, burned or suffocated to death. The cave entrance was almost hidden by the undergrowth and the creepers that grew unopposed up the trees. Ah Min and Jinot stood in utter silence at the entrance for a very long time, mourners paying their respects to the unappeased dead, or perhaps pilgrims at a site made holy by the sacrifice of innocent blood.

"I'm afraid of this place," said Jinot, looking at the cave entrance. "I smell death. I've heard the cave's haunted by the spirits of those who perished in there. People are calling it Ghost Cave."

"Never mind what people call it, I got out of it alive because of you and Enti."

"To be honest, I wouldn't go in now, for the life of me."

"I wouldn't either. I couldn't bear the idea that I might be treading on bones of the dead, and I can't help but think of the two children I carried in there, hoping it was to safety."

Ah Min and Jinot made their way through the shambles of old Mau San to an overgrown path that led to a small hill which overlooked what once had been a thriving community. Jinot followed Ah Min as he skirted the foot of the hill before stopping at a gravestone covered with wild grass. It was the Liu family grave erected by Ah Min and Lo Tai years ago when they had first arrived at Mau San.

"So is this where you buried the things from your village?" Jinot asked.

Ah Min nodded. "We used to come here every year to remember our ancestors and Tang Shan, until the uprising."

Ah Min and Jinot pulled off the weeds covering the tombstone, brushed the dirt from its surface and cleaned up the surrounding ground. Taking from their baskets some bamboo chicken and rice wrapped in leaves, a bottle of tuak and fruit grown in their kampong, they carefully placed them on the tombstone. Ah Min planted several joss sticks in the soil at the front, lit them and then together they both kowtowed three times before the grave.

Finally, carefully arranging a pile of paper ingots and a paper boat in a propitious spot, Ah Min set them alight.

"The ingots are money for the ancestors to spend in the land of the dead. The boat is for their smooth sailing in the underworld, and to ask for their blessings that we may have a smooth voyage back to Tang Shan."

They picnicked happily beside the grave, tucking into the food they'd brought with them and savouring their time away from Tikuan and their daily chores. Above all, they relished being away from the prying eyes of Udet.

35

"They were so in love, your great-grandfather Liu Hon Min and great-grandmother Jinot," Therese says to her grandfather the morning after she had read about their romance and the early days of their marriage. Realizing now that there was indeed a Bidayuh connection, she asked, "Did you know she was a Bidayuh and we both have Bidayuh blood in us, Grandpa?"

"My father had told me so, but I never knew any of the Bidayuh relations."

"That's really too bad. But let's first finish your story. I'm anxious to know what happened to the baby born to your friends in the jungle."

"People are sacrificing their lives in the worst possible living hell and you're thinking of the baby! But I can understand and will come to that," Grandpa says with patience, a sad smile forming on his lips. Therese switches on the recorder.

"In the evening of the 27th of June 1965, some thirty raiders from Kalimantan attacked the 18th Mile police station along the Kuching-Serian Road, killing several policemen and emptying its weapons store. A few civilians between 24th Mile and 26th Mile were also shot and killed; one poor soul was hacked to death with a parang. There had been threats of SCO retribution against any government informants for a while, and some of the killings that night were interpreted as executions of anti-communist supporters and spies. Although no one from our camp was involved in the 18th Mile raid – the evidence pointed to it having been committed mainly by Indonesians from

Kalimantan – the Sarawak Communist Organization was nonetheless implicated, especially in the savagery meted out to the locals."

"That's not good for the SCO. And not good for the guerrillas," observes Therese.

Grandpa nods. "Immediately, the government set up curfews and road blocks along the Sarawak side of the border in the First Division. Then, early in the morning of the 6th of July, just nine days after the raid, and with no previous warning, the police rounded up some seven and a half thousand Chinese locals from bazaars and communities between 18th Mile and 24th Mile and ordered them to leave their homes and move to makeshift camps under police surveillance, promising to resettle them in permanent structures later. The Sarawak government's forced relocation of these Chinese from the Kuching-Serian Road rendered us completely cut off from whatever help and support we had previously received. Our food ration was immediately reduced to the bare survival minimum.

"By July, little Lin Sun was six months old. Li was still nursing him, but she needed the fuel that would boost the engine. She had become very wan and thin, skin over bones. Bong continued to give her part of his daily ration, while fighting his own hunger. At first Li resisted, but for the sake of their child, she ate whatever was offered her, all of her ration and part of Bong's. It was still not enough to sustain a normal adult, let alone a nursing mother. I was sorry to see them struggling so for their child's survival. Li tried offering him soft food time and again, but he would gag and bring it up. He had lost all his earlier baby fat and his arms and legs were very scrawny, like a newborn's, just longer. His big eyes bulged from sunken sockets, accentuated by his bony cheeks and broad forehead. His rib cage too was pronounced and skin hung dry and translucent from his buttocks; you could see the veins beneath. That contented, happy face he'd had just three months earlier had disappeared. Occasionally, he still managed a smile after he had been nursed, but those moments were becoming more and more infrequent, as his mother's milk invariably failed to satisfy and prolonged nursing only left him crying in frustration.

"'I'm hurting, Bong,' I heard Li sobbing one day when we were at camp. 'He sucks too hard! He bites me!'

"'I told you to try giving him some soft rice,' Bong said. 'It's time he started eating rice.'

"'I have tried, but it seems he only wants the breast, my stubborn baby,' Li said, sounding more stressed than ever.

"'I'll starve before I see my son starve,' Bong said.

"'If only he would take even rice water. But he regurgitates it and goes for the breast,' Li repeated. 'If I could produce enough milk, it would be alright.'

"From then on, I saved part of my daily ration of rice and sweet potato for Li. As expected, she initially refused, but for the sake of Lin Sun, she finally accepted it. Whether my meagre supplement did any good, I had doubts. Every night, I'd wake hearing Lin Sun cry. Hunger is a very painful sensation for anyone to bear. For a baby, it must be excruciating, not understanding, not knowing; just instinctively crying its lungs out whenever it felt hungry. For Lin Sun, there was never satisfaction, only the desperate embrace of a mother who loved him and would give her own life that he might live, if only she could.

"The forced encampment of the Chinese population on the Sarawak side of the border, and the increased surveillance by the Malaysian and Commonwealth troops, meant we had to rely mostly on our small subsistence plots of rice and vegetables, and eggs from the hens we had. We supplemented this with whatever we could find in the rainforest; wild game was desperately hunted, but we often had to make do with jungle ferns. Sago palms were very good, whether they were dead or alive. The starch was filling and we would also eat the grubs that infested the dead palms. The natives considered them a delicacy and very nutritious. Bong and I would gather as many of the fat, white squirmy creatures as we could, saving most of them for Li; in spite of her intense aversion to the sight of them, she'd eat them, desperate for anything that might boost her milk supply. It was a most wretched time."

Grandpa Liu pauses for a short while, clearing his throat. "In late August, Commander Koo held a meeting at camp and informed us of the SCO's decision to establish a guerrilla base in the First Division of Sarawak, in the hilly limestone region of Bau. Our camp members were among the guerrillas called to action, to infiltrate into Sarawak territory and build the platoon base. That would be one of our biggest incursions in a long time. Twenty guerrillas from our camp were to take part in the operation, with others from a camp near the border at Serikin, and would be led by some Sarawak-based members of the armed wing of the SCO. To get into Bau meant crossing enemy lines, dodging ambushes by enemy troops and hiding in the rainforest as we made our way to the hilly terrain. Bong was allowed to remain at our base camp on account of Li and the baby; I was among the twenty picked to go. The mission date was the 15th of September 1965."

"Meanwhile, every time I saw little Lin Sun throughout July and August he seemed to have grown smaller and more fragile. He was wasting away," Grandpa Liu says with emotion. "Too weak to respond to us, he had even stopped crying for milk. About ten days before the planned incursion into Bau, I found Li in hysterics, Bong holding her shaking body and the small bundle that was Lin Sun.

"'She's dried up,' Bong told me, his face edged in despair.

"'You mean?' I was unsure.

"'No more milk. She just stopped completely producing the last two days.'

"'And Lin Sun?' I looked at the weak and whimpering baby in Bong's arms.

"'He's starving. We tried giving him rice water, but he's probably too weak to swallow.' Bong was crying as I had never seen a man cry.

"'I should have forced rice water down his throat long ago,' cried Li, looking deranged. 'Where did I go wrong? Why don't I have milk anymore? Oh, what have I done to my child?' She was screaming.

"I took a look at little Lin Sun, and my heart hurt. Yes, it literally hurt as though I was having a heart attack. The bones in his tiny body were all protruding and looked as if they would break through his translucent skin. His eyes were dull, sunken, lifeless. I held out my arms and Bong placed his baby into them. He turned to hold Li again and comfort her. Lin Sun felt so light, his elongated frame could weigh no more than six pounds. I could not bear to look at his face. I closed my eyes and in my mind saw the little cherub smiling and cooing as he had done five months previously. And I broke down, trembling, raining tears on Lin Sun.

"A day later, on the 7th of September, as night fell, Lin Sun drifted into an eternal sleep in the arms of his grieving mother. Bong held Li to him and together they lay curled in a fetal position on their bed in a heart-rending embrace, drowned in their own sorrow. They were holding their dead son between them, covering his withered, lifeless form with kisses and tears. They remained like that till the morning, while the rain pounded mercilessly on the atap roof above.

"They buried little Lin Sun the next day at the foot of a huge tapan tree close to the camp, his tiny body placed in a little makeshift wooden coffin. His funeral was attended by all the comrades who were at the camp. Li was mute and numb, stoical throughout the burial, drained of tears, perhaps even emotion. Bong dug up the earth, fiercely intent on his task as though his life depended on it. He lowered their son's little coffin into the ground and replaced the earth while Li stood quietly by.

"A week later, Bong said goodbye to Li and joined me and other comrades on our mission into Sarawak, heading in the direction of Bau."

36

Like trees that flowered and bore tiny fruit which grew and ripened as the season advanced, so the seed that was planted in Jinot's womb began to develop. Ah Min was beside himself with joy when Jinot in September of 1858 confided the news that she was with child.

"I would like to have a son. In Tang Shan, every family wants to have a son to carry on the family name, and especially so in farming villages where sons can do the heavy work in the fields. A son is considered good fortune. But whether this one is a boy or girl does not matter at all," said the elated Ah Min, putting his arm around Jinot and gently touching her still small abdomen with his hand, "because we will have many more children!"

"The baby will be beautiful, especially because of the Chinese and Bidayuh blood he or she will have." Jinot's smile was radiant; it shone with the joy of expectation. "I'll tell Mother and Enti this evening."

Enti received the news with glee. She embraced her sister, and tears formed in her eyes.

"May you have a safe pregnancy and delivery, and may your baby be healthy and beautiful," she said. Turning to Ah Min, she added, "Congratulations, Ah Min, on being a father soon. If the baby is a boy, I hope he'll grow up to be like you, a man of courage and integrity."

Udet was happy. "Our family line will now live on, thanks to you, Ah Min and my daughter Jinot."

Udet did not look at Enti, but her elder daughter caught her tone of voice, that emotive implication of displeasure that Enti was neglecting her duty of marriage. After all, she was no longer a young girl of sixteen. Back then, Udet had discouraged many of Enti's suitors, but she was becoming anxious with the passing years. Every time an eligible young man from a neighbouring village, approved by Udet, called in the evening at their asuok, Enti would hide in the loft, refusing to come down to give the poor fellow a chance for them to be better acquainted.

Enti had not been short of suitors. She was an attractive girl, perhaps more striking than Jinot, although Jinot's dimpled smile and soft and thoughtful gaze showed off best her sweet, gentle disposition. Jinot had always been the docile one. Udet did not appreciate Enti's strong will and independence, especially when those qualities conflicted with her plans for her daughter's future. Perhaps she subconsciously saw in her older daughter something of her own self. She wanted both her girls to marry men of good physical strength who could help her in the fields, yet would be obliging and respectful to her as the matriarch of the family, and give her robust grandchildren of good blood. Ever since Joto's death, she had looked to her daughters all the more to provide her with sons-in-law who could fill the big void Joto had left. Ah Min answered to her need for such a son-in-law. Her only regret was that he was not a Bidayuh by blood.

It was a peaceful, precious and private time for Jinot and Ah Min in the months of waiting and expectation. And when the baby kicked in Jinot's belly, hiccupped, or turned itself, she would giggle with delight.

"This is an elbow," Ah Min would say when he felt a wiggly bump on Jinot's stomach. "And this is a knee! And here is the source of sustenance for our child," he said, as his hand naughtily wandered to her swelling breasts.

The big moment arrived on April 3rd, 1859, the birth of Ah Min and Jinot's firstborn. Udet, as the bedan of Kampong Tikuan, delivered her first grandchild with the help of Enti. Throughout Jinot's labour, Ah Min waited outside their asuok, pacing the awah as the day wore on, his hands in a cold sweat, his face tense with agonizing concern for his wife's safety and their baby's well-being. Jinot's screams cut him to the bone. The ordeal seemed endless. Then, hours later, after what seemed an eternity, Ah Min heard from behind the door to the asuok the sweetest sound he had ever known in his entire life, the cry of his firstborn son.

37

To everyone at Kampong Tikuan, he was Kuea, a common name for babies until they received a proper name.

"We're supposed to give him his real name within days of his birth," Jinot said to Ah Min.

"Why don't we call him Kuea for now?" Ah Min said to Jinot. "We'll name him properly when he's older. In Tang Shan, when a baby boy is born his parents call him by the name of an animal, such as Ah Chu, meaning pig, or Ah Keu, a dog. This way, the evil spirits will not be jealous of the child, thinking he's just a pig or a dog and not worth harming."

"What did your father and mother call you?" asked Jinot, amused.

"Ah Niu, which means buffalo."

"No wonder you are so strong now!" Jinot laughed.

"Besides, I really want my father to name him when we take him back to Tang Shan," Ah Min said, looking seriously at Jinot.

"That's fine. But what do we tell Mother when she asks why we are not naming him?"

"We'll just say the Chinese believe evil spirits may harm him if he is given a proper name before he turns two."

Kuea was always hungry and nursed constantly; he put on weight in contentment. He was the most lovable child under the sun, not just to his parents, grandmother and aunt, but to all those who came in contact with him at Tikuan. In three months, he had grown very plump and cuddly; he had large round eyes like his mother's, chubby cheeks, as though they were constantly stuffed, and a lighter complexion than both his parents'. More importantly, he had an easy disposition and was always smiling.

When Kuea had been just a few days old, Udet lifted him up and said in Bidayuh, "This boy is mine! Bidayuh blood flows in him. He will grow up a Bidayuh, loyal to our longhouse and our tribe. He will be a brave warrior, my grandson, my pride, my joy in my old age!"

Ah Min noticed the disconcerted look on Jinot's face and was anxious to know what Udet had said. Later that evening, when they were alone with the baby in the loft and while Udet was still out in the awah, Jinot told him. "I'm worried my mother will be very unhappy and angry when we leave. She's becoming too possessive of Kuea. I cannot imagine what she will do to prevent us from going."

"Don't worry. Remember we are not going to leave until Enti marries. The chances are she will marry a Bidayuh and their children will be full-blooded Bidayuhs, not mixed like our son. Your mother will be very happy then, and she will not mind us leaving. Don't worry about the future now. Let's just enjoy our son." Jinot's anxiety subsided as Ah Min held his wife close and little Kuea suckled contentedly at her breast.

Two months after Kuea was born, Ah Min and Jinot moved into their own asuok in the new longhouse that had been completed behind the original. Kampong Tikuan was expanding.

From the time Kuea was born, Jinot talked to him in Bidayuh, while Ah Min talked to him in Hakka. They wanted him to know both languages as he grew up and to be aware and proud of his dual ethnicity and heritage. His first words were in Bidayuh, the language to which he was constantly exposed, but when spoken to by his father in Hakka, he seemed to understand and smiled. He was an agile boy. At ten months, he had taken his first steps independently and by the time he was fifteen months, he was running from one end of the awah to the other, playing with the other children of the longhouse. He was sociable and happy.

One day early in October 1860, when Kuea was eighteen months old, his parents visited the 18-mile bazaar again, taking him in a big juah strapped to

Ah Min's back. It was an outing for the young family a few days before the rice planting was to begin, when everybody would be busy in the fields. The strip of sandy beach on the riverbank at the 18-mile bazaar would make a new and exciting playground for Kuea. He had never seen the Sarawak River, his village being so far away. They made a few stops for rest during the twelve-mile trek through the jungle, but eventually reached the north bank opposite the bazaar. A boat owned by a Malay was kept moored there to take passengers across for a small fee, and as they approached the bazaar landing, they could see someone putting finishing touches to a new wood-framed gazebo on the path which led from the riverbank. It was a hexagonal wooden structure made of red vertical posts with a matching six-panel roof converging to an apex. The plank flooring was already in place and the sides were all open. At the top of the path, a new sign caught their attention: *Kampong Buso*.

Venturing down the street, they passed some Malay houses that had been built since their last visit there two and a half years earlier, on their way home from paying respects to Lo Tai and Liu Shan Bang at their graves in Jugan. There was also now a new row of Hakka shophouses just before the store where they had stopped that previous time. Mr Wen, the store's owner, was happy to see them again and offered them refreshments.

"So how come the bazaar's now called Buso?" Ah Min was curious.

"You know in Malay, the word *busuk* has the meaning of rotten or decomposed. Since the uprising, people have been calling the place Buso because of the dead left in our streets."

"And Mau San is now known as Bau, which also means something unpleasant," said Ah Min.

"I'm afraid, unfortunately, that these names will stick," said Mr Wen.

Leaving the main part of the bazaar, they made their way back to the river. Ah Min took Kuea to the narrow strip of beach and let him run up and down and feel the sand between his toes. It was a new experience for him as his feet touched the cooling water. He giggled at first, a little afraid, then with delight as he soon gained confidence. He piggybacked on his father, as Ah Min swam across to the opposite bank and back. Jinot took shelter from the sun in the newly constructed gazebo, leaning on one of the horizontal rails connecting the posts. She watched her son playing gleefully with his father in the water, her face a portrait of domestic contentment.

"I am treasuring the moment, Ah Min. May the good spirits keep us always together as a family," she said, when her husband and son joined her in the gazebo.

"Of course we will always be together. What can separate us?"

"We mustn't tempt the spirits. When I'm happy, I'm afraid that my happiness may be taken from me."

"I love you and Kuea, and I will not let anything keep us apart, ever. The three of us will always be together."

Jinot looked shyly at Ah Min. "Actually, there will soon be four of us," she said.

"We are? I mean, you are?" Ah Min looked at his wife, wide-eyed with excitement.

Jinot nodded. "For two months, I've not had the monthly flow. I think we will have an addition to our family next May."

Ah Min kissed his wife fervently, while Kuea looked on impatiently, wanting his father to go back with him into the water.

38

"I hope this too will be a boy, for as the years go by I will need all the help I can get with the farming," Udet said, when she was told Jinot was with child again.

Jinot's pregnancy was going well, as had the last. Enti was very happy with the news that another baby was on the way. She also had her own reason to be happy.

"Jinot, this fellow from Kampong Saga has been coming to our asuok in the evenings. Mother is quite impressed," Enti confided in Jinot when she was over at Jinot's asuok.

"And you? Do you like him?" Jinot held her breath.

"He's different from the others. He's kind and considerate, gentle, unassuming. And what makes him stand out, he's educated. He even learned to read and write English when he was living in Kuching. His father was a gardener at the Rajah's residence, but this was twelve years ago, before the uprising, and his father has long left the job." Enti paused a moment, looking a bit reserved. "I've been coming down from the loft to sit with him when he visits."

"That's a very good sign, Enti!" said Jinot, happy for her sister, but also secretly excited for herself and Ah Min as it meant they might be one step closer to achieving their plan of going to China. "I'm glad Mother approves."

"Well, she was anxious about getting me married. She was asking him lots of questions."

"She must really like him then. Tell me more about him, Enti," Jinot pressed.

Enti put on a complying air. "Well, his name is Koper. He's a year older than me. He is one of three sons in his family."

"That's good, that there are other men in his family. I mean, he can be spared. His parents won't need him around when he marries. Will you marry him if he asks?"

"I will consider."

Later that night, Jinot told Ah Min about Enti's new suitor. Ah Min was very excited too. "Our dream of leaving for Tang Shan is going to come true soon, Jinot. By the time our baby is born, Enti will be married, or will soon be. We will wait till the baby is about six months old, big enough to manage the sea journey, then we will leave."

"You will talk to my mother about it when the time comes, won't you?"

"Yes, I'll talk to her. I'm sure she won't object when she has another son-in-law to help her. Besides, he is Bidayuh, and I am not. That's a big plus for Koper!"

"I only hope this will work out as we think."

During the remainder of Jinot's pregnancy, Ah Min kept a small fire in the kitchen of their asuok, which apart from its use for boiling water and cooking also kept the wood and bamboo dry, especially during the rainy season. He spent a lot of time with Kuea, to give Jinot more rest. Ah Min would take him with him into the jungle to find edible ferns, mushrooms and medicinal herbs, Kuea in a large juah on his back, and a special bond was established between father and son.

"Mama?" Kuea asked, using his limited vocabulary.

"Mama resting at home. She is having baby soon," Ah Min would answer in Hakka. He wanted his son to be able to converse with his *gung gung* and *po po* when finally they were able to return to his native China. Kuea had to know some Hakka.

Before long, the rice harvest was upon them. Ah Min worked from the break of dawn to sunset gathering the ripened stalks, conducting the threshing processes of stomping and pounding, then winnowing and finally laying out the rice grains to dry on the tanju. He was doing his job and

Jinot's. Kuea had a good time helping his father with the harvested rice stalks, jumping on them with his tiny feet, and falling into them again and again. To him, it was a wonderful game.

Enti confided in Jinot one afternoon during harvest time that Koper had asked her to marry him, and she had said yes. Moreover, an uncle of Koper's had been to see Udet to negotiate the wedding.

"Congratulations, Enti, and thank you so much!" Jinot said, hugging her sister.

"Why thank me?"

"Because now Ah Min can go back to China with me and our children. It has been Ah Min's dream for a long time. He's staying because of Mother. Now that Koper will be here to help her, we can go."

"When Koper's uncle asked Mother if I could move to their longhouse after our marriage, Mother said she would need both me and Koper to be here with her, since she was a widow who had lost her only son."

"I hope that doesn't present a problem with Koper," Jinot said with concern.

"Actually, Koper and I have talked about it. He knows he has to give in to Mother's wish in order to marry me. Luckily, his parents are reasonable and are understanding of Mother's situation. Koper has already told Mother he would live in our kampong after the wedding. The wedding date is set for the 1st of September, five months from now."

"I'm so happy, Enti. Very happy for you and very happy for us! By the time our second child is six months, you'll be married and Koper will be living in Tikuan. That's when we will leave. But please keep this a secret. Don't tell Mother about it. Ah Min will tell her later, when the right time comes. I just hope she will take it well and let us leave with her blessings." Jinot noticed the uncomfortable look on Enti's face.

"If you and Ah Min wish to go, you should go," Enti said quietly. "Koper and I will take care of Mother."

"Thank you, Enti. You are my best and dearest friend."

That day, Enti and Jinot's conversation took place while they were resting during the harvest in a small bamboo hut that stood at the edge of a paddy field on a path close to the jungle. Jinot had brought some food for the workers in the field, leaving Kuea with a neighbouring woman. The two sisters were alone in the hut. As they poured out their hearts, it had not occurred to them to keep their voices low, until they heard a slight noise to the rear. Immediately, they halted their conversation and looked out. No one was in sight. Perhaps it had just been the rainforest whispering a warning to them.

39

Ever since she was a child, Jinot had been disturbed by the rain. It usually came in the afternoon to the great island of Borneo, especially in the months leading up to the rice harvest. The rain fell like dense, unbroken threads of silk. It was strong enough to carve out deep gullies in the soft dark earth and make leaves tremble in the green lushness of the forest. It spattered, sometimes pounded, on the thatched rooftops of longhouses. It picked up momentum as it splashed on the hillside, like a rapid cascading home.

As she grew older, Jinot had imagined hearing in the thunderous downpour the chant of the tribal black magician who could call up evil spirits to inflict harm on victims. *Black magic could make bad things happen. Black magic could make bad things happen.* The black magician who lived alone in the jungle about two miles from Tikuan was an old Bidayuh woman. She did not belong to the kampong. Jinot and Enti had never seen her, but they had heard frightful stories as children about her, how she could use voodoo spells to inflict insanity or agonizing death on her victims. They referred to her as the witch and Jinot had once asked her mother if she had ever seen the woman.

"Yes, I came across her in the forest one time. You should have nothing to fear from her if you have never done anyone wrong," Udet replied, a wary look on her face. "But you should keep out of her way nonetheless."

The day after Enti and Jinot's heart-to-heart talk in the shelter by the paddy field, Ah Min and Jinot trekked into the jungle to gather midin, as Jinot had a craving for the wild fern. They'd left Kuea napping in the care of their neighbour at the longhouse. Suddenly, they heard distant thunder. Soon the rain would come. They would need to hurry back if they didn't want to get caught in a downpour, but as they turned round they saw in the distance among the trees someone coming from the direction of the kampong and heading into the dark recess of the jungle. Instinctively they stopped, stepped off the path and crouched among the undergrowth. As the figure passed them, they realized it was Udet. She did not see them, so focused was she on making her way to wherever she was going.

Their curiosity aroused, and disturbed as to what Udet might be up to, they followed her stealthily at a distance. After some fifteen minutes, they saw a small wooden cabin through a break in the forest's trees. Udet headed directly for it. Ah Min and Jinot edged closer, staying out of sight off the path. An old woman with long, dishevelled white hair sat on the floor of the canopied verandah. She wore a jomuh, tied at her waist. Her bare breasts hung shrivelled and low, brushing against her distended belly. In her hand was a painted wooden doll. Ah Min and Jinot were looking at none other than the witch of Jinot's childhood.

As Udet approached, the old hag slowly rose and beckoned to her before entering her hut. Udet walked up the few steps to the verandah, bending her head a little at the door, and followed her in.

Ah Min and Jinot squatted down, camouflaged by the jungle's vegetation, waiting for what seemed forever for Udet to re-emerge. They felt a raindrop, then a splatter, and then more as the rain fell in earnest, and were thankful for the shelter of the broad-leaved palms above their heads. Although drenched and uncomfortable by the time Udet reappeared from the witch's domain, they remained motionless as they watched her lift her face to the low dark sky. There was a disturbing intensity in her expression as she walked away from the cabin, back towards Tikuan. The old harridan came out soon after, waving her wooden doll, and then gave out a shrill, long-drawn cry that seemed to resound to the thunder, sending intense shudders through the two already wet and shivering young onlookers.

40

"Grandpa, do you believe in the practice of voodoo?" Therese asks as she is having lunch with her grandfather at a restaurant on the riverfront boulevard. She cannot help being disturbed by what she has read the night before about the episode in the jungle not far from Kampong Tikuan in the time of Ah Min and Jinot.

"Black magic has been practised among most of the indigenous groups of Borneo for centuries. But many Dayaks, both Bidayuhs and Ibans, have become Christians, and so it is not much used nowadays."

"Have you ever come across anyone who's been a victim of black magic?"

"In fact, yes," says Grandpa Liu, geared up to tell a story. "There was this Malay fellow who lived in Kuching by the old mosque. One day, as he was walking close to the city centre, he hawked and spat into the street. Unfortunately, someone happened to drive by in a convertible and was hit by the spittle. Enraged and insulted, the driver stopped his car and yelled obscenities at the man. Since shortly after that day, the poor Malay has been plagued with a strange illness. He began initially twitching his facial muscles and then started repeatedly rocking his head from side to side. As a result, no one would give him a job and he had to live on charity. This happened about twenty years ago. I still see the poor fellow in the city sometimes; he's lean and drawn and shabby-looking, still making strange faces and flinging his head like a derelict. People say the driver in his anger must have had a voodoo spell cast on him."

"I'd call that a bad case of a facial tic," Therese says. "Did he see a doctor?"

"He was probably too poor and ignorant to see a doctor. Besides, if it was really voodoo, no medicine would help. Only the person who had the curse cast on him could have it removed. Want to hear a more gruesome case that involved a friend of mine?"

Therese nods with eager apprehension.

"When this Hakka friend of mine was a young man, an Iban girl he knew fell in love with him, but he was already married and would not return her attention. He began to experience a severe pain in his belly. He then started to vomit and was unable to hold food down. The most startling thing was he began passing live worms in his stools. Doctors could do nothing. No medicine could cure him. He was dying. His wife suspected that he was the victim of black magic. She knew about the Iban girl and went to her and begged her to have the spell lifted, if she had indeed imposed such a curse on him. The Iban girl really loved him and hearing how he was suffering she agreed to have the curse undone. After that, the awful symptoms left my friend and he recovered."

"Hmm! That was probably nothing more than him having parasites in his intestines. He must have eaten some uncooked meat and the eggs hatched into worms," Therese says with a shudder.

"My father once told me that if you believed in black magic, you would be a victim of it because any misfortune or illness that befell you could be blamed on a curse. But if you didn't believe in it, it would not harm you because you would regard any misfortune or illness as the result of natural causes."

"That's so true. These phenomena can often be explained with science."

"Why such an interest in voodoo?" Grandpa asks.

"I've come to the part in the story of Liu Hon Min where there was a voodoo witch who cast black magic on people. It's really quite disturbing."

41

With the end of the harvest, the new life inside Jinot grew to term. On the evening of Gawai, May 1st, 1861, while everyone at Tikuan was gathered in the awah of the old longhouse, feasting and drinking, Jinot started experiencing labour pains. She tried to get comfortable sitting on the raised platform of the awah, but suddenly it felt as if something had popped inside her and a watery fluid streamed from her womb. She turned to Ah Min and whispered urgently into his ear. He got to his feet and quickly but quietly so as not to break up the festivities sought out first Udet and then Enti, who was with Koper. Jinot was at once helped into Udet's asuok, even though Ah Min had their own asuok in the new longhouse ready for the birth of their second child.

Ah Min was at first allowed inside the asuok, where Jinot had been made comfortable on a mat, while Kuea was left in the care of a neighbouring woman. Udet told him to light a fire in the kitchen and then to fetch water from the mountain stream that ran past the longhouse. She began to chant spells to ward off evil spirits which might harm the mother and the baby. Jinot was whimpering, her forehead and face covered in sweat, her pains now increasing in intensity. Udet continued to read her spells, the haunting incantations of a bedan, her voice increasing in volume to a wild crescendo until it drowned Jinot's continual moaning. Enti gave Jinot water from a small bowl and Udet told her to give her betel nut to chew.

As soon as Udet stopped her chanting, Ah Min knelt over his wife, who was very pale and sweating, her hands clenched, her upper teeth biting her lower lip. As she rested her eyes on her husband, she raised one hand to him. Taking her hand in his he bent down closer.

"I don't feel good at all," Jinot said. "I'm scared."

"You'll be fine," Ah Min comforted. "I love you. Kuea loves you. This will be over soon and then we'll have a new child, and Kuea will have a brother or sister. You are so brave, my love."

"Where is Kuea?"

"He's with our neighbour. He's safe with her."

"Ah Min, stay with me."

"Of course I will stay with you."

Ah Min continued to hold Jinot's hand, wiping the sweat from her forehead and offering words of comfort. Jinot's pains grew worse. Udet gave her more betel nut and resumed chanting her spells to ward off the evil spirits. She then turned to Ah Min and said, "You should leave now, Ah Min. Wait outside and we will call you as soon as the baby is born."

"I want to stay!"

"You cannot stay, Ah Min. The husband should not be present at the birth. You remember when Kuea was born, you were waiting outside then," Udet said.

Turning to Jinot, Ah Min reluctantly whispered in her ear, "I'm going out for a short while. I'll be back as soon as the baby is born. I know you'll be fine. I love you."

With a lingering, desperate look at Ah Min, Jinot let go her hand. Ah Min bent down to kiss her damp forehead. As he stood up, turned and slowly left the asuak, Jinot followed him with eyes of despair.

Ah Min found Kuea asleep in the care of the neighbour in the awah. He thanked her and told her to return to her own asuok, and then sat down beside his son on the raised platform and watched him sleep. The chubby Kuea looked serenely contented, oblivious to the nervous tension consuming his father and unaware of the agony his mother was enduring to bring a sibling into the world for him. For Ah Min, the endless wait in the awah was tormenting. The Gawai celebrations were now over and as most residents and guests had turned in for the night, Koper, who had been out on the tanju, came into the awah and sat down beside him.

Ah Min strained his ears, hoping any moment to hear the cry signalling his fatherhood for the second time. But that cry never came through the flimsy walls. All he could hear were Jinot's piercing, heart-wrenching screams, the commotion augmented by sounds of hurried footsteps inside the asuok. Every cry Jinot uttered was like a blade cutting into Ah Min's heart. He had no idea how long it was since Jinot had gone into labour. The night sky was becoming lighter and the cockerels were already crowing. Kuea remained asleep and Koper had dozed off, his head against the awah wall. Jinot's screams gradually subsided. For a while, there was an unnerving silence inside the asuok, and then raised voices. Silence finally fell again.

Minutes later, the door to Udet's asuok opened. Enti emerged. She just stood there crying and shaking, looking distraught and scared. Ah Min was at the doorway in no time. He brushed past her into the asuok and was quickly by Jinot's side. Udet was not there. Jinot had her eyes closed. She was asleep, perhaps unconscious; she wasn't moving. A woven blanket was covering her body. By the light of the oil lamps, he saw blood on the mat on which Jinot lay, blood on the floor around her and blood in a basin nearby. Horrified at the sight of so much of it, Ah Min cried like one driven mad as he dropped down beside Jinot, holding her, caressing her.

"What happened?" he yelled frantically. He brushed aside Jinot's matted hair from her ashen-grey face. He kissed her cheeks. "Wake up! I love you, Jinot."

Gradually, Jinot opened her listless eyes. Her face lit up for a fleeting moment at the sight of Ah Min, and then her eyes closed once again. Just then, Enti re-entered the asuok.

Ah Min cried out, "Do something, please! Help her!"

Enti looked over to Ah Min. She shook her head, crying as though her heart was breaking. "She has lost a lot of blood. The bleeding won't stop. I have sent for the priestess."

"Baby," Jinot managed to whisper.

At this, Ah Min thought for the first time of the baby that Jinot had been carrying.

"Where's the baby?" Ah Min asked.

In a strained voice, Enti replied, "The baby did not live." A pause, and she continued, "You should not see your stillborn child. Bad luck."

"I want my baby," Jinot said, tears rolling down her face.

"It really does not matter, Jinot. The spirit of death has taken our baby and nothing can bring it back. Kuea and I love you," Ah Min said. "You have to live for us. We'll have another baby." Losing the baby would be a devastating blow for Ah Min, but at that moment all he cared about was his wife.

As Enti did her best to mop up the continual slow flow of blood and cleaned Jinot's body with warm water, Ah Min asked, "Where's Udet? I thought she was tending to Jinot."

"She took the dead baby out through the back so you wouldn't see it," Enti said amidst her sobs.

"Was it a boy or girl?" asked Ah Min.

In the same tight voice, Enti answered, "Boy."

The priestess arrived. She asked Ah Min to step back and he grudgingly allowed her to assume his place. The priestess, who had been officiating at the Gawai celebrations, touched Jinot's forehead and proceeded to recite incantations to drive out the evil spirits that they thought were causing her bleeding. She chanted for a long while.

Ah Min was watching Jinot from a step away. Her lips moved and formed the word "Kuea". Ah Min turned to Enti and said, "Bring Kuea to her."

Enti went out to fetch him, and the priestess carried on with her chanting. When Enti returned, Ah Min took the now wide-awake Kuea from her arms and edged close to his wife, brushing the priestess aside. He knelt down so that Jinot could touch her son.

"Mama!" Kuea cried, as soon as he saw his mother, and held out his short fat arms to embrace her.

"Mama loves you very much, Kuea," Jinot said faintly in Hakka to her son, every word she uttered a big physical effort. "Don't want to leave you, Kuea." Kuea placed his cheek next to hers and touched her face with his hand, as if he understood what his mother was saying. Jinot turned her eyes towards Ah Min and said, still in Hakka, "Give Kuea a good life."

"I promise. Do not worry. Kuea will grow up a fine man. He will make you proud." His voice was broken by his crying.

"I want to kiss Kuea," she said, choking.

Ah Min brought Kuea's cheeks to Jinot's lips. Kuea turned his face towards his mother's and smothered her with his kisses. Jinot managed a weak smile. After a while, she said, every word harder to form than the one before, "So sorry I can't go to Tang Shan. Take Kuea."

"Don't say that. We will take you with us in our hearts, my dearest wife. I will make sure you are known and remembered in the Liu family for all future generations." Jinot managed another faint smile. She closed her eyes. When she opened them again, Ah Min asked, "Are you in pain?"

"No pain. Just cold. Hold me," she whispered.

Ah Min lay down beside her, on the edge of the blanket, holding her close, Kuea between them. Kuea seemed to understand the situation. He did not try to wriggle out of his parents' hold, but turning towards his mother, he kept his eyes on her face, as if he sensed she was slipping away from him and he didn't want to let her go. Together the three lay, locked in an embrace, long after daylight had seeped into the asuok.

While Ah Min, Jinot and Kuea lay huddled on the blood-soaked mat, Enti knelt at the foot of her sister, not caring about the blood that was staining her jomuh, and cried bitterly. The priestess had left the asuok, and Udet had not returned. Ah Min had his arms around his wife and son, holding on to that moment that would fill his eternity. Some time lapsed. Kuea was asleep. When Ah Min next looked over to Jinot, he saw that a peaceful, painless sleep had quietly come over her. Drained of her lifeblood, her slow, weak pulse had dwindled to a standstill. Her face was sheet-white, her blue lips slightly parted. Her eyes were open, staring at eternity. Ah Min leaned over the sleeping Kuea, kissed his wife on the lips and gently closed her eyes.

42

The afternoon of Jinot's death, Enti and Udet, who had now returned to the longhouse, washed Jinot's body. The fact that Udet was not present during Jinot's last moments did not trouble Ah Min. He did not think there was anything she could have done, for all her midwifery experience. Jinot was dressed in her best jomuh and Udet then summoned the village pinanuh to her asuok. The pinanuh rolled Jinot's body in a mat and left it in a corner until the next morning. Udet told Ah Min that all of Jinot's belongings were to be gathered and placed with the body.

"We need to burn everything that was Jinot's, so that her spirit will not return to look for them," Udet said. She was dry-eyed and her voice was controlled, as it was when she had received news of Joto's death. It was hard to tell what emotions she was experiencing at the loss of a daughter and a grandson who never survived into the world of the living.

"Everything that had belonged to her?" Ah Min asked. "Can't I keep something of hers?"

"No, unless you want her to come back to haunt us all," Udet replied in an adamant tone.

Then there was the dead baby.

"Where is my dead child? We need to bury him."

"A baby that has died at birth is put in a basket and hung on a tree. As bedan of our kampong, I have fulfilled that duty."

"You left my child to rot on a tree?" Ah Min was beside himself.

"It was painful to me, what I did, for he was my grandson, though he never took a single breath of life." Udet paused, her eyes betraying a sadness that she had not expressed till then. "To have lost Jinot–" Her voice finally broke and she could not continue. For the first time since he'd known her, Ah Min saw tears welling in Udet's eyes.

Ah Min returned to his asuok in the new longhouse and collected all of Jinot's personal belongings to be burned at her cremation; all but two items, which he secretly hid under the mat on which he and Jinot had slept. These were the jade Buddha pendant that had been his mother's hanging from its gold chain and the bark painting of Jinot done by her cousin Sibon.

"Jinot, I am keeping the jade Buddha and the painting of you. I don't want them to be destroyed," Ah Min said aloud, while looking around the asuok as though he sensed her presence. "I don't care if you come back as a ghost looking for them. In fact, I *will* you to return to my world. I already miss you more than any human being could imagine. Let me see you! Let me feel you! You once told me you believed in spirits. Be my good spirit, my ghost, and stay with me and Kuea. We both love and miss you so much."

While Ah Min gathered Jinot's belongings, Enti took care of Kuea, who kept crying and calling for his mama. Even at his young age, he seemed to be aware of his great loss. Enti tried her best to distract him with his bamboo toys, but he would not be consoled.

The next morning, Ah Min led the procession, carrying in his arms Jinot's body wrapped in the mat, with the pinanuh by his side, followed by Udet and Enti and Enti's future husband, Koper, holding Kuea. They reached the cremation ground on the bank of a small stream. Ah Min gently laid Jinot's wrapped body on a stack of dried firewood already prepared for the cremation. Ah Min embraced the wrapped corpse one more time. He put his lips to where her lips would be and let them stay there for a long moment. "Goodbye, Jinot, my dearest wife," he said aloud in Hakka. "Be comforted knowing that Kuea and I will always love you. I will teach our son to keep your memory alive for all our descendants to come." He then asked Koper to hand Kuea to him and he let the two-year-old hug the wrapped body that was his mother for the last time. He stepped down with Kuea from the wood stack, his vision blurred with tears. The shaman who had presided at the annual Gawai celebrations prayed and chanted that Jinot might go to the afterworld in peace and not return to earth to haunt them. Some women from Tikuan sang dirges and songs of farewell.

Presided over by the pinanuh, attendants at the cremation lit the firewood and flames soon engulfed the body lain at its top. Jinot's personal belongings were burned nearby. The fire from the burning corpse emitted a lot of smoke. Instead of rising skyward, the smoke swirled and spiralled above the pyre until it was gradually dissipated by a gentle wind. Ah Min recalled what he had heard, that smoke at a cremation rising towards the sky meant a direct and fast passage for the dead to the afterworld. Smoke encircling around and above the burning body meant the ghost of the cremated would return to earth. For the first time since Jinot's ordeal and death, Ah Min managed a weak smile.

43

In the days following Jinot's funeral, Ah Min saw his wife in every nook and corner of the home that they had built. Her image was in the candle flames when night beckoned him to bed. He heard her voice in the morning twitter of birds and in the pitter-patter of rain on the atap roofing of their longhouse. Kuea's frantic cries for his mother added an unsustainable weight to Ah Min's already burdened heart.

Despite his young age, Kuea was able to communicate in simple Hakka with his father.

"Where Mama?" Kuea asked, looking at his father.

"She's here with you, although you cannot see her. You can feel her here." Ah Min touched Kuea on the chest.

"Mama here?" asked Kuea, pointing to his own heart.

"Yes, Mama is here, in your heart."

Kuea looked down at his chest and could not see Mama there. "Mama coming home soon?" he asked.

"Mama has gone to a faraway place. Mama won't be coming home soon, but she is watching over you."

Kuea could not understand. To a two-year-old, only the tangible and visible, nothing else, were real. Especially at night, he cried for his mother, no matter how much Ah Min comforted and cajoled. Ah Min was aware that mourning alone would only deepen his anguish and dull his brain. He had Kuea to think of, to care and live for. "Give Kuea a good life" was Jinot's dying request, that and "Take Kuea" to Tang Shan. By the end of the fourth day after the funeral, Ah Min's mind was made up. There was nothing left for him at Tikuan, only Kuea and the bittersweet memories of Jinot, which he would take with him for ever, no matter where he went. He would leave Tikuan with Kuea, leave Sarawak, and journey back to China as soon as he could. His parents and sister were in their village in Dongguan, struggling for their livelihood, with his brothers gone to fight with the rebels against the Manchus. Now was the time to go home. Jinot would want him to.

Ah Min resumed his work life at Tikuan for the while, tending mostly to Udet's fruit trees and pepper and cocoa crops, and helping with building jobs at the kampong, leaving Kuea in the care of a neighbouring woman at his longhouse. Since the day he and Jinot had seen Udet going to the old woman in the jungle, he had not wanted to leave Kuea alone with her. Ah Min mistrusted her. He could not forget the chilling intensity on her face when she'd left the witch's hut. Had she suspected his intention of leaving Kampong Tikuan with Jinot, Kuea and the new baby to return to Tang Shan? Was she going to resort to black magic to prevent them from going? Ah Min had planned on Enti's husband being able to replace him in the family, so that he wouldn't be indispensable. However, he had not taken into consideration the importance of his children to Udet. That she loved Kuea, there was no doubt. Kuea was a sunny, lovable child with eyes like two black glinting marbles and round, plump cheeks, although by now he had lost much of his baby fat. Anyone, least his grandmother, must have a heart of stone not to love him. But Udet's fondness for the child only added to Ah Min's anxiety as to what she might do to keep them at Tikuan. He looked for an opportunity to discuss with Enti and Koper his plan of returning to China, and when they came by to his asuok one evening for supper, two weeks after Jinot's funeral, he told them of his intention.

"Enti, I know Jinot told you that we planned to leave Sarawak and return to Tang Shan. With you here, Koper, I can leave Tikuan with Kuea and have peace of mind knowing Enti and Udet will be in your care. I really want to go home."

"You have our support, Ah Min. Yes, I knew you had wanted to go back to China. You should go, and the sooner the better. This is no life for you here, or for Kuea. Your parents need you in China. They too should be able to see their grandson and hold him," Enti said, tears forming in her eyes. Ever since Jinot's death, Enti had become very labile. She seemed to have been stripped of her former self-confidence and assertiveness. She looked forlorn.

"How do you think Udet will react?" asked Ah Min.

"She will be angry and sad, but you have to live the life you want," Enti said.

"This may be unwarranted, but I've been troubled ever since Jinot and I saw her going to that wooden hut in the forest. I'm worried she may use black magic to keep us here."

Enti looked away for a moment. Then addressing Ah Min, she said, "Don't worry about Mother. As a widow with no son in the family, she probably wanted to explore using voodoo spells as a protection against her vulnerability. Mother won't want you to leave for she values you very much, but with Koper to help her in the fields and all the work at the kampong, you can be spared. She will not have a voodoo spell cast on you to keep you from leaving. As for Kuea, she will never harm him in any way, for she loves him dearly." Then she added, "However, it's best to avoid any unpleasant confrontation with her, so don't tell her about your plans of leaving and there's no need to say goodbye."

"Wouldn't she be more upset if we just left without a proper farewell?"

"Goodbyes are painful. Don't make it worse for yourself or for my mother."

"You know your mother best. I'll do as you say. But I have a few important tasks to take care of before we can go, including booking our passages."

"Do whatever you need to do. And when you are ready, then leave."

Shortly before sunrise the next day, while Kuea was still sleeping, Ah Min trekked into the jungle to the foot of the tapang tree where he and Jinot had buried the bag of gold coins some three years earlier. He dug up the coins, returned with them to his longhouse and hid all but four of them under the bamboo floorboards of his asuok. He picked up Kuea and left him with the woman in the next asuok, telling her only that he would be going downriver for a couple of days on business and asking her to take good care of Kuea while he was gone. Kuea would spend that night and the next with the neighbour.

Returning to his own asuok, Ah Min wrapped the four coins in cloth and put them in the jacket pocket of his samfu before setting out for Buso. Soon after noon, he reached the riverbank across from the village, but instead of crossing the river to the bazaar, he asked the Malay boatman, who was at his usual spot on the bank, to take him downriver to the 16-mile bazaar. The 16-mile bazaar had also by now acquired a new name, Siniawan, which, according to the boatman, came from the words "sik nyaman" meaning "not pleasant" in a Malay dialect.

Ah Min stopped at Mr Yong's teahouse. The teahouse owner expressed his shock and deep sympathy over Jinot's death. Ah Min asked Mr Yong if he could give him Sarawak currency in exchange for the four gold coins, as he recalled he knew someone who would trade them.

"You are lucky today! I don't normally keep so much money on me, but I have recently sold my pepper farm because I'm getting too old to look after it properly. I still haven't decided what to do with the money, so it is here, under lock and key!"

"I am very thankful," Ah Min said, looking earnest. "I have another big favour to ask of you, Mr Yong. I am leaving Sarawak soon to go back to Tang Shan with my son. I made a promise to Lo Tai that I would not leave without him. I want to take his remains with me."

"It's been four years since his burial. I imagine all that is in his grave are his bones. I can ask the grave-diggers here to gather them for you."

"I'd be most grateful. But since I'll have my young son with me and a lot of belongings, bringing back Lo Tai's ashes will be better. Can you arrange to have his remains cremated? I will pay well for the service. I'm going to Kuching now to make arrangements for the boat passage, but I'll be back tomorrow."

"You're lucky again! The funeral facilities that serve the nearby kampongs and bazaars are here in Siniawan. I can arrange to have this done in a day, since there is no new burial taking place today. The ashes will be in my shop waiting for you when you return," said Mr Yong.

"I believe Jinot is guiding me every step of the way," said Ah Min.

From Siniawan, Ah Min got on a longboat to go downriver to Kuching, reaching the capital in the evening. In 1861, the town of Kuching extended for three-quarters of a mile along both banks of the Sarawak River; it had recovered from the Chinese Rebellion. A good number of new shophouses had been built on the south bank, although they were closed for the night by the time Ah Min arrived. He spent the night at an inn on the riverfront, but as soon as businesses opened the next morning, he went to the shipping agency Jarong Jawa on Gambier Road to book a passage out to Singapore on the next available boat and from there on to Hong Kong. He was told a vessel would be leaving Kuching in a week's time, on May 28th. He purchased cabin spaces for himself and Kuea with some of the currency Mr Yong had given him for the gold.

With his business completed, Ah Min hired a tambang to take him back to Siniawan. It was mid-afternoon by the time they docked and the boatman, a friendly middle-aged Malay named Ahab, said that because of the hour he would spend the night there as it would soon be too dark to return to Kuching. Ah Min arranged for him to take him further upriver to Buso the next morning. He then went directly to Mr Yong's teahouse.

On a table in Mr Yong's private parlour was an eight-inch-square black lacquer box.

"I got a Taoist priest to chant at his grave, before it was dug up. The coffin had disintegrated. In this climate, you'd expect it so. His bones were collected and cremated. Take him home, Ah Min."

Ah Min thanked Mr Yong profusely and paid him for the service. At Mr Yong's insistence, he spent the night at the teahouse owner's shophouse instead of at an inn. Early the next morning, Ah Min took his leave of him.

"I wish you and your son a safe journey to Tang Shan. If you ever come back, come see us. But if I don't see you again, I will know you are doing well back home in Tang Shan. Farewell, my friend." Mr Yong embraced Ah Min.

As arranged, the boatman was waiting at the water's edge to row Ah Min upriver to Buso. Before he went ashore on the river's north bank across from the bazaar, Ah Min asked Ahab to meet him and his young son at the same place on the north bank on the morning of May 27th, one day before they were due to leave Kuching for Singapore, and to take them to Kuching in his tambang, promising him generous payment.

44

It had been arranged that Koper would meet Ah Min and Kuea at four o'clock on the morning of May 27th at the junction where the footpath from Kampong Tikuan crossed the dirt road that eventually joined up with the road to Lundu. He would have a horse to take them to the boat landing across from Buso.

In the days before his planned departure, Ah Min packed his personal belongings, including the box containing Lo Tai's ashes, the pouch of gold coins, the piece of bark with Jinot's portrait, now rolled up, and the jade pendant, into two big juah that Jinot had woven. It saddened him that he could not say goodbye to his neighbours at the longhouse, but he could not take the chance of word getting to Udet that he and Kuea were leaving. In spite of Enti's assurance, he was still wary of Udet, afraid that she might resort to black magic to keep him and Kuea at Tikuan, especially Kuea. He was sorry and felt a genuine guilt that she would not be seeing her grandson again. That the old lady loved Kuea, Ah Min had no doubt; when Kuea was in her presence, she had always shown a softness that she gave to no one else. The evening before he planned to leave Tikuan, Ah Min took Kuea over to Udet's asuok to play with the other children in his grandmother's longhouse. They remained there for a considerable while, in the awah and out on the tanju, and when it was time to take Kuea home, Ah Min told him to say goodnight to his *sumuk*. He did, and then, as if he sensed it was a long goodbye, gave his grandmother a big squeezing hug. Udet uttered a heartfelt laugh. Ah Min looked away.

"Goodnight, Sumuk," Ah Min repeated after his son. Without looking Udet in the eye, he gathered up Kuea and left her longhouse to walk back to his own.

Enti had said her goodbye to Ah Min and Kuea the night before, when she dropped in at their asuok. She was crying hard as she kissed and hugged Kuea. She was not there when Ah Min took Kuea over to visit Udet on the last night, having purposely gone to call on a friend in a neighbouring kampong to avoid arousing her mother's suspicion should she succumb to tears on seeing Kuea again.

Before the first cock's crow broke the dull silence of the night and before any hint of a lightening sky signalled the approach of dawn, Ah Min strapped the two juah to his back, one beside the other. With the sleeping Kuea in his arms he left his asuok where he and Jinot had spent their happiest times and stepped quietly down the trunk ladder. He knew as he turned his back to the kampong that he would never see it again and trekked somewhat sadly along the footpath from Tikuan to its intersection with the dirt road. The load on his back was great and the sleeping Kuea felt heavier than usual. Luckily, he only had a quarter of a mile to walk before reaching the crossroads where Koper would be waiting.

The night air was refreshing, the only time in the day when the temperature felt reasonably comfortable. Kuea was draped weightily on his shoulder and Ah Min tightened his hold on his son, his most precious belonging. Together, father and son would brave the world, confront all odds and make a life for themselves. Jinot's spirit must be with them. He would always have a part of her with him. Who said the spirits of women dying in childbirth would return as malicious banshees? Not Jinot. Her ghost would return, visible or invisible, but always as a gentle and kind spirit, full of goodness and love, as she herself was in life. She would protect their son, and their descendants to come. His thoughts of Jinot made his trek less burdensome and before he knew it he had come to the crossroads where Koper was waiting with two horses, one which he'd borrowed, as he would accompany Ah Min to Buso. They rode at a steady pace, with the awakened and excited Kuea seated in front of his father, making stops to stretch their legs and let the horses rest.

Ahab and his tambang were waiting for them at the Buso landing when they finally got there at around seven in the morning. Kuea happily let the boatman help him on board, but before Ah Min boarded the tambang himself, he embraced Koper warmly, saying, "We will not see each other again, but may good fortune shine on you and Enti."

Reaching Kuching in the early afternoon, Ah Min checked in at an inn at the Main Bazaar before setting out to stock up on non-perishable food for the sea journey. He put Kuea in one of the juah, strapped it to his back and walked down Gambier Road, now wearing workers' pants instead of his Bidayuh loincloth. He purchased a sack of rice, mung beans for germinating on the voyage, a supply of preserved cabbage and salted eggs. Not to go home without presents, he bought a catty each of black and white pepper, something homegrown from Sarawak. All his purchases he placed in a jute sack the rice-shop owner gave him. The shopkeeper, a Hokkien immigrant, kindly offered to keep the sack in his shop for the night and have it carried on board the junk the next morning before it set sail for Singapore.

With his shopping chores completed, Ah Min finally had time to rest and stroll along the waterfront with Kuea, still in the juah, past the many shops and teahouses. Scenes of his first day in Kuching twelve years earlier when he had arrived with Lo Tai on the fish-eye boat, *Nam Wah*, flashed back. Who could have predicted that his intended five years in Nanyang would stretch to twelve and the tragic events that were to take place in Sarawak would overturn his plans and change his life forever?

The fish-eye boat now taking Ah Min and Kuea from Kuching to Singapore and then north-east across the South China Sea to Hong Kong was the *Toishan*. True to his word, the Hokkien store owner delivered the sack of goods soon after Ah Min and Kuea had boarded the junk the next morning. Kuea was fascinated with the boat, especially when his father pointed out the larger-than-life eyes painted on the bow. Instead of the cheaper deck space he'd had on his outbound journey with Lo Tai, Ah Min had paid for cabin space below; he did not want to subject Kuea to the elements or damage his belongings, especially the box containing Lo Tai's ashes and the painting of

Jinot. As for the bag of gold coins, Ah Min kept it wrapped in a cloth pouch which he wore all the time tied round his waist.

At eleven-thirty on the morning of May 28th, 1861, the *Toishan* sailed out of Kuching waters towards the mouth of the Sarawak River delta. She then glided full sail into the wind, westbound for Singapore, taking Ah Min and little Kuea with her.

45

"There was so much tragedy in the life of Liu Hon Min, Grandpa. His wife, Jinot, died in childbirth. My heart is breaking at the thought of his young son losing his mother. I cried reading about that last night. I also feel so sorry for Li in your guerrilla story when Bong went on such a dangerous mission immediately after the loss of their baby," Therese says. "I wish he could have stayed behind when she needed him most."

"State before family. The common good before personal attachment. This was our guiding motto, our uncompromising principle." A bitter smile forms on Grandpa Liu's lips, his expression etched in disillusion. "That was a defining day and it was to change our lives forever. Let me begin from when we were transported in a cranky old Indonesian army truck from Entikong to pick up twenty more comrades on our mission. Their camp was about five miles south-east of the border with Sarawak and two of its SCO members were to be our guides all the way to the intended guerrilla base in the Bau region.

"We wasted no time in trekking to the border that morning. We each had a backpack containing ammunition, an army blanket and food for a day. And we each carried a rifle. Our commandant on the mission was a Hakka named Ong Lip Kuen; he'd led many successful cross-border raids of defence positions and border settlements, and boasted of having killed many enemy troops, including a handful of Gurkhas, in border skirmishes and ambushes.

"It was only mid-September, but the rains had come sooner than expected that year, making the track more difficult. Avoiding the Malaysian checkpoint at Serikin, we headed on foot across the unmarked jungle border. Our only enemies so far had been the uncooperative weather and the extremely muddy forest floor. We'd had twenty hours of nonstop downpour prior to our mission and trudging through the rainforest in those conditions was a terrible ordeal and an ultimate test of endurance, to say the least. My army uniform and jacket were soaked and my boots leaked, meaning my feet were wet and very uncomfortable. We continued to pick our way through the forest in the approaching dusk and although I could still make out occasional patches of light through gaps in the canopy above, the only sounds we heard were the perennial call of frogs and crickets – louder now because it was wet – and the scrape of our boots on the muddy ground. But we were in Sarawak!

"We had to stop for the night before total darkness engulfed us and each set out to find a tree in which to shelter from the mud and any enemy soldiers. I chose one with a few lower branches and clambered up to where I would be shielded by their foliage. I anchored myself on one of the bigger branches, my backpack between me and the trunk, and my rifle slung across my shoulders on my front. To prevent myself from falling if I dozed, I tied my right thigh to my anchor branch with a rope. By the time I was settled in my far-from-comfortable position, night had fallen.

"I must have slept quite soundly, for I was awakened by birdsong and the noise of movement below. Dawn had broken and was visible through the leaves, though it was still quite dim in the forest. I peered down and saw five or six Gurkhas, recognizable by their uniforms, tracking stealthily below, each man carrying a rifle. Not a sound was made from above. We dared not move and kept our weapons slung across our shoulders. Using our same track, the Gurkhas passed among our trees, two of them stopping to look around carefully before proceeding further. We finally breathed again.

"The distance from the border to our intended base was about seven miles. This target campsite was on a densely forested hill two miles south-west of Bau and about two miles west of Serikin Road, the main road connecting Serikin to Bau. We set off again. It was a rainless morning, but the heat and humidity were still with us and gave no relief. By ten in the morning, we were almost there and had only about another mile to go.

"It had been quiet for the last mile or so, unearthly quiet, not even the twitter of birds or the rustling of leaves, a dead silence within the forest. It seemed almost unnatural and I had an uncomfortable sense of foreboding, as if every movement we made might trigger an explosion, every step we took might be our last. Then I heard a chirp in the trees to our right, soon to be followed by another to our left, as though it was an answering call. Before I could indicate any concern to my comrades, a gunshot shattered the earlier silence, sending a flock of birds fluttering from above. One of our men in the front of the file collapsed, and Ong shouted an order for our group to disperse and take cover. A volley of shots followed, and more men fell. Keeping low, I scrambled behind a large tree.

"I crouched in the undergrowth for a few moments and then blindly crawled directly away from the firing. I did not dare to stop, but kept going to increase the distance between myself and the enemy. There was no time to think, no time to pause. My uniform was repeatedly snagged on the thorny vines and I got badly scratched in trying to free myself. The gunfire gradually lessened and finally stopped. I remained crouching and took out my pocket compass. I was heading north-east towards the town of Bau. My best hope was to continue in that direction and take refuge in one of the Hakka bazaars. Deciding I was now far enough away from the scene of the ambush, I stood up and ran as fast as I could.

"I hadn't got far when I heard the unmistakable sound of footsteps behind me. I dropped down again and looked back. Three of my comrades were on the path, and to my great joy and relief one of them was Bong. We regrouped in silence and then immediately set off again towards Bau.

"Another ten minutes of fast walking took us out of the protection of the forest onto a country road. We had bypassed any bazaar that might have been in the vicinity and had reached the town's limits. To lessen the chances of being seen, we took a small gravel road that led to the old section of Bau, what had been Mau San.

"Mau San looked deserted. Not a soul in sight. On our right, three old wooden houses lined one side of a dirt path running from where it joined the unpaved road to its far end in a forest. Another path sloped upwards to the left. We took the path on the right towards the forest, edging carefully past the houses in case they were being used as cover, but they seemed deserted. The remains of an old temple were further on to the left of us, and beyond those was the rainforest. Across from the temple ruins were the remnants of a flag pole, about eight feet high, with what was left of its posts planted in the earth. Bong sat down at the foot of the pole, leaning his back against it. He looked haggard and dishevelled, his jungle greens covered in mud.

"'That's what's left of the Mau San flagpole destroyed by the Rajah's men when they chased the Hakka miners back here during the Chinese Rebellion,' I told the others. 'The Rajah's men massacred the entire population of Mau San, the miners and their families.'

"'How come you know so much about the history of this place?' Bong asked, making an effort to get up from the flagpole.

"'I was here on a school trip with my students,' I said. 'It's sad that so few Chinese know about those tragic events.'

"We walked down the path back towards the houses and the intersection with the unpaved road. There was no answer when we knocked on the door of the house closest to the flagpole. We then tried the second house. No answer there either. We were approaching the third when we heard the grinding sound of heavy tires on the gravel road. Any second and a vehicle would appear. Frantically, we ran back towards the temple ruins, intending to make for the undergrowth and forest behind. The truck had come to a stop and we heard the stamping and shuffling of boots. They had seen us. Without a second's elapse, shots were fired.

"I was the closest to the temple and made a dash for the forest. I turned to look back for a split moment, just in time to see Bong lurch forward and hit the ground halfway between the flagpole and the temple. He crawled a few feet, but then stopped, his face buried in the dirt. To go back for him would mean sure death for both of us. I had no time for second thoughts and I ran as fast as I could through the undergrowth, putting as much distance between Bong and myself as was possible. I knew the troops would come after me and my two other comrades if they were still heading for the forest. I did not see them, but they could have been running towards another section of trees. Then I heard more shots behind me from the right. They might have picked off another of the men. My heart was pumping to the point of bursting, but I kept running for dear life. As I ran, I heard shouts; they were getting louder. They were gaining ground on me.

"Suddenly, the forest seemed to have come to an abrupt end and I found myself at the edge of an expanse of water. I immediately knew then where I was. This was Tasik Biru, the Blue Lake, once a mining quarry. I was at a dead-end. To go back into the forest would mean running straight into a bullet, but to go on around the lake would mean I'd have no proper cover. The lake seemed the lesser of the two evils; it at least had some vegetation around its edge. I turned left and made my way along the fringes of Tasik Biru, staying close to the forest rim. I heard more shots. If there had been one comrade left other than myself until then, I was now probably alone against a whole platoon of enemy troops. I had no plan, only to try and dodge the fire for as long as my strength would sustain me. I knew any moment I would succumb to exhaustion and then the end would be inevitable.

"Every so often I could see the shimmer of water to my right where the vegetation thinned. Another four hundred yards of running and in front of me was an open field. If I went straight across that I'd be a sitting duck, but to continue around the lake would mean returning to where I'd started out and a probable encounter with troops left to guard any escape. I zig-zagged as fast as I could across the open field, looking for somewhere to hide.

"Ahead was an old mine. Perhaps I could conceal myself in one of the shacks till night fell. I would worry about tomorrow after some sleep. Then all hell broke loose! I felt a sudden thrust and my arm seemed to explode. I saw red. Blood. Another shattering impact. This time, it got me in the leg. I fell to my knees. The pain was excruciating. I had to stand up, I had to stand. If I fell I would never get up again. With the most painful effort, I managed to get back on my feet. Hide. I had to hide. Thirty yards in front of me was a low, rocky mound, a hill heavily covered with trees and creepers. I ran into the protection of the undergrowth, working my way round to get away from my pursuers, until I saw in front of me an unexpected shadow of hope."

The arrival of three of Grandpa's bridge buddies rudely interrupts his story at its eleventh hour. They have come to get him for their weekly tournament. All else must wait.

46

Kuea was a resilient little boy and remained well the entire journey on the sea from Kuching to Hong Kong. Ah Min, however, came down with a fever and had stayed below for a few days. Kuea endeared himself to the other passengers; in fact he provided relief in the long and tedious, sometimes hazardous, voyage. It was not often that such a small child, and one so engaging, would make that journey from Nanyang; although occasionally children migrating with their parents would make the voyage in reverse. Kuea pined for his mother still, but the many activities on the boat provided him with distraction. He loved watching the deck-hands at their work, trimming the sails, swabbing the planks and reefing the main to keep the boat afloat during an approaching storm. The action on board was all a game to him. Ah Min strapped Kuea to his back whenever they were on deck. He could not risk losing him overboard to the engulfing waters of the South China Sea.

After thirty-five days of endless sea and sky, with only a brief call into Singapore, they reached Hong Kong. The young British island colony offered many attractions to those passing through: the great hustle and bustle at the waterfront, brighly painted rickshaws bobbing along the quay, shops selling a myriad of goods and food products from all over the world, and above it all Victoria Peak surveying its harbour filled with steamers and junks. But Ah Min's heart was not in them. He just wanted to set foot on Dongguan soil again, to be home and embrace his aged parents and his sister after twelve long years away. There was so much to say, so much for him to hear.

He was particularly anxious to have news of his brothers, but at the same time longing to present his parents with his precious gift, their grandson. If only Jinot could have been with them; she would have made a beautiful and pious daughter-in-law.

As soon as the *Toishan* dropped anchor in Hong Kong's busy harbour, Ah Min and Kuea transferred to a river junk which would take them the more than sixty miles up the Pearl River to Dongguan. As the junk eventually neared Dongguan town, the water shimmering in the noonday sun, Ah Min strained his eyes, looking for familiarities, anything that would trigger a sense of home. There was the same old cement pier from where he and Lo Tai had bade their farewells, their eagerness for a new life in Nanyang dulled by the mixture of apprehension and sadness at their leaving. The same waterfront shops were there also, just looking older and shabbier. The same open market, with its midday crowd of shoppers. Had it really been twelve years since he'd been gone?

Ah Min engaged a coolie on the waterfront to carry his belongings, keeping for himself the juah which held Kuea and now also the gold coins. They walked out of the commercial district of the town towards the enveloping countryside. They had to cross the narrow, raised footpaths of several paddy fields to reach his village of Cheong Cuan. Ah Min's heart was pumping fast, his eyes scanning the landscape for the stream and its old stone bridge, the stand of high bamboos and the crumbling village wall. From a distance, the village was immediately recognizable, but a new high wall had replaced the centuries-old earthen barrier he'd known as a child. The masonry of the arched entrance on the further side of the bridge had also been reinforced and a formidable iron gate, reaching almost to the arch, complemented an inner double-panelled wooden door. The gate and door stood open. As Ah Min walked through, followed by the coolie, he was stopped by a guard who emerged from a sentry hut inside. Ah Min quickly identified himself.

"You are Liu Pak's son from Nanyang? I knew he had a son in Nanyang, but I was very young when you left here. Welcome home! Does Liu Pak know you are coming back?" asked the young man, looking almost as excited as Ah Min.

"No. My father will be surprised. Hey, what's all this heavy fortification?"

"You might not have heard in Nanyang, but Punti clans have been attacking us Hakka, raiding our villages and killing our people. We need to be on the alert all the time."

Ah Min remembered the animosity that had existed between the Hakka and the Punti when he was growing up. He wanted to know more, but first he was anxious to see his family. Bidding goodbye to the sentry, he continued into the village.

He passed the schoolhouse, the temple with its ancestral plaques, the noble house of the village's richest man and finally reached the narrow lane at the end of which stood his family home. He literally ran towards it, with Kuea bumping up and down in the juah at his back, leaving the coolie to follow with his heavier load. Ah Min's heart was bursting with excitement. He knocked on the red painted wooden door and waited. He knocked again, this time more purposefully, and heard footsteps in the inner passage and then the door being unfastened. The next moment, the door was pulled back and there stood a young woman. It was his sister, Siu Chun! She had been fifteen when Ah Min left. At twenty-seven, her classic features of beauty were still there – the small but expressive eyes, the finely curved lips, a gently pointed chin, perhaps enhanced with her maturity – but something had dulled her once fresh vivacity; she looked pensive, even despondent.

"Siu Chun? I'm Ah Min, your brother. I've come back from Nanyang!" Ah Min cried out in one breath.

It took Siu Chun a good long moment to register what she had just heard. Then she broke into a spasm of tears and laughter, hugging herself, perhaps embarrassed to throw her arms round Ah Min who looked more a stranger than her big brother. "Pa! Pa! Ah Min has come back!" she screamed, stamping her feet for joy.

A grey-haired elderly man emerged from an inner room and shuffled over.

"Pa!" Ah Min cried out, and could not continue. Drowned in emotion, he embraced his father, sobbing uncontrollably. Then, stepping back a small distance, he awaited his father's reaction. The old man stared at Ah Min, stunned and in disbelief. Then his face softened as his eyes showed recognition of his son who had been gone for twelve years, and tears streamed down his weather-beaten face like run-off in the paddy streams after heavy rain. He tried to regain his composure, his lips forming the words: "Ah Min, you are back!"

A movement behind him reminded Ah Min that his son was still strapped in the juah. Quickly he crouched down, untied the strings and lifted Kuea out.

"Pa, this is your grandson. I have brought him home to you and Ma." Ah Min peered into the house, looking for his mother.

Liu Pak touched Kuea on the head with trembling hands. Kuea shrank from his touch, looking shy and afraid, and clung to his father.

"Kuea, this is your gung gung. Say Gung Gung," Ah Min told his son, but Kuea hid his face on his father's shoulder.

"Come in with my grandson," the old man beckoned, all smiles.

Ah Min took Kuea into the house. The coolie had meanwhile also arrived. Ah Min took the juah, paid him well and sent him on his way.

"Where's Ma?"

"Your ma is no longer here. She'd be so happy to see you and your son." There was a sadness in Liu Pak's words.

Ah Min understood. "Am I too late?"

"She died two years ago, from a growth in her belly. I'm sorry to tell you such bad news when you have just come home."

Ah Min looked around the sitting room and his eyes fell on the family altar against the far wall. A plaque hung above it. Two candles were burning on the table, a bowl containing a few oranges between them.

Ah Min went over, knelt in front of the altar and cried. Kuea followed him, grabbed his jacket and seeing his father cry and perhaps sensing the emotional tremor of the moment started to cry too.

"Ma, I'm an impious son. I failed to give you any joy in life. And now that I've come home and brought you your grandson, I am too late and you cannot see him."

"Do not grieve, Ah Min. Your ma can see her grandson. The spirit of the dead lives and can do things we cannot imagine. Seeing you are back and have a son, she'll be comforted in her afterlife. She will protect him from harm." Liu Pak put a hand on Ah Min's shoulder. After a moment, he asked, "Where is your wife?"

Ah Min looked up and said through his tears, "She too passed away, giving birth to our second child. The baby did not live."

"Why, oh why is our family beset with so much misfortune?" Liu Pak wrung his hands.

"Jinot was a beautiful woman and a good wife. We were planning to leave Nanyang and come back with our two children, but fate was unkind." From the other juah, Ah Min produced the bark painting of Jinot and showed it to his father and sister. "This was painted by Jinot's cousin as a wedding gift to us."

"She's very beautiful," said Siu Chun.

"The painting is a good representation of her, but it cannot capture the beauty of her spirit," said Ah Min. Looking at his son, he said, "Kuea is all that I have left, my only consolation. He's travelled all the way with me from Nanyang. He's a tough boy. I know you'll love him."

"I love him already. What a good-looking fellow. Look at those big eyes and long ears, like a little Old Man of Longevity! What name do you call him?"

"Kuea."

Liu Pak's face drew a blank. Ah Min continued, "It's a Bidayuh name commonly used for babies. My wife was from the Bidayuh tribe of Sarawak, in northern Borneo."

"I see," said Liu Pak, looking thoughtful.

"Well, Pa, Kuea is now two. He should have a proper name. Will you do us the honour of giving him a real name?"

Liu Pak's face brightened. He thought for a moment and said, "Nan Sun, to mean he was born in Nanyang."

"Liu Nan Sun. I like the name. It speaks of his roots. His mother must like this too," Ah Min said. "From now on, he will be called Nan Sun."

Nan Sun acted shyly towards his grandfather at first, but he took to his aunt, Siu Chun, in no time, following her to the wood stove where she boiled water to make tea. Soon the family sat together at the table, drinking tea and eating rice cakes that Siu Chun had baked in their humble oven.

"Siu Chun, I have nothing much to give you from Nanyang, for I left in a hurry soon after my wife died. But here's one of the baskets she wove.

She was a skilled weaver of rattan and straw goods. Keep this as something from your sister-in-law." Ah Min emptied the juah he'd been carrying and gave it to his sister.

Then he untied his pouch of gold coins and laid each coin on the table. His father and sister stared in amazement.

"Half of these coins are ours, Pa. The other half I will give to Lo Tai's family."

"Lo Tai did not come back with you?" Liu Pak asked.

"He died in Nanyang. I've brought his ashes back to his family. It won't be an easy task to bring such sad tidings," Ah Min said quietly. "I have such a long story to tell you. It will take days, even weeks, to tell you all that happened in Nanyang."

After Siu Chun and Nan Sun had gone to sleep, Liu Pak and Ah Min talked long into the night. Ah Min asked about his brothers.

"I have not heard from Ah Yan and Ah Yee since they left to follow Hong Xiuquan. I don't know if they are dead or alive, and I'm afraid we will never know," sighed Liu Pak. "This is a bad time for us all. The Manchus are weak and corrupt and don't care about the people, but Hong Xiuquan is no saviour. His rebellion has left so many dead, fighting for his so-called Tai Ping Tian Kuo, the Heavenly Kingdom of Peace, indeed! The poor are dying of famine and disease, while he sits comfortably in Nanjing living a life of selfish pleasure and corruption. Ah Min, we have little food here. Our farms are not producing enough for subsistence." Liu Pak's face was red with anger as he spoke about the sufferings caused by Hong's rebellion. "If he was really for the people, why didn't he rout the Manchus while his forces were ahead? Now it's too late. The Qing army is turning its attention to suppressing the rebellion." Liu Pak bit his lip, looked down at his feet and shook his head sadly. "I'm afraid your brothers are dead, why else haven't I heard from them? Not a single word in ten years! They probably died fighting their way to Nanjing, or were killed in battle against the Manchus after they got there."

"They were young, Pa, and could easily be convinced they were doing right by a rebel leader who promised liberation from oppression and poverty. Once in a while, there comes a leader who has the welfare of the people at heart, and will fight to the death for the common good. Unfortunately, Hong is no such man. If it's any consolation, Ah Yan and Ah Yee did what they felt at the time to be their duty for their country. We should be proud of them."

Liu Pak wiped a tear from the corner of his eye. Ah Min noticed how much his father had aged in the twelve years he'd been gone. He would be seventy-seven now. Time and physical hardship had been unkind to him, but Ah Min knew that the loss of most of his family, more than his chronological age and bodily stress, was the main factor in making him look older than his years.

"I heard about the fighting between the Punti and the Hakka," prompted Ah Min, changing the subject.

Liu Pak shook his head slowly. "After you left, the bad feelings between the two got worse, and eventually there were open conflicts and battles in Guangdong along the river delta, especially in the Taishan area, but also around here. A lot of Hakka were killed and in retaliation they went after some Punti, killing them. Punti hooligans then raided many of our villages. They took young girls, raped them and sold them to brothels in Macau. I'd die before I'd let them do that to Siu Chun."

"I'll kill them if they touch Siu Chun."

"The Punti will always think we Hakka have usurped their land, even though we settled here from the north several hundred years ago," Liu Pak said. "It's a terrible tragedy that we are fighting our own kind. We are all inhabitants of Guangdong Province. Most Punti don't think that way." Then, his face lit up and he said, "But tonight I am very happy because you are finally home, and I now have a grandson. Our bloodline will continue with your son. We will not die out."

47

Breaking the news to Lo Tai's father and mother of their son's death was one of the most dreaded ordeals for Ah Min. Leaving Nan Sun with his grandfather and aunt the morning after his arrival home, Ah Min walked to Lo Tai's house across a neighbouring paddy field. Situated near the edge of the village, it backed onto a fishpond and a cluster of bamboos. In the juah he carried was the black lacquer box containing Lo Tai's ashes and the pouch holding half the original number of gold coins: twenty-seven of them. The burden on his back was extremely light compared to the weight in his heart as he knocked on the door of Lo Tai's house.

The elderly Liu Sheung Hung and his wife recognized Ah Min almost at once. It did not need much time and many words before they realized their son was never coming home. Seeing the black lacquer box that Ah Min took out of his juah, they broke down in a spasm of heart-wrenching wails that was most unsettling for Ah Min, as he stood helplessly by. Lo Tai's mother suddenly dropped down onto the hard floor, pulling her hair and writhing in utter anguish, and Ah Min, glad to do something, knelt down and helped her to a chair, while Lo Tai's father embraced the box that contained his son's ashes and washed it with his tears. When their initial outburst of grief had finally abated, Ah Min presented them with the pouch of gold coins, saying, "Lo Tai wanted you to have these."

The pile of gleaming gold was an effective and unexpected distraction and a tangible consolation. They stood staring at the coins in surprise and total disbelief.

Ah Min kindly kept the coins' true origin from Lo Tai's parents, letting them retain the illusion that their son had indeed made a fortune from hard work in Nanyang. He summarized the events leading to their son's death, stressing all the while Lo Tai's selflessness, integrity and sense of loyalty that had made him stay behind and fight alongside his fellow miners in their struggle against foreign suppression and domination.

"Lo Tai was a hero among the Hakka people in Nanyang. He gave his life for the cause of freedom for them. He will be remembered in the whole of Nanyang for generations to come. You should be very proud of him, and not grieve too much for his ultimate sacrifice."

The old couple was somewhat comforted.

"How is Ah Lan?" Ah Min asked after a while.

Lo Tai's mother shook her head slowly. "She waited for Lo Tai for eight years," she said. "Her folks finally forced her to marry a farmer's son in a neighbouring village. She now has a son and a daughter."

Ah Min felt a deep pang in his heart. If they had left in 1856, before the rebellion, Lo Tai would have come home and it wouldn't have been too late for him to have married his childhood sweetheart. But Ah Min would not have married Jinot, nor would he now have Nan Sun with him. This was the eternal mystery of hypothesis versus outcome, or was it human endeavour against the hand of fate?

As Ah Min left Liu Sheung Hung's dwelling and made his way home across the paddy field, his juah felt a lot lighter – as did the burden in his heart.

48

Ah Min was heading home from the neighbouring village of Hong Cuan with his father and sister, Nan Sun in his juah at his back, after attending the wedding of a relative there. The walk to Cheong Cuan was a little over two and a half miles; it was mainly across paddies and dirt paths, but also cut through a forest of deciduous trees and tall undergrowth. The wedding banquet had lasted till late. The relatives in Hong Cuan had asked them to stay the night, but Liu Pak wanted to get home so he could go to the village temple the next morning, the first day of the eleventh moon. Ah Min had been back for six months.

"There have been no incidents lately with Punti gangs around here. Things are pretty quiet these days. We'll be fine," Liu Pak had assured his hosts at Hong Cuan. "Besides, it's a clear night and we have moonlight to guide our way."

"Big brother, do you miss Nanyang?" Siu Chun asked, as they walked towards Cheong Cuan.

"I do. I miss Jinot and our happy times together. I also miss my friends who died in the rebellion, especially Lo Tai and Jinot's brother, Joto."

"Even though I love Nan Sun very much, I know I can never take his mother's place. But I will do my best," Siu Chun said.

"Nan Sun is lucky to have you to take care of him. But, Siu Chun, you are now twenty-seven, late for marriage, but not too late. You should marry and have your own home," said Ah Min.

"I'm contented where I am, especially now that you are back, and with Nan Sun."

Liu Pak walked beside them quietly, as if deep in thought. Perhaps he too was thinking of marriage for Siu Chun now that Ah Min was home to help him on the farm. He could seek the assistance of the village intermediary to arrange a potential match for her. Twenty-seven was a late age for marriage, as Ah Min said, but still a reasonable age. Siu Chun had grown into a good-looking woman, and if it were not for her adamant desire to remain company for her father and mother, helping them on the farm and in the home, she would already have been wedded to one of the many suitors who'd come knocking on her door.

They had gone about half the distance between the two villages and had just entered a group of trees away from the open paddies when suddenly about ten yards in front of them a dark figure emerged, and then another. Siu Chun gave a short gasp of alarm and they all stopped in their tracks.

Ah Min immediately unstrapped the juah containing Nan Sun and set it down behind him.

"Siu Chun, hold Nan Sun and stay behind me and Pa," Ah Min commanded.

The two strangers stepped closer. They were men of medium build, and by the light of the moon that filtered between the trees Ah Min could tell that they were young and strong.

"Kind of late to be going somewhere, hah?" one of the men said with a sneer.

Punti for sure. Not good.

"We are going home after a wedding. Please allow us to continue on our way," Ah Min said, sounding as courteous as he could make his voice.

"Not so soon. I see you have a young lady there. We'd like to be acquainted."

Not good at all. Ah Min felt for the handle of the knife he carried in a sheath at his belt. He would only use it as a last resort.

"Kindly allow us to go on our way as it's late. We have a small child here," Ah Min said, a slight tremor in his voice that bothered him.

The two men began to move towards them. It was time for action, as words were useless. In a low voice, Ah Min ordered Siu Chun to take Nan

Sun and run back in the direction of Hong Cuan. He handed his father the knife and together they braced themselves for physical confrontation with the two Punti hooligans.

As Siu Chun turned and ran with Nan Sun, the Punti thugs tried to get around Ah Min and Liu Pak and give chase. Ah Min lunged at one of the men, while his father tackled the other. From his years of strenuous labour in the mines of Sarawak, Ah Min had amassed enough raw strength to fight and beat any reasonably strong opponent. He was able to stun his man with a few blows on his chest and head. As the man lay recovering on the ground, he heard a terrifying cry from his father and saw the glitter of metal in the moonlight. Immediately, he ran over to his father and hurled himself at the man who was stabbing at Liu Pak. Mad as a wild animal, Ah Min wrestled with the man from behind with his bare hands, trying to force the weapon from him. The man held on to his knife as he elbowed Ah Min and tried to turn around to face him. They were on the ground, rolling and grunting like two wild boars. As the Punti tried to stab him, Ah Min pushed hard and deflected the knife, its sharp blade plunging into his opponent's neck. At once, blood spurted everywhere, bright and profuse, and the man gave out gutteral retching noises. Ah Min left him and ran to his father, lying not far away heaving hard and clutching his stomach. By then, Siu Chun had run back with Nan Sun to where Liu Pak lay.

"We need to stop his bleeding and take him home quickly," said Ah Min.

"What about the men?" Siu Chun asked, frantic and distraught.

Ah Min looked over to where he had left his own opponent stunned, and realized he was no longer there.

"I think I killed one. Too bad the other got away," said Ah Min. "No time for him. Pa needs attention." Ah Min took off his cloth jacket and tied it tightly around his father's gaping wounds.

"He'll go back and tell his gang," said Siu Chun in hysterics.

"Nothing we can do. We need to take Pa home as quickly as possible. I'll carry him and you take Nan Sun."

Siu Chun put Nan Sun in the juah and strapping it to her back started straight away in the direction of Cheong Cuan. Ah Min recovered the knife he had given to his father, which was now lying on the ground, and lifting

Liu Pak onto his back, he headed as fast as he was able towards their village in the steps of Siu Chun.

Liu Pak lay at home for two days, never quite regaining consciousness after the attack. He had been stabbed several times in the stomach, and despite all the attention and herbal applications the village doctor gave him he succumbed on the third day. He died with his son, daughter and grandson at his side.

"There's no justice in this world! I'm glad you killed that murderer and I hope he is rotting in hell. I hate the Punti! I hate them all!" Siu Chun wailed with uncontrolled grief.

"Killing Pa's murderer was a necessity at the time, but it can't bring Pa back." Ah Min put his arm around his sister to comfort her. "Siu Chun, we still have each other and now we have Nan Sun also. Life must go on, if only for my son's sake. Pa and Ma will watch over us."

Liu Pak was buried in the family plot beside his wife. The day after the funeral, the village headman called on Ah Min and Siu Chun.

"I know this is not a good time to say this to you, while you are mourning your father, but for your safety, you should leave Cheong Cuan, in fact leave Dongguan, at least until the trouble with the Punti has blown over. I know that fellow deserved to die, but the one who got away will make up a different story. You should leave as soon as possible."

"There are several villages which are reached through that wood. We did not tell them exactly where we were going. The Punti will have a hard time tracking us down," said Ah Min.

"It is a matter of time before they find you. As long as you remain here, you are jeopardizing your lives, and the lives of all our villagers. Ah Min, take my advice and leave, the sooner the better."

"Where can we go? This is our home, and our parents are buried here!" cried Siu Chun.

The village headman was silent and looked over to Ah Min.

Ah Min was slow to answer, and when he did, he said in a determined voice, "There is nowhere we can go in China. We are seeing the last days of the Qing Dynasty. The country is cursed with poverty and famine, decadence and injustice. This is no place for my son to grow up. I will return to Sarawak with Nan Sun." Turning to his sister, he said, "Siu Chun, come with me."

"Are you serious, Big Brother? You've only just got back after twelve long years! What about Pa and Ma's graves? Who will pay respects to them every first and fifteenth day, and at Ching Ming? Our roots are here and this is our home. It has been so for over five hundred years!" Siu Chun was in tears again, as she looked defiantly at Ah Min.

"I will ask a villager to take care of your father and mother's graves and burn incense and paper ingots for them on all the days of remembrance," the village headman said assuringly.

"We will be forever grateful for that," Ah Min said. He took out two gold coins from an inner room in the house and presented them to the village elder, who looked at them wide-eyed. "These should pay for the care of our parents' graves for a long time," Ah Min said. Turning to his sister, he continued, "Siu Chun, be sensible. We need to leave. Do so for Nan Sun and the villagers here, if not for yourself. I will return to Sarawak with Nan Sun, but I cannot leave you behind. We will take a junk to Hong Kong, from where it should be easy to get a passage on one of the boats bound for Singapore and Kuching."

That night, they packed their essential belongings, their parents' ancestral plaques and the remaining gold that was Ah Min's share of the loot. Ah Min took also the bark painting of Jinot that meant so much to him. By dawn, the three of them were on their way down the Pearl River to Hong Kong, no goodbyes said to friends and relatives, no farewell except a silent one in their hearts to their buried parents and ancestors and the village that had been their family home for more than five centuries.

Three days later, they boarded a fish-eye junk that soon hoisted its sails and keeling slightly was on its way to Singapore. Standing at the bow of the *Dong Fong* with Nan Sun in his arms, Ah Min said to his sister, "I do not think we will see China again in our lifetimes. From this day forward, Sarawak will be our adopted country and the home of our descendants for generations to come. Nanyang may not be a land of gold and fortune, as I had thought when I left China the first time, but with honest hard work and perseverance we will overcome our sadness and sorrow, and all the hardship that awaits us there, and build a new life for ourselves. We will make it work."

49

Across Sarawak, in towns with a large Chinese population, Chap Goh Mei, the fifteenth day of the Lunar New Year, marked the last day of the Chinese New Year celebrations. It was a day of offering, thanksgiving and supplication to the Taoist gods, and a day of festivities, colourful processions and lion dances.

Chap Goh Mei fell on February 20th in the year 1913. Nan Sun started out early that morning from Buso for Bau, a four-mile trek through jungle using dirt paths. Ever since his father had taken him there to see the lion dances in 1862, the first year they returned from China, with the exception of the year after the big fire of December 1909 that had swept across the town and destroyed it, Nan Sun had travelled every year to Bau for the festival. While he was alive his father went with him, and sometimes also his aunt, Siu Chun. When Nan Sun married, his wife, Siew Han, would join them, and later their son, Yiu Jo. After his father's death in 1912, Nan Sun decided to continue the annual family tradition of going to Bau.

That year, 1913, Yiu Jo, who was nine at the time, had come down with a fever a day or so before Chap Goh Mei and Siew Han had stayed at home with him. As for Nan Sun's aunt, Siu Chun, at seventy-eight she had for the last several years found the long trek too strenuous for her. So Nan Sun, for the first time, went alone.

He took the jungle trail as usual. Although it was a convenient shortcut, it was not a sensible route for a solitary traveller. There had been robberies along the trail from time to time resulting not only in the loss of personal possessions, but injuries to the victims and sometimes those waylaid being killed. Nan Sun took the chance, thinking that because of the festival it would be safe. As fate would have it, halfway along the path a man suddenly appeared. He had a cloth tied over the lower half of his face, so Nan Sun knew instantly that he was up to no good. Nan Sun had nothing of consequence on him, only the shirt on his back, his walking sandals and some small change in one pocket. The ruffian nonetheless grabbed him and immediately searched him, finding just the coins. Nan Sun sensed the man's frustration. He had heard of cases when robbers, annoyed because their victims had no valuables, knifed them and left them where they lay. No sooner did he think it than he felt the touch of steel on his chin, a sharp point tracing the contours of his throat. Was this how his life would end? What a senseless way to go! He'd not now see his son grow up, and all because he took a foolish risk. This was the grim result of him tempting fate. Too late for regrets. Let it be quick.

Quick it was! The action that ensued as the assailant was pushed off balance took both of them by surprise. Nan Sun saw the sudden brandishing of more metal, this time carried by a new arrival on the scene, a much taller and bigger man. The would-be robber quickly regained his balance, turned and ran, avoiding any contest with Nan Sun's rescuer, who chose not to give chase.

"I cannot thank you enough," Nan Sun said to the man, looking shaken, though not injured except for a slight laceration below his chin, and some buttons torn.

"I'm glad I came along just then," his rescuer said. He was a decent looking man of about fifty, bare-chested with tattoos on his arms, brown-skinned and wearing a loincloth. He was clearly a Dayak, but also spoke decent Hakka. "You saved my life! I'm so thankful to you," Nan Sun repeated.

"No need to thank me. I just happened to be in the right place at the right time. Fate as you may call it!"

"I'm Liu Nan Sun of Buso. I was on my way to Bau to attend Chap Goh Mei." Nan Sun extended his hand and the Dayak shook it.

"Tomen, from Kampong Tikuan. I'm on my way to Bau too. We'll walk together the rest of the way. There's advantage in company."

"Kampong Tikuan!" exclaimed Nan Sun, staring at his benefactor.

"Yes, why?" Tomen asked, surprised at Nan Sun's reaction.

"My mother, who died when I was two, was a Bidayuh from Kampong Tikuan."

"I've never seen you at our kampong!"

"I left the kampong with my father after my mother died, and I have not gone back since."

"That's very interesting. Tell me more."

"It's a long story, but I will give you a summary as we walk. My father came from China to work in the mines in Mau San. He told me he met my mother through her brother who was also a miner. He married my mother and they lived in Kampong Tikuan until she died giving birth to her second child. The baby did not survive either. After their deaths, my father took me back to China with him. I was only two then, and have no recollection of the kampong and sadly none of my mother. Unfortunately, my father was involved in a clan war just a few months after we arrived in China and he had to leave again with me and my aunt. We came back to Sarawak and he bought a store in Buso. We've lived there ever since."

"And all this time, you or your father never came to Tikuan?"

"Ever since I was old enough to understand, my father kept telling me not to go near Kampong Tikuan because he was afraid my Bidayuh grandmother might try to keep me there with her, possibly using voodoo to do so. She's probably long dead now, but my father never went back to Tikuan all the years he lived here. He said the kampong would bring back too many sad memories for him. He missed my mother till the day he died."

"That's some story. I wonder which family your mother came from."

"My father wouldn't tell me my grandmother's name. I didn't even know if we had other relatives living in the kampong. All I know is my mother's name, Jinot."

"Never heard of her," said Tomen.

"You were probably not born when she died," said Nan Sun.

"You said your father had passed away?" Tomen asked.

"Just last year."

"It's hard to lose a parent, no matter how old you are. My mother died three years ago," said Tomen, "and I'm still mourning her."

Nan Sun and Tomen were early for the procession when they reached Bau, now a flourishing town reborn from the ashes of Mau San. Since the fire of 1909, which had wiped out the town for the second time, new shophouses had been rebuilt on the main street and on side streets which had been added.

"You come to Bau often?" Tomen asked.

"Not anymore, but I rented a room above a shophouse in town when I was attending secondary school here. My father wanted me to have a good education. I even learned English here," said Nan Sun. "My father said knowing English would get me far in life. In fact, he sent me to Kuching for more English studies in my final year of secondary school."

"You were lucky to have that opportunity. I never had a formal education, but my father could read and write English and he taught me English from the time I was very young."

"Looks like we can practise English on each other!" Nan Sun laughed. "But first, since we are now in Bau, the least I can do is to treat you to some Hakka food."

"I never refuse Hakka food or Hakka hospitality!" Tomen said.

They walked down the main street of Bau. Tables were being set up as altars at intervals along the centre of the street and on these were huge brass urns with joss sticks planted in them and trays brimful of fruit, dumplings, cakes and buns. They picked a teahouse a short way down a side street and ordered kolo mee and tea.

"So you are here to attend Chap Goh Mei too?" Nan Sun was curious that a Bidayuh would journey a long distance from his longhouse to Bau to attend what was intrinsically a Hakka festival.

"I'm actually here to buy some herbal medicine for my father who's very ill. We have our own medicine man, but he couldn't do much. I've heard there are some special Chinese herbs which are very good for bowel ailments," said Tomen. "Maybe you can take me to the right shop?"

"I'll take you to a herbalist after the procession," said Nan Sun, glad that he could do something for Tomen. "You have a family?"

"Yes, I'm married with two sons and one daughter. And you?"

"I have only one son. I married when I was twenty-eight and I had him when I was forty-five. Actually, my wife and I had four other children before him, but none of them survived beyond five years. My son is now nine and I'm fifty-four! Sometimes, I feel like I'm taking my grandson out!" Nan Sun laughed.

"I'm sorry you lost four of your children. But the important thing is you still have a son to help you when you are old, and to carry on the family name," Tomen said.

Nan Sun liked his new friend Tomen. Apart from the fact that he had saved Nan Sun's life, Tomen seemed a decent person, filially pious towards his parents. He was outgoing and looked confident.

The sounds of gongs, drums and cymbals coming from the main street signalled the start of the procession. Thick crowds had lined both sides of the road. It was already mid-morning. Nan Sun and Tomen had by then finished eating their pork noodles and went out to the main street to watch the goings-on.

Brightly decorated floats meandered their way down the processional route, each representing a local business or organization. These were interspersed with large mascot lions in colourful and glitzy array, manoeuvered by humans hidden under their gaudy, furry folds, marching and dancing to a jarring ensemble of gongs, drums and cymbals and escorted by members of the clubs and societies they represented. The lions stopped at every altar set up on the street and danced a jig or performed a stunt. Spectators cheered and clapped. Shopkeepers nearby presented them with lucky money offerings in red envelopes.

"I've watched this almost every year for the last fifty years. I still enjoy it. Wait till the medium arrives!" Nan Sun shouted to Tomen above the noise.

The Taoist medium came in an apparent trance, carried in a sedan chair, the seat of which was made of multiple knife blades, sharp sides upturned. As his sedan stopped at every altar on the street, the medium alighted and approached the table with its offerings where Taoist followers were seeking his intercessions to the gods, which he would make with brush strokes of black ink on red paper.

"Think that would help my father?" Tomen asked, not totally convinced.

"I am a cynic about this sort of thing, but there are lots of devout Taoist followers who think the medium is a living saint and can work miracles," said Nan Sun.

"I'd give a lot for my father's recovery," said Tomen. "But I think he'll fare better with the Chinese herbs."

Throughout the procession, Nan Sun and Tomen managed to stay together in the crowd. When the procession and lion dances had ended and everyone was helping themselves to the food on the tables, Nan Sun said to Tomen, "Surely it will be too late for you to go back to your kampong tonight. You are most welcome to spend the night at my house in Buso. I'd like my wife and son, and my aunt, to meet you."

"I was planning to sleep in Bau tonight. But I'll accept your kind invitation if it's not too much trouble for you and your wife," said Tomen. "It will shorten my journey in the morning."

"It's settled then. They will be happy to meet the man who saved my life."

Nan Sun first took Tomen to a Chinese herbalist in town. Tomen explained his father's condition as best he could and the herbalist dispensed enough doses of a mixture of herbs to last a month. Tomen paid the herbalist without hesitation, although it was a sizable sum he charged. Taking the package and the herbalist's instructions, Nan Sun and Tomen walked the four miles back to Buso, reaching the bazaar in the late afternoon. Nan Sun's shophouse was the third furthest from the dirt path sloping down to the river. Above its entrance was a sign with two Chinese characters, "Ho Ho". The store sold a variety of local food items, from dried and smoked meats, rice, sago, cocoa, sugar and spices, to fresh vegetables and fruit. Buso's children loved the store for the sweets it kept.

To Nan Sun's relief, Yiu Jo's fever had broken. Siew Han prepared a sumptuous Hakka meal that included steamed chicken with rice wine, braised duck with spices and soya sauce, and lui cha in honour of their Bidayuh guest. Nan Sun's aunt, Siu Chun, helped Siew Han in the kitchen. Siu Chun was still alert in mind but had become very bent; she had lost quite a few inches in height. Over the years, she had assumed matriarchal status in the household. She had never married and helped her brother bring up Nan Sun.

"I am very grateful to you for saving Nan Sun's life," Siu Chun said to Tomen, after Nan Sun had gone to change his torn shirt. "Make Buso your rest stop any time if you are travelling this way. You are always welcome."

After supper, the family sat with their guest in the living room at the back of the store. Tomen noticed the bark painting on the wall of a beautiful Bidayuh woman in a jomuh.

"Who's that lady, may I ask?"

"That's my mother. It was painted by a cousin of my mother's. See the green trinket she's wearing on a chain?" From under his white cotton vest, Nan Sun fished out a jade Buddha pendant hanging from a gold chain around his neck. "This is what she's wearing in the painting. My grandmother from Tang Shan gave it to my father when he left for Nanyang, and my father gave it to my mother as an engagement present. My father had been wearing it all these years after her death, and he passed it on to me before he died. Fortunately, I wasn't wearing it today when I went to Bau."

"Tell Tomen about the ghost," Siew Han prompted her husband eagerly.

"Ghost?" Tomen was all ears.

"Well, yes, there's a female ghost pacing inside the gazebo down by the river on moonlit nights. But she harms nobody. Just a creepy presence. She's been haunting the gazebo for years."

"Nan Sun's father believed it to be the ghost of his wife, Nan Sun's mother, because she seemed to be wearing a black jomuh like a Bidayuh woman," Siew Han said. "But every time someone dared to get close to the gazebo, she vanished, so we never saw her face."

"Had your father tried to get close?" Tomen was enthralled.

"My father had actually once got to within five yards of the gazebo before she vanished, but she was looking out to the river so he couldn't see her face. After that, my father said we should let her be. He was convinced it was my mother and he was content to see her ghost from a distance. He didn't want to scare her away."

"Whether she's your mother's ghost or not, I think something's troubling her. Unfortunately, nobody will know what it is or how to help her," Tomen concluded.

50

One day late in September 1913, when the sun had set but the western sky was still washed with a pale tint of red, a man in his early fifties, scantily clad in a loincloth and trekking sandals, and with a juah on his back, entered Buso just as parents were calling their children in for the night. The man walked up to Ho Ho, the country store, and knocked on the wooden panelled door, as the store had been boarded up for the night. Nan Sun's aunt, Siu Chun, opened the door and was pleasantly surprised to see Tomen. It had been seven months since he and Nan Sun met on the day of Chap Goh Mei, when chance brought them together and he saved Nan Sun from an unthinkable fate.

"Can I see Nan Sun?" he asked nervously, as soon as they had exchanged greetings. He seemed anxious but not obviously worried, eager but not overly excited.

Siu Chun invited him into the sitting room at the back of the store and went through the kitchen to the back door to call Nan Sun in from the yard. Nan Sun came in to find Tomen looking at the bark painting of Jinot.

"Welcome, my friend. So happy to see you again!"

Tomen turned to face Nan Sun. "I've come to bring some sad news. My father died five days ago," Tomen began.

"I am so sorry," said Nan Sun with sincerity, "so very sorry."

Tomen looked serious, hesitated, then said, "Shortly before he died, he told me he had written a letter to me, which he'd put inside a Chinese ceramic jar at home. He said I was to read it only after his death. Well, two days ago, I found the letter and read it." Tomen stopped again, as if it was hard for him to find the right words. Then quickly from his juah he took out several sheets of folded paper covered by hand in English and gave them to Nan Sun. "Please read. They will explain everything."

Nan Sun's impression of Tomen from their first encounter was that he was a man of confidence, quite unlike the Tomen who had now come to Buso to break the news of his father's death and ask Nan Sun to read his letter. Feeling uneasy about Tomen's change in manner, Nan Sun nonetheless took the letter, sat down at the table and by the light of a kerosene lamp proceeded to read it.

December 12th, 1912

My dear Tomen,

I am writing this letter in English for you and for your descendants, as I believe English will be the common language in future for both Bidayuh and Chinese. It is my intention that you read this letter after I die, because I cannot bring myself to tell you the truth while I live.

Your mother, Enti, had a younger sister, Jinot, who died giving birth to her second son, a healthy baby. While Jinot was unconscious, bleeding to death, and her husband, Ah Min, was still waiting outside the asuok, your grandmother, Udet, climbed out through the back window and left Kampong Tikuan, taking the newborn baby to a Bidayuh woman who had given birth earlier in a neighbouring kampong. She asked the woman to nurse the baby for the while. She bribed her heavily to keep the baby a secret and threatened a voodoo curse on her if she told anyone. The fact was Udet had previously overheard Jinot talking to Enti about Ah Min's intention to return to China with his family, and the very idea of their leaving her troubled her most deeply. When Jinot lay dying, Udet was afraid Ah Min would take both his sons to China after Jinot's death. She could keep the baby if Ah Min was told the baby was stillborn.

But Udet could not hide the truth from Enti, who was assisting her in the asuok during Jinot's labour. Before Udet took the baby out of Kampong Tikuan, she made Enti swear to secrecy about its survival. She threatened that if Ah Min ever found out that his second son was alive, she would inflict a voodoo curse on him to prevent him from reclaiming his second son and take his first son from him as well.

Not long after Ah Min left for China with his first son, I married Enti. She confided in me what happened the night of Jinot's labour and death. Over the years, Enti and I were childless, but we were nonetheless blessed with a child, Jinot's second son, whom we adopted as our own. You are that son, Tomen.

Without looking up from the letter, Nan Sun paused in his reading. He closed his eyes, as though deep in thought. Gradually, a tear formed and rolled down his cheek, then another. Tomen stood by, all the while watching nervously Nan Sun's reaction as he read. When Nan Sun finally opened his eyes, brimful of tears, and looked towards Tomen, Tomen said, in a low, trembling voice, "Please read to the end."

Udet was happy that we took you as our own. You would be with her at Kampong Tikuan, a comfort in her old age, and you would carry on the family line. Udet loved you, Tomen. You were indeed her grandson, Jinot's son. And even though she later heard your birth father had returned from China with your older brother and they were living twelve miles from our kampong, she left them alone. Ever since I married Enti, I had replaced Ah Min as the man in the family. And while Udet would have wanted your brother too, for she had loved that boy dearly, Enti pleaded with her to let the poor motherless child be with his father. She convinced Udet that she could never win the boy's affection and she should be content with having you, Tomen. As the English saying goes, "a bird in the hand is worth two in the bush".

After Udet's death in 1895, the threat of the voodoo spell on Ah Min no longer existed. We could have reunited you with your birth father and brother, but Enti and I loved you too much to let you return to Ah Min. And so, over the years, you knew only us as your parents, and honouring and loving us as such.

Enti and I were blessed with three grandchildren, gifts from you and your good wife. But always there was the shadow of guilt looming in our conscience. We had taken Jinot and Ah Min's son for our own, and would not give him back after Udet's death when the fear of the voodoo curse had disappeared. Now Enti is gone. I alone hold the secret of your birth. I still have the chance to redeem myself, tell you the truth about your birth parents, and go to Buso and tell Ah Min, if he is still alive, the truth about the son he believed to be dead. I can still right the wrong committed over fifty years ago. Both Ah Min and I are now old men. Time is running out on us. If I am to tell him about you, I should do so soon. But not only am I old in years I am also weak in will. I cannot bring myself to take that first step on the road to Buso and confess a wrong done to my brother-in-law all these years. I am now the respected patriarch of a family. I will not give it up.

However, it is not my intention to perpetuate this wrong. So I am writing this letter. The Chinese jar I bought from a Hakka boat hawker will be a safe storage place for it until I die. I will tell you about this letter when I am near death, and ask you to read it when I am gone. Only then will my conscience be cleared and my sister-in-law Jinot's spirit be appeased. Forgive Enti and me, my dear Tomen, for keeping you as our own son all these years.

For the last time, I will sign off as

Your loving and devoted father,
Koper

Nan Sun folded the letter, stood up from his chair and turning towards Tomen, who was standing the whole while watching him read, said in an unsteady voice, "Now I know Pa and Ma had sent you to save my life that day. Welcome home, my brother."

They embraced, and standing beneath the bark painting of Jinot let their tears flow freely without reserve.

"If only they were here," said Tomen, looking up at the portrait of his birth mother.

"They *are* here. I can feel their presence."

"To think we have lost fifty-two years!"

"We will make up for them. There's still time," Nan Sun said. Seeing Tomen's face full of the deepest loss and longing as he gazed on his mother's picture, Nan Sun took down the painting and gave it to his brother. "I think it's time this portrait of our mother was in your safe keeping."

Later that moonlit night, when Nan Sun and Tomen walked together down the main street of Buso towards the river and came to the gazebo, the ghost was not there. They stepped inside onto the gazebo's wooden floor.

"I don't think we will see her again. What troubled her has been set right. She is happy at last," Tomen said.

"But her spirit will be with us and our descendants. She'll always protect us from harm," Nan Sun said with conviction.

51

"I finished reading the story of Liu Hon Min last night," Therese says, as soon as she steps into her grandfather's house. "It sheds a whole new light on our ancestry."

"You mean the Bidayuh side of our family? My father did tell me about my great-grandfather marrying a Bidayuh and that they had two sons, my grandfather Liu Nan Sun and his brother who was raised a Bidayuh."

"Tomen. His brother's name was Tomen. They were both sons of Liu Hon Min and his Bidayuh wife, Jinot, your great-grandparents. In fact, the two brothers did not know about each other's existence until they were in their fifties. I read about that in the last chapters of the manuscript, an amazing surprise ending."

"You know more about them than I do. All I know is that a terrible accident during my father's time split the two families. This would not have been recorded in the manuscript as it happened a few years after my grandfather, Nan Sun, died."

"What accident?" Therese quickly interrupts, recalling what the Bidayuh, Miseng, had told her.

"I had a brother who was five years older than me. His name was Ka Chi. When the accident happened I was only three and had no recollection of it. My father told me about it much later. The tragedy occurred in 1944, during the Japanese occupation. A Bidayuh cousin who was about eighteen was visiting us in Buso. He offered to take Ka Chi to Kampong Tikuan for a few days to go fishing and do some jungle trekking. Ka Chi, who was then eight, begged our father to let him go. My father finally agreed, but impressed upon the cousin that he must take good care of him. While at Tikuan, they were crossing a rope bridge after a heavy rainstorm when the bridge gave way, throwing Ka Chi thirty feet into the water below. The Bidayuh cousin managed to cling to the rails, but by the time he'd got himself to the riverbank, my brother had already been swept out of sight. The river was exceptionally high. The cousin and his friends searched the banks and eventually finding my brother's lifeless body washed up on the shore brought him back to Buso. My parents were distraught beyond words. My father blamed the boy for Ka Chi's death and swore never to have anything more to do with the family, and as I got older he made me swear to the same."

"Have you ever told my dad about the accident and the rift between the two families?"

"Not really. All my life I've had no association with our extended Bidayuh family and I did not think your dad needed to know about them, or would care. They wouldn't mean anything to him anyway, especially now that he's in Canada, just as they don't mean anything to you."

"But they do, Grandpa. After reading all about Liu Hon Min, I feel strongly akin to them and that our lives are intertwined with theirs. I'm sure that Liu Hon Min and Jinot would want us to be reconciled. You don't know how their two sons, Nan Sun and Tomen, were separated and reunited. That's why I really want to read their story to you. As for the present rift, the accident that caused your brother's death happened a long time ago. Your father is gone now. We should get to know the Bidayuh side of our family and be reconciled with them."

Grandpa Liu is taken aback at Therese's words.

"I don't know about that. I'd prefer to let sleeping dogs lie, so to speak. Not resurrect the past and bring back painful memories. After all, the Bidayuh relatives have become so remote. I've never had contact with them and they don't know us or care if we exist." Grandpa Liu hesitates for a moment, and says with finality in his voice, "I really have no intention of reviving our kinship. Now if your recorder is ready, I'll tell you the rest of my story."

52

"What I had come to that gave me that faint glimmer of hope was the entrance to Ghost Cave." Grandpa picks up on the recollection of his escape from the pursuing troops.

"Ghost Cave? That's the cave where Liu Hon Min hid and was saved by the two Bidayuh sisters when he was running from James Brooke's men after the Chinese Rebellion failed. It's all in the manuscript!" Therese cannot hide her excitement, something more than common curiosity boosting her adrenalin.

"How about that! I never knew, but I had known about Ghost Cave ever since I was old enough to be scared by ghost stories. Everybody around Bau knew that the cave contained the skeletons of hundreds of women and children who had died in there over a century ago, smoked out, asphyxiated as they say, by the White Rajah's men. As a young boy, I was scared by rumours of people hearing terrifying, chilling sounds of crying and wailing in the cave. There was even an account, whether true or not I don't know, of a farmer going in looking for swiflets' nests and stumbling upon a chamber full of horror-stricken, ashen-faced women holding their babies and screaming and closing in on him like mad banshees. In terror, he ran out, leaving his torch and nets inside.

"Anyway, with bullet wounds in my arm and leg, and being pursued by British and Malays, I felt I had no choice. Shutting my mind to all the awful tales I had heard, I parted the bushes and crept in through the cave's low entrance. My pursuers must have seen movement in the bushes for another shot rang out, just missing me but hitting the stones above the cave's mouth. I hurled myself forward into the darkness.

"I groped my way for a few yards and then fumbled for the torchlight in my backpack, which I was still carrying. I turned it on and could see enough to know I was in a small chamber with a roof I could touch if I extended my arm. A collection of bats hung above me. The air was cool and smelled of damp. Water was dripping slowly from the roof and had formed puddles on the ground. I then became conscious of a haunting, hollow, whispering sound from an underground draught. I flashed my torch around and could see an opening in the wall opposite the cave's entrance. I limped over, squeezed through and found myself in a narrow defile. I had by now become very aware of the pain in my leg, but I continued to drag myself down the passageway in the hope of finding an exit. It was a blind hope really, because if there had been any exit why hadn't the women and children escaped? Like them I was doomed. It was just a question of whether I'd be captured or killed on sight.

"The passageway eventually came to an end and I found myself now in a big chamber, much, much larger than the first. I flashed my torch on the rough ground and shivered when I realized I was staring at bones, skeletons of the dead of a hundred years. These would be my companions in my final hours.

"I was totally exhausted and in a lot of pain. My wounds were still oozing blood through my uniform. I sat down against a wall to take stock of myself; my left arm felt numb, but the pain in my right thigh was sharp and raw. What was I going to do? I took some deep breaths and then with considerable effort repositioned my rifle, which had been over my right shoulder, against my good leg and backpack and aimed it at the passageway. I would shoot at anyone who emerged from there until I had no more ammunition, until my last breath. I turned off my torch and waited in the darkness.

"For a long while, it was quiet in the chamber. There was no sound coming from the passageway, only the faint wheeze of moving air and the drip of water from the roof. In what I assumed were to be my last hours, I let my thoughts drift… I had always believed in spirits, the spirits of our ancestors, those that protected us from harm. I also believed in unrequited spirits that roamed the earth to vent their grievances, or to avenge themselves for wrongs done to them in their lifetimes. It was perhaps strange that a professed communist should believe in the supernatural, but I had always dissociated my support of communism as a political and sociological ideology from the inner yearnings of my soul. The cave breathed ghosts, even though they were not visible to my naked eye. They should have no grievance against me. If anything, they should feel some camaraderie; I was facing a similar end, though on a different platform of time. A strange notion it was, to think I was in friendly territory in Ghost Cave. It was almost comforting. Against my conscious will, my hands gradually relaxed their hold on the rifle and my eyes began to close. I drifted off into a deep, dream-filled sleep.

"A beautiful woman, draped in a black sarong and with long flowing black hair was beckoning me. I was still in Ghost Cave, which had become miraculously lit up so that I could see her clearly, but the bones which had been on the ground around me were gone, as was my pain. She took me by the hand. She felt light as a spirit, but had the strength of a man for she literally pulled me up. Still holding me by the hand, she led me to an opening in the far wall, hidden in the folds of the rocky chamber. I would never have noticed it. She eased through the gap, taking me with her, and we made our way down another even narrower passage. Having left the chamber, we were now in complete darkness, but I could sense the air becoming fresher. Gradually, the passage began to lighten and I could see my way.

"The woman turned to me. I can never forget that face, her serene beauty, the subdued smile, the love in her eyes. Then, in a sudden burst of light, she vanished. I was alone once more in Ghost Cave.

"It was still quiet in the cave. My enemies had not followed me in. Perhaps they knew that sooner or later I would emerge waving a white cloth, or else die in there from injury and hunger. They would not wish to risk being shot at entering the cave. And they were right about my hopeless predicament. I had no way out but through the way I had gone in. Unless…

"When I woke fully, I was confused. I was still where I had fallen asleep, but the lady in my dream had seemed so real. I could feel her soft but firm hand. She was like a breath of fragrance in the dampness of the cave's surroundings. Perhaps she was an angel taking me to heaven, as I had sometimes read in Christian stories when I was a child about what happened to the good when they died.

"A strange thought then struck me in what I was sure had to be my last hope, wild as it might seem. The pain in my leg had subsided while I'd slept, but as I made an effort to stand it returned twice as fiercely. In my dream, I recalled being led along the wall to the left for about ten yards before reaching the hidden gap. I turned on my torch, slinging my backpack and rifle on the shoulder of my uninjured arm, and limped in that direction, groping my way and feeling every crack and crevice I saw.

"About thirty feet from where I'd begun, I sensed a draught and at the same time felt a break in the rock. I was overcome with emotion; it was as though I'd been given my life back again. Without hesitation, I slid sideways into the gap and inched my way down the narrow passage, my sixth sense telling me it was a tunnel to the outside, to life."

Therese stays very quiet. Seeing tears welling in her eyes, Liu Ka Ming pats his granddaughter gently on the back and says, "For a long time, whenever I thought of my miraculous escape from what had seemed a certain death, I too cried tears of gratitude. Since then, I have become a believer in a *force* that controls our lives in the grand scheme of things."

"Funny how a traumatic event can change one's life and belief," Therese says, dabbing her cheeks.

Grandpa nods.

"I'm now almost at the end of my story. It was late afternoon by the time I got out of Ghost Cave, and in case the British and Malay troops were still watching the front entrance, the only one they would know about, I hid in the forest till it was dark. I then made my way slowly and very cautiously into Bau. A Hakka family that owned a carpentry shop in Bau took me in as soon as they saw my bloodied state and called in a local doctor to tend to me. He cleaned up my wounds and removed a bullet lodged in my right thigh. I stayed in the attic of the carpenter's shophouse for three weeks while the family nursed me back to health. I have remained grateful to them ever since."

53

"I left Bau in late October 1965 because I didn't want to get my kind hosts into trouble. I was also anxious to rejoin the guerrilla force. A guerrilla base had been established near Gunung Gading, two miles from Lundu, on the Sarawakian side of the border. I was able to secure a westbound ride heading for Lundu and ultimately reached the base. By late 1965, the combined Malaysian and Commonwealth anti-communist forces had tightened their search for guerrilla camps and were staging ambushes in Sarawak, as well as in Indonesian Kalimantan for over half a mile inland. They were assuming the offensive in their operations to stamp out our activities, especially in the First and Second Divisions.

"On November the 5th, we set out through the rainforest to destroy a defence position near Sematan, close to the border. It was a strategic post, sandwiched between the border and the coast. We were two miles past Lundu when we were surprised by Malaysian and British jungle patrols. This time, there was no escape. They shot and killed two of our men. The rest of us, fourteen in all, were captured. We were trucked to Kuching the following day.

"I was interned at the 6th Mile detention camp on the Kuching-Serian Road. From the camp, literally a prison, I was allowed to send word to my family in Buso. The letter I wrote to them was one of the most difficult tasks of my life. How would you explain yourself to those who loved you for having broken their hearts?"

"A very difficult task indeed," Therese agrees.

From his shirt pocket, Grandpa takes out a letter, written in Chinese.

"My mother gave it back to me before she died. She had saved it all those years. She said it was the best thing she had received in the three years since I'd left home. She saw that as a message of love and hope from me. I'll translate for you.

20th November 1965

Dear Pa and Ma,
    I hope you are well. I am sorry for having left you without saying goodbye. I am also sorry for my long silence, but where I was, I could not write to you. I had taken part in communist armed activities in Sarawak and was captured earlier this month. I am now being held at the 6th Mile detention camp for an indefinite period. I am allowed two visitors once a week. Please come. I miss you and want very much to see you.

Always your son,
Ka Ming

"My letter, like all letters written by inmates at the camp, was screened before it was mailed to my parents. During the following week's visiting hour, I had a visitor – my mother. As soon as we saw each other, we both broke down. No reproach from my mother, just concern for my health and well-being. Boundless and unconditional was a mother's love. For the rest of my internment at the detention camp, she visited me every week without fail and brought me snacks that I liked, and paper and pens, sketchbooks and drawing materials. I was allowed books too, but only in Malay and English and they had to be inspected and approved. I asked my mother to bring me some English fiction, such as Rudyard Kipling's and Joseph Conrad's classics. Those were my best form of escape. You have remarked how impressed you are with my command of English. Well, the many English classics I read while in detention were my teachers."

"How long were you in there?" Therese asks.

"Two years and one month, but it seemed an eternity. Living conditions were abominable. The camp consisted of single-storey, longhouse-type buildings. These had aluminium roofing, which accentuated the insufferable, clammy heat of the interior. Our sleeping quarters were very cramped, about forty beds in each room separated by small lockers where we kept the few belongings we had. The beds were just hard boards covered with mats. Needless to say, men and women had separate quarters. We took our meals in the mess hall, three meals a day of rice, boiled vegetables and sometimes a piece of fatty meat. I was always hungry. One day, I passed by the kitchen and saw workers washing rice with their feet. That helped take a lot of my hunger away!" Grandpa smiles, and takes a sip of his tea. "When conditions became too impossible and our petitions for improvements were ignored, I joined other inmates in a much-publicized hunger strike. Our terms were to get rid of the aluminium roofs, give us adequate medical attention and let married couples who were interned at the camp meet periodically in privacy. The hunger strike lasted thirty days and we only ended it when the authorities finally agreed to our demands. Within two months, new tiled roofs replaced the aluminium ones; inmates deemed seriously ill by our prison doctor were sent out to local hospitals for treatment; and a small section was set aside for married couples to meet once every fortnight."

"Did your father ever visit you while you were at the camp?"

"No, never. He couldn't get over his disappointment in me and the shame he felt I'd brought to the family." He pauses with a sigh.

"I could have been released from camp any time if I had agreed to act as an informant and provide details about my comrades and confess to having been misled into communism, a proposition unthinkable to me. That was why I stayed there for so long. I was released on December the 15th 1967 and only then because the camp was overcrowded and they needed to make room for new detainees. On my release, I had to report to a police station every week for the next two years.

"When I stepped out of prison a free man, my father was there with my mother, ready to take me home." Grandpa wipes a tear from a corner of his eye.

Therese's cheeks are flushed. "That's an incredible story, Grandpa. So many died in the armed struggle. So much courage, sacrifice, tragedy." She pauses and then asks, "By the way, what happened to Li, Bong's wife?"

"I'm coming to that. After I recovered from my injuries and joined the guerrilla camp near Lundu, I found out that eighteen of our comrades on that deadly mission to Bau had been killed in the ambush, including Bong and the other two who escaped with us to Mau San. Those who survived managed to cross the border back to Kalimantan. Our casualty count that time was the highest on any one mission. Word of which comrades had been killed of course reached our camp at Entikong. So Li must have received the news of Bong's death soon after the failed operation. I could not imagine how she took it, especially so soon after the loss of her child. I wish I could have been there for her, but then again, no one could have done anything to lessen her grief."

"Have you heard from her since?"

"Yes. A year after Bong's death, the Malay government made radio and television broadcasts, and distributed flyers, offering an amnesty to communist guerrillas who would lay down their arms and return to the life of law-abiding citizens in Sarawak. I was still in the detention camp at that time. But when I was released in late 1967, I heard from a mutual friend of Bong's and mine that Li had taken the amnesty offer and returned to Kuching."

"Did you see her after your release?" Therese asks.

"Yes, I got in touch with her again. I was relieved to find that she had found a way to cope, for she was able to talk to me about Bong and the baby and wanted to know about Bong's last moments. I tell you, it was so hard for me to talk about it to her, that instant of seeing Bong fall and not being able to help." Grandpa's voice wavers.

"You made the best decision under the circumstance, Grandpa," says Therese.

"Li told me that after her return to civil life she went with a friend to a church in Kuching and was eventually baptized as a Catholic. She said her new faith had pulled her through her tragedies."

"I'm glad for her," says Therese. Giving her grandfather a questioning look, she adds, "I'd like to meet her while I'm here, if that's possible."

Grandpa Liu puts his arm around his granddaughter. "Sadly, Li died of cancer in 1993. She was your grandmother."

For a moment, Therese remains mute, as if she has trouble understanding what she has just heard. Then with a tremor in her voice, she asks softly, "You mean you married Li and... and you and she had my dad?"

Grandpa Liu nods, and tears and smiles mingle as he embraces his granddaughter. "I guess I had been subconsciously in love with her for a long time, even when she was married to Bong. I was happy I could give her a good life after all that she had been through."

"And you gave her a son, my dad, to fill the place of the one she lost," says Therese, between sobs. "Oh, I wish with all my heart I had met her."

"She was a beautiful and gentle woman, and she would have loved you so much, her granddaughter. But you were only two when she died. Your father came home for her funeral, but you were too young then, so you stayed in Canada with your mother."

"Does my dad know all this about his mother?"

"Strangely, I have never told him. He has known all along about my stint with communism and my life as a guerrilla, but I didn't want to tell him about his mother and Bong, and the baby that died, while she was alive. You see, Li never mentioned Bong or their baby again after we were married. It was as if she had sealed that sad chapter of her life in the deepest recess of her heart. I didn't want to bring back her pain. I should have told your dad when he came home for his mother's funeral, but I was too upset over Li's death at the time. I never thought I'd be telling you first. Perhaps you can bring his mother's story to him."

54

"Going back to the manuscript, Grandpa, it was strange, perhaps uncanny, that you hid in Ghost Cave where your great-grandfather Liu Hon Min had taken refuge when he was trying to escape from James Brooke's men. Except that the cave didn't have that name in his time. What's more, he was rescued by two Bidayuh women who got him out through an opening at the back. One of them was your great-grandmother, Jinot, and the other her sister, Enti. I bet it was the same exit where you got out."

"This is really news to me! And if it was the same exit, it's an extraordinary and incredible coincidence."

"You can say that!" says Therese. "But then again, perhaps the spirit of Jinot was watching over you and showing you the way."

"If so, she must have been a hand of fate, the force I said earlier."

"True, you can look at it that way," Therese agrees. Much as her grandfather can accept her theory as a possibility, Therese senses a reasoning based on his acquired faith, an objectivity that lacks the emotional kinship she herself feels about her Bidayuh ancestry. As an afterthought, she says, "In the manuscript, there's mention of a painting of your great-grandmother, which is now at Kampong Tikuan, the longhouse that once was her home. I really want to see it. Grandpa, would you go with me to Kampong Tikuan? Just once?" Seeing her grandfather's negative response, Therese pursues, "I know you don't want to have anything to do with our Bidayuh relations, but can you please do this one thing and go with me while I'm here?"

"This will mean stepping into the territory of our Bidayuh relations, people I've never personally known. How do you explain to them the purpose of our visit? That we are there just to take a look at a painting? It's awkward. It's embarrassing. I don't think this is a smart thing to do."

"It won't be awkward or embarrassing." Therese hesitates, and then continues, "I have a confession to make, Grandpa. One of the Bidayuh cousins has been in touch with me since I've been in Kuching. He found out about me coming to visit you from my blog. In fact, he is hoping for reconciliation between his family and ours."

"You never told me about this. How do you know who this guy is, that he's not some bad element in town looking to take advantage of a foreign girl?"

"Before I read *The Life and Times of Liu Hon Min*, I thought he was bullshit also; I didn't believe him. After reading the manuscript, I've had a total conversion. I think that he and I almost certainly are related, that we share the same ancestors. Some of the things he told me concerning his forebears are actually mentioned in the manuscript. He couldn't have known about them unless he'd had the facts from his family. We share the same past history. His great-great-great-grandmother, Jinot, is also mine, and is your great-grandmother. I want to see her portrait. Please, please?" Tears well in Therese's eyes and trickle down her cheeks. Gradually, she sees a softening in her grandfather's face.

55

Miseng looks nervous when he stands on the threshold of Liu Ka Ming's house and Therese introduces him to her grandfather. Grandpa Liu invites him in and asks his Malay servant to serve tea. Therese's grandfather assumes a courteous disposition towards Miseng, who addresses him awkwardly as Liu Pak, a generic Chinese greeting for any elderly man, not necessarily implying family ties. Liu Ka Ming avoids talk of their common ancestry, but keeps the conversation to the present, showing some interest, feigned or otherwise, in Miseng's studies in Kuching. Therese, on the other hand, keeps watching with nervous anxiety Miseng's and her grandfather's facial expressions, hoping for some intimation of acceptance of kinship between them. Her grandfather's stiff politeness is unsettling to her. Before long, however, they have boarded a taxi, crossing Batu Kawa Bridge, then along Jalan Batu Kawa, the highway that takes them out of Kuching in the direction of Tondong and Bidayuh country of the interior.

"The original longhouses of Kampong Tikuan are the same as they were in the 1850s when Liu Hon Min and Jinot were here," Miseng tells Therese and her grandfather as they proceed further into their car journey, referring for the first time since his meeting with Liu Ka Ming to their common ancestors. "A third longhouse was added, meant for our own residents when it was built, but in the last fifty years many Bidayuhs have moved to the towns. So we use it for tourist homestays nowadays. Sooner or later, we all give in to the temptations of the big cities."

"I admire the ones who stay behind. Without them, your traditions would die out. It's a toss-up between progress and heritage. In this day and age, I'm afraid there's little space for the noble savage," says Therese.

"I don't know how noble we are, but my folks who still live in the kampong are happy, wanting little, needing little," Miseng says. "They live on rice cultivation, subsistence farming and selling handicrafts. We now have good government representation, unlike the days when we were governed by the White Rajahs, or even the British colonial government."

Surrounded by the lush green vegetation of a tropical, hilly rainforest, Kampong Tikuan is a community of multiple wooden or bamboo houses on stilts, some connected by a common verandah of split bamboo flooring, some as single, separate living quarters in close proximity to one another and erected on various levels of the hillside. Cutting through the old baruk, from the ceiling of which a basket of skulls still hangs, Miseng takes his visitors into his longhouse, one that answers to its name with twenty-eight individual asuok. It is the original longhouse, the first built in the kampong, according to Miseng. His paternal grandparents live in the asuok where Miseng's father had also lived with his family before they moved to Bau. That asuok was where Miseng was born.

Therese and her grandfather bend their heads slightly and step inside the asuok, where they find themselves immediately in the company of Miseng's parents, paternal grandparents and sister. The men are bare-chested, wearing shorts, the women in their modern native costume of black blouse and calf-length skirt with red trimming. Miseng's parents and sister are visiting from Bau. His father and sister speak good English and welcome their guests kindly. The rest of the family embellishes their limited English with smiles and friendly gestures. Liu Ka Ming responds with stiff civility, which Therese tries to soften with her broad smiles and excessive show of warmth.

Therese and Liu Ka Ming are invited to sit on the matted bamboo floor in a circle with Miseng and his family.

"Grandpa, before we see the painting, I think it is common courtesy we share their meal. It would be very impolite not to," Therese whispers to her grandfather, who nods solemnly, looking out of place and remains reserved after the initial greetings. They are brought plates of bamboo chicken and rice, and tekesom, the fermented pork dish, as well as the sweet alcoholic drinks tuak and tepui. For dessert, they are served a variety of fruit from the family's garden, rambutan, miniature bananas, pineapple and durian.

"You can tell I have my roots here in Sarawak, for I love durian. Many of my friends in Canada cannot stand the smell of it," says Therese, licking her fingers after putting one segment of the soft pulp into her mouth.

"If you love it, you cannot have enough of it. But if you hate it, it smells like cats' poo," laughs Miseng.

"I still have to hear of someone from Sarawak not liking durian," Grandpa Liu speaks up for the first time, still not relaxed, but savouring a big piece of the fruit offered him by Miseng's mother, Kala.

Miseng's grandfather says something in Bidayuh which Miseng translates into English, "Grandfather says his own grandfather, Tomen, told him our Chinese ancestor, Ah Min, and his Bidayuh wife, Jinot, had lived in this asuok." Grandpa Liu nods in acknowledgement, but remains silent on the subject.

"I believe both their sons, Tomen, who was your grandfather," says Therese, addressing Miseng's grandfather, "and Nan Sun, who was my Grandpa Liu's grandfather, were born in this asuok," says Therese. All eyes are on her. Seeing their look of wonder, she adds, "I know about their story from a journal handed down from Nan Sun."

At the end of the meal, Miseng says something in Bidayuh to his family, to which his father, whose name is Rigop, responds in English, "Of course you should see the painting of Jinot, our beautiful ancestor." He gets up and beckons to Therese and Grandpa Liu to follow him up a trunk ladder to the loft of the asuok. Everyone follows.

Hanging on the wall of the loft to the right as one reaches the top of the ladder is the bark painting of Jinot, a young native woman in a black jomuh, her long black hair cascading down her bare shoulders, a green trinket glinting from a gold-coloured chain around her neck, the jade Buddha, its reflection of light breathing life into the still portrait. With cold hands, Therese ushers her grandfather closer to the painting. Therese notices the medium on which the portrait was painted, a piece of dried bark. The painting has a few not-too-prominent cracked vertical lines here and there, but it is otherwise quite well preserved. Therese fingers the jade Buddha she is wearing, her eyes focused on the faithful replica of it in the painting, tears welling up at the sight of the little green Buddha her great-great-great-grandmother was wearing; two women traversing time and space to touch in that moment of enlightenment.

Liu Ka Ming stands motionless in front of the portrait for at least a minute. Silently, biting her lower lip, Therese turns her attention on her grandfather, while the rest of the entourage looks wonderingly at them both. Grandpa Liu stares at the painting without a word. His expression is solemn, as it has been since his arrival at Kampong Tikuan, his lips pursed tight. He begins to blink and Therese detects a faint weakening in his guard, a gradual relaxation of his taut facial muscles. Tears begin to form in his eyes, until they can no longer be contained and start rolling down his furrowed cheeks. He turns to Therese, and nods. Regardless of their company, Therese hugs him knowingly and they cry in each other's arms.

"She was with me in Ghost Cave," Grandpa Liu manages to whisper hoarsely into Therese's ear.

His face wet with tears, Liu Ka Ming looks around at everyone who has gone up to the loft, his uptight countenance giving way completely to an expression of warm acceptance, as he opens his arms to embrace Miseng and every member of his family.

Later, Liu Ka Ming and Therese are introduced to other members of their extended Bidayuh family who are still at Tikuan, twenty-three of them. They are told more than a hundred and fifty other members of the clan live and work in Kuching and surrounding towns.

56

Therese and her grandfather spend the night at Kampong Tikuan. The next morning, Miseng and his father, Rigop, drive their guests back to Kuching in the family car. Rigop is driving, and at Therese's request they take the longer route along Jalan Bau-Lundu to Bau. Just before reaching the modern town of Bau, they swing down a small country road to the old section, Mau San. The road leads to an open paved area in front of a recently built small temple. Across from the temple is a canopied stage. The place looks deserted.

"This was the way the gold miners during the White Rajah's time walked from the town to the mines, except there was no road then, only a muddy footpath," Rigop explains.

Rigop leads Therese and her grandfather along another small paved road to the right of the temple, between a few wooden bungalows. About eight hundred yards from the temple, they come to a monument, a three-tiered charcoal-coloured granite platform, topped with a marble plaque on which are engraved in gold a number of Chinese characters, which Grandpa Liu translates:

In Remembrance of the Hero Liu Shan Bang
Father of Mau San, Martyr Against Colonial Tyranny
With Ultimate Integrity, Never to Submit

30th September 2006

"A little late for this, isn't it?" Therese asks with a cynical look.

"Better late than never," says Rigop. "I'm Bidayuh, but I feel very strongly for his cause and for the rebellion, partly because our ancestors fought and died in it. Look over there." He points to the right.

About twenty yards from the monument is a small gazebo-styled structure, open on all sides, in the centre of which are planted the lower segments of two old wooden posts with some faded red paint on them.

"What's left of the Mau San flagpole," Miseng remarks.

They walk up to it. The bases of the posts are anchored into tiled flooring covering the earth beneath. Beside the posts is a small altar. A couple of charred joss sticks are planted inside a ceramic urn. In front of the altar, on a metal pedestal, is a slate plaque with Chinese writing.

"It says that Liu Shan Bang called his men to arms against the White Rajah at this spot. Here many Mau San inhabitants were killed by the Rajah's men," says Grandpa Liu. Then in a tight voice charged with emotion, he looks up. "It was also here that my friend Bong and I stopped to rest for a moment in our escape from the Malay and British anti-communist troops in 1965. In that moment I saw Bong killed at the hands of the enemy."

Before returning to Kuching, they make one final stop: Ghost Cave. Lying within the premises of a functioning gold mine in modern Bau and hidden from the public eye, access is restricted to those with passes to enter the grounds of the mining operation. Rigop, who was known to the mining officials from his days as chief assistant to the Pemanca of Bau, easily secures permission for them all to go in.

A worker at the property takes them up a short path to the cave, which is inside a small hill densely covered with trees and creepers, the opening to the cave overgrown with vegetation and hardly visible but for the canopied wooden altar built across it. No one has entered it in years, the guide says. Who would want to go into its dark, eerie recesses, where the spirits of the dead are said to still wander? Time has not softened its ghostly reputation, only accentuated it with lingering tales of hauntings.

"According to what I read about Liu Hon Min, there's an opening in the back of the cave. The Bidayuh sisters Enti and Jinot went in through the narrow gap and got him out when he was trapped in there and almost killed by James Brooke's men," Therese informs, not sure if Miseng and his father know about the rescue.

"If that was the case, the secret opening must still be there, but I suppose it would be hard to find now with all these trees and creepers," says Miseng, proving his ignorance of the fact until now.

Therese looks over to her grandfather who has remained silent since entering the cave vicinity. He looks serious, his eyes betraying an unfathomable sadness mingled with gratitude. Finally he says, "I was hunted by British and Malaysian border troops in the Sixties and I hid in that cave. I thought my life would end in there. I found that secret passage to the outside, with a little help, and got my life back." At his own mention of a little help, Grandpa looks over to Therese and they share a knowing smile, but neither Miseng nor Rigop seems to have followed the inference.

"Very strange," Rigop remarks. "In all my years in Bau, I have never heard of there being another exit from the cave. The front entrance is the only way in and out as far as I know."

In a slow, deliberate voice, Grandpa Liu says, "The other exit may well be a phantom doorway only opened to those whose destiny is meant to be framed by it."

Mystified by Grandpa Liu's words, Therese steps back from the cave entrance to take in the foliage-covered hill that embraces Ghost Cave: its human bones, silenced screams, heart-rending tragedies and stark secrets – and yet, a haven for life.

About Women in Publishing Society

WOMEN IN PUBLISHING SOCIETY (WiPS) was established in Hong Kong in 1990 to bring together professional women working in publishing-related fields and offer them support, mentoring, continued education and networking opportunities. Its members come from many nations, but all live or have strong connections in Hong Kong. While English is not necessarily their first tongue, they all write in that language. They are a dynamic group of poets, memoirists, novelists, editors, designers, teachers and artists who share a love of the written word.

Since 2001, WiPS has published an annual anthology, *Imprint*, of its members' work. The growing popularity and success of this title encouraged the Society in 2013 to offer a literary prize, the Saphira Prize, for unpublished writing. An independent international panel of judges chose Elsie Sze's exceptional manuscript as the winning entry. *Ghost Cave* has been project managed, designed, edited and typeset entirely by WiPS members.

www.hkwips.org

Printed in Great Britain
by Amazon